The
Quiet Woman

Michael Bealey

Dedicated to my pops
John Michael Bealey

ACKNOWLEDGMENTS

Firstly, I must thank my partner Helen for her gracious support and patience when helping with editing. Without her ability to extract the gremlins left by my poor spelling and basic lack of academic accomplishment, I could not have completed this book.

A big thank you must also go to the several individuals who gave me invaluable feedback whether requested or not. You know who you are.

A swelling thank you to Lele Bobeszko for her enthusiastic support and feedback, along with an over-gushing review of this my first novel.

Thank you to my talented daughter Charlie for her excellent cover design.

1 ARRIVAL

Looking down at the speedometer Alex conceded he was driving way too fast, again. Taking his foot off the gas he physically shook himself to force transition into a more chilled state. After all, this was just what he needed following a crazy, emotional and very stressful month. The split, although not totally unexpected, had been messy and overly confrontational. Retreating back home into the Peak District to spend some time gathering himself was definitely the way to go. And there was always the possibility of - her, the girl behind the bar in The Quiet Woman public house. He'd thought of her occasionally over the last year or so. Her smile, calm confidence and gentle manner, a stark contrast to the cursing fury of abuse Michelle had left him with. Was it possible she could still be there? It had been over a year since he'd been back to Sterndale for his father's funeral. Willingly distracted he was more relaxed now and driving the meandering country road in dreamy contemplation.

That was until in the middle of a tightening right-hand bend, a speeding black Alfa Romeo careered alongside with little room for manoeuvre. A flush of adrenaline rushed through him, raising every hair and shooting from every pore. For a fleeting moment his heightened senses capturing the scene brought him face to face with the driver of the derailed vehicle. Fear stricken and battling for control, the desperate soul made no eye contact. It was obvious to Alex even within this rapidity the driver had clearly lost control and it was he who must avert the inevitable. Twitching the wheel towards the roadside and braking violently, he slid to a halt narrowly avoided a collision, and the Alfa was gone.

'What the...! Bloody idiot,' he blurted, slapping the wheel and setting off the horn.

With the screech of tyres and smell of burning rubber still filling his senses he moved off quickly, realising the precarious position the car was now in. Accelerating hard he checked his rear-view mirror before glancing over his shoulder nervously several times expecting to see another vehicle upon him before he was clear of the blind bend. Breathing deeply, he fought to relax again, the anxious tension building in his neck and shoulders. Although his anger with the Alfa driver was beginning to eat into him it was tempered by the relief of avoiding a serious accident. It was only a few miles now to the cottage.

Approaching the village of Sterndale the low autumn sun blazing through the windscreen blinding him momentarily. Slamming down the visor, he sat back high and straight in his seat to get the best view of the road ahead. Alex knew these roads well. This had been home for most of his formative years. He'd learnt to ride a motorcycle and passed his driving test around here before heading off to University. Familiar places from his childhood passed by as though in miniature. Strange, how even though he'd been back many times his perception of the place was still through the eyes of that young boy, unaware of the wider world outside the confines of the village limits. He quashed a building sense of resentment that rose within him. He had no time for that, not right now.

Passing the post office and the village store on the left and the church on the right, the road opened onto the square where, set back from the main street stood the shadowy facade of The Quiet Woman. A few cars and a couple of motor bikes were parked outside, along with a brim-full builder's skip. A double-take tied a knot in his stomach as his eyes returned to one of the vehicles. It was the Alfa that had nearly run him off the road, he was certain it was the same car. He had toyed with the idea of going into the pub before heading for the cottage, just to see if she was still there behind the bar. Beautiful, vulnerable and every bit a barmaid from the waist up through the curves of her ample breasts to her masses of cascading blond hair.

'Calm down mate,' Alex checked himself. Now though there was the added obstacle of a potential scene if he was to confront the driver of the black Alfa. Not normally being one to start any kind of affray, that wasn't going to happen, was it? He reluctantly concluded.

His mind made up, he pulled onto the car park alongside the offending black Alfa and jumped out ready for anything, if only a distracting alternative to a lonely evening in at the cottage.

On approaching the pub door, he took a moment to compose himself. He was just calling in for a quick drink before heading to the cottage. To all and sundry that's how he wanted to be seen and probably would be seen, as that was actually what he was doing, with one or two added agendas. Scanning the interior of the pub Alex felt almost comforted that the place hadn't changed, being pretty much what you'd expect of a country pub in the midst of the Derbyshire Peak District. It was in reasonably good repair, comfortable and spacious with a well-proportioned open fire roaring away on one wall. Amongst the usual pub décor of paintings and cluttered shelves were a menagerie of various stuffed birds and animals both in and out of display cases. Maybe not that acceptable in this day and age, but not particularly out of place here. Alex remembered the landlord, Bill Palmer, was renowned locally for his taxidermy skills. He'd heard several stories of him over the years reconstituting local folks' deceased pets to more permanent static companions. A practice that obviously split opinions locally, as well as being the subject of many unsavoury jokes.

The smell of pub grub was in the air, along with a lingering odour of what Alex thought he recognised as stale beer. Taking a quick glance around the room he noted a few couples eating at tables and at the far end of the bar two rough, out dated Hells Angel type bikers, motor-cycle helmets in hand. At the other end of the bar a familiar face was chatting with the barmaid; it wasn't her though, it wasn't Anna. Alex covered an amused smirk with a manly chin scratch. The familiar face, last seen gripped with fear was, without doubt, that of the black Alfa driver. From his appearance Alex guessed he was probably of North African or Egyptian origin with geek-ish good looks and a strangely endearing persona. As he approached, he tuned into their conversation. The guy was obviously making an attempt at chatting up the barmaid with some pretty rubbish lines. Regardless, with his doubtless confidence and huge warm smile, he was stealing her attention with giggling embarrassment.

Stepping up to the bar a few feet from the bikers Alex nodded at a middle-aged man he recognised as the landlord. The ruddy faced publican seemed not to recognise him as they made eye contact.

4

'What can I get you then mi Duck?'

'I'll just have a pint of the Marston's please and a bag of Quavers,' replied Alex, spotting the modest crisp selection behind the bar.

Alex didn't really expect to be remembered as he'd not spent much time in the pub in recent years. Strangely it seemed to him that the landlord had always been there and didn't appear to have aged much in the last twenty plus years.

Taking a glass, the barman sniffed loudly and began pulling the beer. 'Here on holiday are you sir?'

'I'm here for a bit of a break, yes. I used to live round here when I was younger.'

'Did you now sir?' replied the landlord taking Alex's money in one hand and delivering the pint glass to the bar top with a wipe across a towel.

Alex didn't reply, feeling unsure how to respond to what had sounded a little condescending.

The landlord tilled Alex's money and returned with his change. 'Well then, enjoy your break, hope to see you in here again sir.'

'Thanks, I'll no doubt be calling in again.'

Returning the change to his pocket Alex turned to find a seat away from the bar, only to be stopped suddenly when his cheek collided with well-worn leather, the smell of which filled his nostrils briefly before they were flattened firmly against it. He jumped in shocked surprise. The shattering sound of breaking glass followed. In that same instance he was being dragged by his jacket collar face to face with one huge, indignant, hairy biker.

'You little shit, you spilt my beer!' A gravelly voice murmured menacingly in his face.

'Sorry mate, it was an accident,' pleaded Alex. 'Let me buy you another drink.'

'This isn't your lucky day buddy boy, I'm in no mood for prats like you,' Mr Gruff continued.

At this point the landlord saw fit to intervene.

'Now come on gents there's no need for this to get ugly, let me get you another drink.'

'Butt out barman!' The other biker jibbed as he leant over the bar with the obvious intent to scare the landlord. 'Keep your bleeding beak out chum if you know what's good for you.'

The landlord froze raising his hands submissively.

'Now just calm down gents. I don't want to have to call the police.'

'Oh yeah, and how long will it take 'em to get here from - Leek is it? Half an hour! If you're lucky,' replied the biker laughing. 'I'd have you spitting teeth before they can find their car keys buddy, now butt out!'

The bar was silent as the alarmed clientele looked on, no one willing to challenge the aggressive ruffians. That was until the barmaid thought she'd have a go. Addressing them firmly with a warm southern Irish lilt.

'Now look here you two! There's no need for this just take another drink and let him be.'

The second biker then turned his attention to the barmaid, 'Shut your pretty little paddy face missy, I'll just as well slap you too if need be, right?'

Alex was in a very firm grip and keeping quiet so as not to aggravate the situation.

'Me and you are going to take a little walk outside buddy boy,' the biker snarled down at him.

Was this a scene from a Clint Eastwood movie? Alex questioned to himself. He could only dream of putting up a fight, but that wouldn't be a battle he'd have any chance of coming out of well. It was then that a surreal intervention unfolded from the unlikely direction of the Alfa driver.

'That is enough gentlemen,' he began. 'Let this man go or you will have found more trouble here than you have bargained for.'

His seemingly misplaced but confident challenge was met with roars of hysterical laughter from the bikers.

'And what's a 2p fart like you gonna do then boy? Don't make me laugh.'

At this our unimposing protagonist picked up two bar stools and began flailing them deftly around his head like something from an old Kung-Fu movie. He wielded the stools with such lightning speed and precision, they took the form of formidable and deadly weapons. The bikers looked on with complete amazement as our hero ended his routine by placing the stools on the floor and mounting them into a lunging position with arms at Kung Fu fighting readiness.

'Can I suggest you leave now gentlemen and bring a close to this hostility? I have no desire to hurt anyone tonight.'

'Up yours, you little shit,' groaned the biker restraining Alex. Pushing him to one side he lunged forward. At this the bar stool mounted adversary dropped to the floor and in one almost imperceptible movement the seat of one of the stools connected swiftly, firmly and precisely with the chin of the attacking biker. Stopped abruptly in his tracks the big daft idiot fell to the floor with a good old tree felling thud.

Thundering fat twin cylinder motorbikes could be heard popping and snarling out of the car park, down the road and out of the village. The fallen biker had been helped hastily to his feet and out of the pub by his mate. Having chosen not to continue the confrontation they left the threatening sentinel like figure of our hero in a silent pose, stools still in hand. The rants and curses of the embarrassed aggressors faded into the sounds of their bike exhaust notes, and they were gone.

All was laughter and celebration back in The Quiet Woman, where Alex found himself face to face with the driver of the black Alfa in a spontaneous high five.

'Thank you,' Alex declared.

'Ammon is my name, and you are most welcome my friend.'

'Yes, well, thank you. I'm Alex and that was some display of martial arts you put on there.'

'It is nothing; it is my heritage,' Ammon replied.

Alex didn't question further as the landlord was now in the midst of offering free drinks all round to the jubilant victors of the fray.

After the excitement had subsided Alex and Ammon sat together at the bar, on the very stools that had briefly become the deadly weapons wielded with such redeeming effect.

'So where are you from Ammon?' enquired Alex.

'I am from Manchester now, but I was born in Egypt, in Dahab on the Sinai Peninsula. I came here with my family about ten years ago. Are you on a holiday?'

'I am, yes, a bit of a break away from it all. And you, are you on holiday?'

'Yes. I too am trying to get away from it all. Some troubles back home. Just needed to get away. I am staying in the pub here. Got a room upstairs. How about you? Where are you staying?'

'I'm in a cottage just outside the village. It's actually a family place, left to us by my late uncle.' Alex found himself opening up to Ammon and offering a little more information than he probably normally would.

'You come from round here then?' asked Ammon.

'I do, yes. Not been back much though, for a long time. Left to go to Uni and that was it really.'

'Have you got family here?'

'Ha!' replied Alex wryly. 'I do yes, just my mother. We don't really get on too well these days.'

'That is not good my friend, we all need family. They are the ones who know us best and know our needs.'

Alex shook his head with a distasteful smirk. 'Sorry mate, not my mother. She knows her own needs alright but, I'm just... never was... good enough I suppose.'

'So sad, my friend. I see it gives you much pain.'

Alex saw an opportunity to change the conversation as the barmaid moved away to serve a customer. 'The barmaid seems to be taking an interest in you mate. I think you're in there.'

'She is beautiful is she not my friend. I have been here for two nights and not managed to get any interest until now,' whispered Ammon.

'I'm not surprised after that display with the bikers, she's gonna be all over you now. Where did you learn that stuff?'

'I come from a long line of Saracen warriors my friend. Proud fighting men with a great code of honour and age-old fighting tradition. My grandfather taught me many things from an early age; that and my mother, her family are circus performers, I learned many useful tricks there too.'

'That's an interesting background you have there,' Alex acknowledged. 'By the way, is that your black Alfa in the car park?'

'It is yes. It is very fast; in fact, too fast for me I would say,' replied Ammon.

'I'd say as well! You nearly drove me off the road on a blind bend on the way here.'

'Oh no! I am so sorry my friend, was that you? I am so very sorry. Oh, my God,' pleaded Ammon. 'It is an automatic and I am not good with it yet. I pressed the wrong pedal and had to go along side you in the bend. It was so very frightening my friend. I am so, so sorry. There are some things of which I am good at but driving is not one I can say.'

'You can definitely say that again.'

They both laughed and clinked glasses acknowledging a cheer.

'Are you going to ask that barmaid out then, or what?' pushed Alex.

'I shall, yes, I need the right moment though,' Ammon whispered back shyly.

'There was a barmaid here when I was back last year, called Anna. I was hoping she would still be-'

'Anna!' interrupted Ammon. 'I have heard her talked about. I heard she went missing and left all her things and possessions in her room. A great mystery my friend. Vanished without a trace.'

'Poor Anna. I wonder what happened to her. That's terrible,' Alex recoiled, puzzled and shocked by the news.

'I think we should investigate this mystery and get to the bottom of it. Maybe even find her my friend. What do you say?' announced Ammon with building excitement.

'Come on, we should leave that sort of thing to the police. We haven't got a chance, where would you even start?'

'From what I heard the police have not got any idea either. There has been nothing done for weeks I was told,' insisted Ammon.

Alex took a deep breath and shook his head. 'It's a nice idea but come on where would you start with a thing like that?'

The pair chatted on into the late evening until Alex insisted it was time to get over to the cottage and sort himself out. They parted with a promise to meet up again the following evening for more beer and chat. He felt an immovable smile take to his face as he walked out to the car, Ammon was an interesting guy and they'd connected surprisingly quickly over that evening. Without a doubt he was glad he'd called in at The Quiet Woman, tainted though it was by the news of Anna's disappearance. The unexpected loss lay heavy in the pit of his stomach. The circumstances of her disappearance felt sinister and fateful.

After a short drive down dark narrow roads the car headlights illuminated the front of Willow Tree cottage. A quaint little eighteenth century former hunting lodge nestled amongst perfectly groomed and manicured flora. Gardens kept pristine under the passionate eye of his mother, who was far more converse with nurturing shrubs and flowers than her own flesh and blood. A rising bitterness riled him momentarily but he shrugged it off with deeply sought abandon.

'Key under the plant pot, which bloody one?' Alex muttered to himself. There were so many now cluttering the drive. Alex suspected mother must be having an affair with the guy from the local horticultural society. She had flirted around him so obviously at his father's funeral, it would be laughable, if not so hurtful. Alex had long felt sympathy for his father, never being able to understanding his parents' relationship. He was a quiet man, reserved but focused, mainly on his passion for woodworking. After retiring he'd spent a lot of his time in his workshop, one of the outbuildings at the rear of family home. The man had long given up to nods of 'yes dear' and acceptance of the one-sided conversations held by his wife. She answered for him on occasions in an almost comedic dual narrative that seemed to be more about her thinking out loud than any meaningful attempt at communication.

The cottage was kept immaculate by mother as a retreat for the family, well, in particular Alex's older brother and sister. They had both earned themselves high powered jobs, Michael as a commercial lawyer in the city and Carolyn as a political analyst for the BBC. And good for them, Alex had thought. He had no quarrel with them, they were brighter than he and had worked hard to get where they were. Alex had always felt like the runt of the litter being more of an artistic persuasion than academic. A trait far from the comprehension of mother who had once summed up his career as a freelance photographer as 'messing about taking pictures'. She had spent a life of do-gooding, on the Board of Trustees of the British Red Cross, no less. Alex imagined the later as a gathering of sunken chested, horn rimmed spectacle wearing old girl guide mistresses, wielding hockey sticks and screaming 'off with his head' in the shrillest Alice in Wonderland's, Queen of Hearts fashion.

Kettle on and a brew before bed, it was getting late and the day had been quite eventful. Alex was surprised at actually feeling some building excitement for the next few days but struggled to reconcile this with recurring thoughts of Anna. An unpleasant notion continued to tug at his sensibility. A beautiful girl goes missing leaving all her possessions behind, it doesn't sound like it could end well. Ammon was surely crazy to think they could play at private investigators and find her or any suspects or motives. That was a matter for the police and whoever it may concern...

2 WHOEVER IT MAY CONCERN

Alex glanced at his watch in exercise mode to check his run duration. It was a lovely crisp autumn morning and he was feeling pretty good considering. Waking to a string of vicious emails from Michelle with more demands for him to collect his stuff from the flat hadn't been a good start to the day. He'd replied as briefly as he could, resolute he was not going to get drawn into any more bitter exchanges.

This was prime running country for Alex. He knew several trails around the area that kept him off the roads for the majority of a good circuit. It was one thing he missed in Manchester, maybe he'd been living in the city long enough he considered. Having access to this out of his back door was like a gym and psychotherapist rolled into one; it maintained his sanity, gave time to think and recharge the batteries. Running down the side of a walled garden he vaulted a fence and onto a track that led back towards the village.

'Hey Mr, this is a private road, the right of way is back there.' A half-recognised voice hailed him.

Alex looked up to see a girl perched on a five barred gate patting the cheek of a fine-looking black horse. It was Madeline Gresham, an old class mate from high school.

'Well look who it is, Alex Hidde back in town,' she jibbed with pleasant surprise.

'Hi Maddie,' Alex replied with a not so well masked reluctance.

His memories of Maddie were of a confident and popular young girl prone to making fun of him at any and every opportunity. Surely she had grown up?

'I heard you were back for your father's funeral last year. What you back for this time?' enquired Maddie, seemingly wanting to make conversation.

'Just a break really, just getting away from it all for a couple of weeks. What brings you back to the village? Last I heard you were married to some dot com computer bloke in London,' he replied with a tentative half interest.

This pretty young girl from school had become an attractive and seemingly self-assured woman, whose presence unnerved Alex as it had back in the day. He couldn't help but note her mature, pleasing figure and masses of tethered curly ginger hair trailing down over her shoulder. She was both threatening and teasingly interesting in uncertain measure. This minor revelation opened him to feelings of self-consciousness as he tried to supress his heightened sense of exposure.

'Well Mr Hidde, my Mum died earlier this year, so, I came back to clear the house, sell up and move on. But having moved back into the house again I'm not sure what to do now. The marriage went to shit, as they do. The arse hole made a break for the door one day, so I shut it behind him and that was that. I don't actually have to do anything right now, or ever as it is. I've had it with men, I've come into a lovely fat inheritance so… might just go travelling and sod everything.'

Her nonchalant delivery was accompanied by a shallow somewhat sexy gaze that made Alex feel even more uncomfortable. Maddie sensed his awkwardness which fuelled her want to have some fun with him; she couldn't resist it.

'So you're on your own again then Alexi-poos?' she cutely quizzed.

'Just been through a bit of a messy break up, yeah.'

'Back here running away from the shit then are you?' Maddie interrupted with a ridiculing giggle.

'You always had a hard time keeping a girlfriend didn't you Alex? Pauline Walton for one made an arse of you, didn't she? Actually, she found me on Facebook not long ago, reminded me of the time you wet your pants in primary school. There was a puddle of pee under your chair and you just sat there, you poor thing.'

'Aw come on Maddie that was bloody primary school—'

'She also reminded me she caught you playing with your todger in class,' she laughed mockingly.

'I was not… at all, my flies were down and I zipped them up and, caught my, myself, in the zipper—'

'Yeah, yeah Pauline reckoned you were having a tommy tank.'

'That bloody hurt that did—'

'Yeah and you let out a little girly scream didn't you poppet?'

'Oh, come on Maddie! We're not in the playground now, we've, well, I've grown up some since then,' he replied realising he had allowed himself to fall into her trap and, no, he still couldn't get the upper hand sparing with this girl. Flustered, he sought a calm mature response but anything he tried twisted his tongue and choked the cool delivery he craved so desperately to hit back with.

Maddie laughed raucously, making him feel familiarly small.

'Oh, how bloody hilarious Maddie, isn't it time you just grew up!' Alex snapped.

'Don't get cross with little old Maddie, especially when I know so much more I can tease you with.'

Alex had already turned and begun running down the lane. He couldn't help but shout out behind him, 'See you around Maddie,' with a parting tone not remotely disguising his 'not if I see you first' intentions.

'Aww Alex don't go getting all stroppy, just having a bit of fun with you,' Maddie laughed in her contented victory.

No, Maddie hadn't grown up Alex reflected. Why all these years later did he still allow her to make fun of him like that? He decided he would forget the meeting and just get on with – what was he going to get on with, just getting on with – it, he proposed. Sniggering to himself he allowed a secret hope that he'd see her again, flitter across his future path.

Alex stared at the image of his father in a photograph he had taken some years before. He had decided he was going to give it to his mother as some sort of peace offering. Even as he'd printed and framed it, he contemplated it probably wasn't the best of ideas and now he was walking up the path to his mother's house bearing it as a gift. Slipping it back into the decorative gift bag he resigned himself to the shallow superficial encounter that was probably about to follow. The photograph had been taken in the garden where his mother and father could be seen tending some very beautiful, blooming hanging baskets. It was a pleasing composition that Alex thought captured the personalities of both subjects in a setting they enjoyed. He hoped the stunning cascades of flowers filling the frame would be the thing his mother might be drawn in by. He had never shown his parents the picture, so, here goes nothing.

'Oh, so you are here then Alex? When did you arrive?' his mother began with her usual interjected brief pauses, which were never quite long enough to begin a response.

'Err yesterday. I got here—'

'So you and Michelle have separated then have you? And where are you living now? You can't stay in Willow Trees indefinitely you know. Your sister is coming up with that lovely Simon Montjoy from the Today in Politics programme she's working on. He does bring those programmes to life you know, what a charming man he is. They'll be celebrating some end of production thing so I'm organising a bit of a do. When are you leaving?'

Alex stood with his mouth half open in readiness to respond, watching his mother flitter this way and that as she filled the air with anything but empathy.

'Mother, I've just got here. A couple of weeks at most, I should think. Then I'm going back to Manchester. I'll need to get back for a shoot mid next month so—'

'Good they're coming up end of the month, twenty-eighth I think she said.'

'Next month! The twenty-eighth of next month?' Alex eagerly checked.

'Yes that's right; so you'll be gone by then, that's fine.'

'Mother you haven't seen me for a year and now I'm here you're asking me when am I leaving.'

'Oh no, I've seen you since then. I've got a W.I. lunch meeting at twelve thirty, what was it I was going to look up? Oh, do you remember George my dear, George Chapman; he's the chairman of the Horticultural society, a lovely man; he's in hospital at the moment having a gall stone removed,' As she spoke, she crouched down to move some magazines around on a book shelf. Whilst doing so she let out a squeaky little fart but carried on as if nothing had happened. Alex could not help but giggle.

'It's not a laughing matter Alex, he's been in some terrible pain recently.'

'I wasn't laughing at that Mother, you erm—'

'I should think not Alex. George has been very good to me this last year. He's given my Sternbergia a new lease of life at Willow Trees, have you seen them?'

'That's the yellow ones isn't it?' Alex replied cheekily,

remembering her telling him once.

His Mother turned and looked at him with a spark of surprise then continued unabated.

'Yes, aren't they just spectacular? He and I are taking a trip to the gardens of La Cervara in Santa Margherita in Italy, as soon as he can travel again that is. He actually knows the family who own the property so it will be a very exclusive visit. I'm very excited. Just wish he'd hurry up and get better then we can make the travel arrangements.'

'I'm sure that will be lovely for you Mother,' Alex replied as enthusiastically as he could manage with eyes raised to the ceiling in despair.

'I brought you this Mother, thought you might like, this.' He handed her the brightly decorated gift bag containing the photograph. She hesitated momentarily before taking it from him, seemingly not approving of the rapping.

'Is it one of your photographs,' she seemed to state rather than question, as she pulled the frame out of the bag and studied it briefly.

'Oh you've captured my Petunias ever so well there Alex, yes lovely.'

She didn't sound overly enthusiastic but it was a better reaction than he had expected and maybe she was even making an effort.

'And Father, I thought you might like it because—'

'I'm not sure where I could put it. I'll have to think about that, but thank you Alex, it's lovely, I'll put it … somewhere.'

She looked around at the walls sparsely adorned with her particular taste in art, mostly flowery subjects with bright vibrant colours.

'Would you make some tea dear while I look up... what was it? Yes, do make some tea Alex.'

It was obvious she was somewhere else as she wandered off tapping her pursed lips with a recollecting finger.

Alex sloped off down the hallway towards the kitchen dragging his hunched frame along like a petulant teenager.

'Do I have to? Captured her Petunias eh, bloody hell, good job she didn't have her Clematis on show ho ho ho.'

He tried to kid himself that he didn't care anymore but when life pinched his thickened skin, it still hurt.

Tea made and delivered to a coaster somewhere on the queen bee danced route his mother navigated around the house and Alex was heading out into the garden towards the outbuildings. One of the buildings was his father's domain, his cave where his wife never visited. After all it was the place, he "played around with bits of wood". He did play around with bits of wood, but he was undoubtedly a talented woodworker spending a lot of time out there, who could blame him?

Alex paused outside the workshop. Looking in through the cob web dusted glass door panels it occurred to him that mother's tidy perfection stopped at this threshold and it was very possible that she had never been in this place, ever? Turning the key Alex pushed the door gently until it jerked open, evoking memories of a visit early the previous year when he'd entered the workshop to talk with his father for the last time.

Taking a deep nasal breath, he stroked his hair back and rubbed his neck, it was just enough to compose himself as he looked around. It wasn't the tidiest of workspaces but there was a sense of order in here. Tools had their place and he just knew they were cleaned and sharpened. It was obvious that nobody had been in since his father's death, and the connection he felt with him was precipitously heart wrenching. He tried to choke back the inevitable tears but had to allow himself some release for a few moments before throwing back his head and smiling. These were good memories of a man in his favourite place using the skill and creativity Alex hoped he had inherited. He knew pushing down those emotions would not help him resolve anything long term, but it was far too disturbing and painful to contemplate right now.

On the shelves behind the workbench Alex noted some pieces of unfinished work. One in particular caught his eye, a house name plate. Crafted on a beautifully grained piece of natural oak the carving of the letters was fluid and perfectly proportioned. Reading out the wording to himself with gathering intrigue, 'Hidden Haven,' he wondered who it could have been made for, finding it strange that it incorporated the family name, Hidde. He went to return it to the shelf but it lingered in his hands and in his curiosity for a few more baffled moments.

Crouching to look under the work bench his eye was immediately drawn to a pile of magazines; in particular the cover of the top one. For a moment the scantily clad female figure adorning the cover shocked him into thinking he'd found his father's stash of porn titles but thankfully it was just one of his old photo mags in amongst woodworking and gardening issues.

At the back of the room stood a large old wooden office cabinet.

Pinned on the double door frontage Alex browsed an array of notes, photos and sketches; various projects he assumed his father had in progress or was planning to start. He opened one of the doors not expecting to find anything more remarkable than another set of chisels or more of the old wooden woodworking planes that his father cherished so much. What he certainly did not expect to come across was one of the most beautiful acoustic guitars he had ever seen. He carefully took it out, sat down with it across his lap and strummed a few chords. He was amazed to discover it wasn't actually that far out of tune. Looking into the guitar's body through the sound hole he could see the maker's name, John Bailey, along with his signature and a dedication – For my forever friend Sarah. Did it or should it still belong to this Sarah? Could his father have bought it? The old man had played some guitar but only classical, as did his brother Michael, who was at one time a disciplined and talented player but this was steel strung with a beautiful slim neck and rounded fretboard. Whose guitar was this? It was without doubt an expensive bit of kit that somebody is probably missing he thought. Somebody who hasn't returned to collect it after his father had repaired it perhaps. He could take it, couldn't he? Alex returned the guitar to the cabinet and closed the door concluding he would make that decision another day. There and then he decided he must lay claim to the contents of this workshop soon, before it was lost to him forever. No one else in the family would possibly have any interest, so it was for him to find a good home for anything that was worth saving.

After another brief encounter with his life narrating mother, Alex drove back to the cottage, grabbed his camera bag and headed out across the fields up towards the coppice of trees know as Hunters' Wood. The afternoon sky was building into a potentially dramatic and moody backdrop, a welcome distraction from the events of the day. With a limitless autumn pallet to play with, nature could just be about to lay on a feast for the photographer's eye and Alex was certainly tuned in to that opportunity. With one of his cameras mounted on a tripod ready to capture the moment the light was just right, Alex surveyed the scene. Beams of sunlight were beginning to cut through a band of darker clouds gathered over the village and distant hills, a few more minutes would be the make or break of this shot. From here he could see down towards the square, and to the rear of The Quiet Woman. Taking up his big lens mounted on another camera body he could make out the sign of the pub clearly. It had been repainted at least a couple of times that Alex could remember but always the same subject; a headless woman with her hands together in front of her covered with what appeared to be a handkerchief. The words "Soft words turneth away wrath" curved over and through where her head should have been. Several stories came to mind relating to the headless woman but he considered most of them as made up to spook the gullible. Alex took the opportunity to inspect the building through his long lens picking up the figure of the landlord engaged in some building work in one of the first-floor rooms; hence the waste skip he remembered seeing in the pub carpark. He was a busy man he thought; working as a landlord and doing his own improvement projects. Ever vigilant Alex returned his attention to the changing canvas before him, in a moment of perfection the light, sky, clouds and autumn colours held hands and sang a song of sweet composition. He clicked off a few frames and it was gone. That was landscape photography; hours waiting for moments of pure magic. His experience told him he didn't need to look at the image on the rear screen of the camera to know he'd captured a special little gift from Mother Nature.

Looking like rain soon, Alex grabbed his kit and headed off back to the cottage and a well-earned cup of tea.

The rain came as he sat at the kitchen table with a large mug and a couple of rich tea biscuits. Snow Patrol's 'Run' filled the room from the digital radio on the window sill as Alex looked out through the cascading raindrops across the fields to the distant views of the woodlands and the high moorland beyond. He contemplated the losses in his life, his father, and recently his relationship with Michelle. As his focus drew back to the droplets of water on the window pane, he felt a longing for a relationship that worked, a soul mate; was that possible, where would he find someone like that?

What was he going to have for dinner? Something he could put in the microwave he supposed, as anything he put near the Aga at the cottage usually ended up looking like a burnt offering on the outside, whilst raw and inedible on the inside. You know where you are with a microwave, not that that meant he ate rubbish! He hated ready meals or in fact anything that he felt had been over processed and definitely nothing from one of those sections in the supermarket where you tended to see obviously single, middle aged guys filling up their trollies for the week or month. Pub food was another option he thought, at the Quiet Woman where he was going to meet up with Ammon later. Truth be told he didn't really want to go out, maybe he'd just spend some time in alone in front of the TV. No, that could end up beginning a downward spiral, anyway, it could be an interesting meeting.

3 AN INTERESTING MEETING

Alex chuckled to himself as he tucked into his scampi and chips, sat in a corner at the back of the bar in the Quiet Woman. The food menu was as dated as the décor he mused to himself. It was good though, proper homemade chips, and the scampi was far better than he'd expected.

He looked around the bar to see if there was anybody he recognised; there wasn't. He didn't really expect to see anyone. There were a couple of local looking farm workers sat on the stools, stroke, Kung Fu weapons at the bar, laughing loudly about someone and his runaway tractor. The landlord also seemed to be in on the joke. The barmaid was different from the previous evening, a middle-aged woman with the stereotypically required cleavage but wearing a permanent scowl, although she did seem pleasant enough when engaging with the clientele. It was reasonably busy for a week night thought Alex. A young girl flitted across in front of him waiting on tables, he glimpsed her name badge, Siobhan. She was very efficient, not sparring many pleasantries but friendly and smiley. With a comical mechanical clunk, the ancient jukebox on the wall burst into life; Follow You, Follow Me by Genesis. Alex chuckled to himself again; this place really is behind the times. What was that old gem still doing on a juke box? The landlord tapped along on the bar following a drum fill and it duly made sense. It was a young guy that was stood at the music machine, leaning against it with his forehead while he selected a few more tracks. He slammed his coins into the slot with a downward spin as though he was familiar with the machine and expected the coins to be rudely rejected. They were not, falling through the internal mechanism with audible certainty.

'Aah! Alex my friend,' Ammon entered from the guests' quarters of the pub. 'Let me get you a drink.'

'Hey Ammon. How are you?'

'I am good, thank you. What are you drinking?'

'A Guinness please, I'll have another Guinness if you don't mind thanks.'

Ammon walked over to the bar and was warmly welcomed by the landlord, drawing attention to the reserved Ammon who looked around with an uncomfortable smile.

'What have you been up to today then?' Alex inquired as Ammon returned to the table with the drinks.

'Well, I have a story to tell my friend. You know the barmaid from last night? Well I went with her to her martial arts class today. She is called Evelyn. I asked her if she would like to go out with me last night and she invited me to go with her today.'

'That's great. Well done mate!'

'Well it was fine until the instructor wanted to fight with me. He is a thug my friend and should not be teaching his ways to good people.'

'What happened?'

'He wanted to show me up I think, so I told him I did not want to fight with him. Then he said let us just do a little demonstration of some moves then. He told me the moves he wanted to show and then approached me. He did not do the moves he said and so I went with it without resisting him but stayed on my feet. I do not think he liked that, he came at me very hard. I tried to put him down gently but he resisted and broke some of his fingers. It was terrible my friend. I took Evelyn by the hand and we left. I told him he should stop his lessons if he did not abide by the spirit in which these teachings had been handed down for generations. She has agreed not to go back to his classes.'

'What an absolute loser. He got what he deserved then I reckon.'

'Maybe my friend, but why do I keep coming across these people?'

'It's the fight for good versus evil, don't beat yourself up,' consoled Alex.

'Evelyn told me more about the missing girl Anna. She told me that there is some guy in the village that is claiming to have seen a body when he was walking, he says it is her. She says he is a crazy guy though so she is not sure how much is true—'

A familiar voice, for the second time that day, cut across Ammon,

'Are you talking about the barmaid who disappeared, Anna, are you?'

'Maddie! What brings you in here?' Alex greeted sinking back into his chair.

'Don't be like that Alexi-poos. It seems we might have something in common after all you big grumpy trousers.' Maddie noted his standoffish body language but persisted, smiling and gave him a sexy wink.

'Ammon this is Maddie, we went to school together. Maddie this is Ammon, we met in here last night.'

The two greeted each other with a nod of the head and an inquisitive smile as Maddie drew up a chair to the table and put her half-emptied pint glass on a spare mat.

'I knew Anna.' said Maddie. 'She was a lovely girl and I'd like to know what happened to her. She just disappeared and the police don't seem to be doing anything about it.'

'Another one who wants to play amateur detective then—' started Alex.

'Well come on my friend this is serious and we might be able to make a difference,' interrupted Ammon with rising passion now he had an ally.

'Yes, Alex. This girl was my friend she would never have left without letting me know. I'm worried about her,' pleaded Maddie. 'I've heard the same thing as you Amman—'

'It's Ammon not Amman,' Alex corrected firmly.

'Sorry, Ammon,' she continued directing her conversation to Ammon.

'I've heard the same as you, the guy who claims to have seen a body in the Peak while he was out running. I think I know who the guy is as well.'

'We must find him and talk to him, find out where this sighting was made and go and check it out,' Ammon insisted, sharing his attention from Alex to Maddie as if he was following a tennis ball rallying between them.

'Come on guys this is getting a little out of hand here, isn't it?' Alex attempted to interject. They both looked at him with the same "do you not get this" gaze.

'This is a matter for the police and, not for us to get involved in, isn't it?' he continued, sensing he was actually probably wrong, and they should, and he did want to find Anna, if they could, and hopefully alive.

'Who's the crazy guy then?' he relented with little grace.

'That's more like it Alexi-poos. He's an old dry stone waller, and a well-known fell runner—'

'Arnold Pinkston!' Alex spurted out, cutting across Maddie who was left with her mouth open.

Ammon raised his arms excitedly, 'You know this man Alex?'

'I only know his name. He was a big name in fell running years back. I read a book about local runners and he was one of the greats. Unrecognised at the time of course, but one of the greats.'

'He is supposed to be a bit bonkers these days though from all accounts,' added Maddie with a doubting tone.

'He was bonkers then by all accounts!' Alex concurred. 'He was famed for running downhill faster and way more recklessly than anyone then or since.'

'At this moment that is all we have to go on though isn't it?' Maddie summated. 'There is a body somewhere out there and it could be Anna. I need to know if it's her or not.' Maddie finished to silence with her now empty pint glass hammered down on the table.

The three of them looked up from the glass and around at each other. Although Alex had been initially resistant there was now a tingle of excitement in the shared venture they had all implicitly signed up for.

'Another drink boys?' said Maddie.

'She is a feisty one my friend,' chuckled Ammon as Maddie wandered off to the bar. 'Is she an ex-girlfriend?'

'No, no. We went to the same schools growing up around here. I certainly wouldn't call us friends either. I'm just not sure about this mate.' Alex contemplated as he stared across towards Maddie at the bar.

'Maybe she is just as lost as we are my friend,' Ammon voiced softly.

'What makes you say that?' Alex whispered back, quite puzzled as Maddie approached carrying three pints skilfully in her hands.

'Hey that is some trick lady,' applauded Ammon taking two of the glasses off her and setting them down on the table.

'A lady hah!' Maddie proudly repeated. 'Did you hear that Alex. It's not what you're thinking is it you big Oscar Grouch.'

Ammon burst out laughing. 'Ha ha, Oscar Grouch! That is Sesame Street isn't it my friend? Oh so funny,'

'What's with the name calling Maddie eh? We're not at school now. Can you give it up please?' protested Alex.

'Ok, sorry, I'll try not to do it again. Mr Monkey Bollock head,' replied Maddie, serious until the very last syllable upon which she burst into laughter accompanied by Ammon who was struggling to hide his amusement.

'Very funny, very funny,' drolled Alex starting to see the funny side and maybe what he saw as a touch of intended endearment.

'Ok. Where does this Arnold Pinkston live?' Alex began, getting into planning mode. 'That's the first move. We go see him and see if he can tell us where he saw the body. If we can't get a location then we still have nothing to go on.'

'I'm going to try get in touch with Anna's parents and maybe get some clues as to her state of mind around that time; if there was any communication of any sort,' chipped in Maddie.

'I will check all the newspaper stories and see if there is any information of use in there,' offered Ammon.

'How long are you here Ammon?' questioned Maddie. 'Do you have a job to go back to?'

'I work in my family's business; or maybe I did that is.'

Alex and Maddie looked on as Ammon sighed an awkward reluctance.

'My family business sells security systems. I am, was, manager of the sales and marketing. I have fallen out with my father who will not let me move the business on in the direction I think we need to go. I do not think it will survive if we do not move with the times. He will not see it, even though sales are falling every quarter. He is stubborn and resists change on any level. I told him we must change or I will not be part of my family's downfall. In a big fight he told me to go, and here I am. Not sure what to do now, he does not answer my calls or emails or anything.'

'Sorry mate. That sounds tough for you,' sympathised Alex.

'Families can be such screwed up places to be, can't they Alex?' declared Maddie. 'We know that one, don't we? Well, mine are gone now but you've still got your crazy mother haven't you?' she continued reflectively.

Alex returned a strained smile, shaking his head in resigned recognition. He wasn't exactly sure what Maddie's history was but he knew she'd had some difficult times losing her father in her teens.

From his dejected slump Ammon jumped up and set off across the room to the bar to order more drinks without asking what they wanted. He returned with a huge smile on his face and a tray full of brimming shot glasses.

'Drink my friends, for tomorrow we go in search of the truth,' he roused.

They downed that batch with rising frivolity and then another followed. A few more empty glasses later and Maddie was getting visibly drunk and looking for some fun.

'Who's he think he's looking at the squinty eyed bastard?' she declared looking across at a stuffed fox behind Alex. 'I'm going to punch him in the face if he doesn't stop starring.'

'You can't do that Maddie he's on our side!' Alex proclaimed defensively. 'I'm bringing him in as a consultant on the case. He's a master of great wisdom and cunning you know.'

'You could have fooled me. He doesn't move much does he?'

'That's cos he's in deep thought, and he never moves at all when he's in deep thought.'

'Not even to have a crap? That's amazing int it? I knew a badger like that once.'

Ammon looked on in stunned surprise, tittering hysterically as this comic exchange was played out before him.

'Just how cunning do you reckon he is then?' questioned Maddie.

'Oooh, I should say very, very cunning indeed. In fact, he is so cunning that that isn't actually him. He's in the Bahamas, in the sun, wearing a panama hat and sipping a chicken broth cocktail through a straw and that is an elaborately cunning model of him left there to fool us.'

'Now you're talking bollox Alex, I'm just gonna punch him anyway,' Maddie lurched forward with a fist clenched but quickly lost her balance and was caught by Ammon as they fell about in fits of laughter.

Their drink fuelled fun was brought to a sobering and abrupt halt when they collectively became aware of the landlord looming over them wearing a particularly stern, disapproving face.

'I'd thank you not to touch my exhibits if you don't mind. There's a lot of hours of work I've put into that fella. And if you could just keep the noise down please eh?'

'We are so very sorry, we will calm down now Mr Palmer,' chirped up Ammon in a very humble tone.

'Well that's ok then,' replied the landlord. 'Seeing it's you Ammon I'll let it go this time.' With that he turned and walked off back to the bar with his wagging finger still raised over his shoulder like a smoking gun.

'Mr Palmer!' questioned Alex with some surprise.

'Yes! I am staying here, and he has been very kind to me since the incident with the bikers. William Palmer is his name; most people call him Bill,' replied Ammon trying to dignify his position.

'Well, I think he can go get stuffed!' tittered Maddie.

Alex followed, 'Yeah, and when he's gone and got stuffed, he can go and get stuffed some more, the bar-steward.'

'Now you are sounding bonkers the pair of you,' said Ammon raising his arms in despair.

'It is funny though isn't it Ammon?' poked Maddie.

'Yes it is, I have to say. It is so good to laugh for me right now,' replied Ammon with a big smile spreading across his face.

Alex sat up straight in his chair, grasped both knees firmly and pronounced, 'Talking of bonkers we have a job to do tomorrow; finding Arnold Pinkston.'

4 FINDING ARNOLD PINKSTON

Alex was scared and running through the dark prison complex that had become his home… after what, why? Red alert lights flashed as an alarm was sounding. A search light caught him from a guard tower and a gunshot rang out. Alex felt the bullet whistle past his head and thud into the earth behind him. He was carrying his ball and chain. The ball had spikes and he was trying to hold it so the spikes did not cut into his body. What was going on? How had it come to this? He turned a corner and only just manged to stop on the edge of a huge drop. He teetered there, arms flailing looking down into the depths. There was a body down there. It was torn and twisted. He was fighting to keep from falling as the ball and chain fell from his grasp and dragged him helplessly over the edge down towards the gruesome decomposing corpse…

Alex sat up with a start. His mobile phone was ringing, he had one mother of a head ache and his mouth felt like something small and furry had been sleeping in it during the night. He picked up the phone and answered with a croaky partially, formed hello.

'Hey Mr Croaky! Geez you sound rough. It's Maddie. I've managed to get into Anna's Facebook account and I've sent her mum a request to contact me. I'm hoping she can write in English. You don't know any Lithuanian do you?'

'What do you mean you got into her Facebook account Maddie?'

'I got into her Facebook account.'

'I got that much but—'

'I hacked it you big drip! What do you think?'

'Hacked it! How did you do that? Isn't that illegal?'

'Umm, might be, but hey, I got in and hopefully we'll get a reply today. You didn't know I was a computer whiz did you Alex? I had a proper job in another life you know; I was bloody good at it too!'

'Well that's great, but if this gets found out and the hacking thing, then you're on your own.'

'Oh go boil your head Mr Goody Pants, bye!' Maddie hung up abruptly.

Maybe he hadn't been as encouraging as he could have been reflected Alex still in a waking daze.

'What the hell was that dream about?' he puzzled as he rubbed his eyes; they were gritty and gummed up and he was struggling to keep them open.

'So Maddie is taking this thing seriously then,' he continued talking to himself as he dragged his reluctant frame out of bed. 'What the hell are we getting into here? I don't want to find Anna dead! That's something for the… the police, or something.'

He made his way to the bathroom checking his phone for the time on the way.

'Half past eight! Oooh my head hurts. Shower and breakfast. Come on dude let's get going.'

He thought about a run and then thought again, maybe later.

Sat at the table in the kitchen Alex munched on a bowl of his favourite crunchy cereal in front of his laptop computer. Checking out the images he'd taken the day before, he thought about printing up the best ones and seeing if he could get some interest from the local shops to maybe sell a few. One in particular he was very taken with; a classic Peak District shot with a magnificent sky and a wonderful ocean of saturated autumnal colours, full of mood and character. That's what he hoped the viewer would see anyway.

'Arnold Pinkston,' he muttered to himself, remembering he had probably committed to finding him during the craziness of the night before.

He reflected for a moment. He and Maddie had actually had some fun together. She had poked fun at him a couple of times but not in her usual cutting way. The thing with the fox had been totally spontaneous and they had bounced off each other in a way he wouldn't have expected. She is nuts though, and he couldn't see how they were actually going to get on together through this mad venture she had succeeded in dragging him into. He'd only come here to get away from the painful split with Michelle. What actually was there to go back to now though; where was his life going? He caught himself before his negative train of thought continued its inevitable downward spiral.

'Ok Arnold Pinkston, why not? Let's have a go at finding you matey.' He searched the internet for any clues as to where Arnold may be living but found nothing more specific than near Buxton, in the Peak District. He tried the telephone directory services but nothing. He then looked up local running clubs; maybe someone in a club would know of him.

'Dark Peak Fell Runners; that's got to be worth a go.' It was the top search result after he had added 'fell' to 'running clubs Buxton' in the search bar of the web browser. On the contact page he found a phone number for a guy called Jack Rydalsh, the club chairman. Alex scribbled the name and number on a post it note and contemplated how he would broach the subject of Arnold with this guy Jack.

'Ok, let's give this a go,' he punched the numbers into his mobile and waited.

'Hello,' a voice answered on a slightly crackly line.

'Hello is that Jack Rydalsh?'

'It is yes.'

'Hi, I wonder if you can help me Jack. I'm a photographer and I'm doing a study of personalities in fell running around the country and I've come across an interesting character called Arnold Pinkston. I was wondering if you might know anything about him.'

'Oh that sounds interesting, there've been some real personalities in fell running and I should know, I've known a lot of them…'

It appeared Jack was a talker, as he was soon into anecdote after anecdote about the fell running legends he'd had the pleasure of encountering over the years. Alex voiced surprise and laughed in all the right places in an attempt to gain empathy with Jack.

'...Arnold Pinkston you say. Well Arnold and I go back a long way —'

'You know Arnold then?' Alex interjected with a hopefully excusing excited tone.

'I do indeed. We go back a long way Arnold and I. We travelled together to meets around the country and ran together on many occasions me and Arnold. He was untouchable in his day was the man. Took some of the Lakeland trophys away from under the feet of the locals up in Cumbria there on several of the classic races.'

'Do you still see him Jack?' Alex managed to get another question in as Jack took a breath.

'Not so much these days. You know he's not a well man; I mean he does have some mental health issues I believe they call it these days. Although, he was always a few shillings short of a pound. If you'd seen him running downhill like I did you'd think he had more than a screw loose.'

Alex laughed then quickly cut in, 'Does he still live locally Jack?'

'He does yes, and what did you say your name was?'

'I didn't. Err Bradford,' Alex winced, Bradford, that was a bit shit he thought as he scrambled for a made-up name.

'Brian Bradford's the name. I'm a freelance photographer and I've always had a great passion for fell running, so, wanted to put the two together and make something erm… interesting for… fell runners.'

Bugger! Even more shit he thought anticipating Jack blowing his pathetic cover story.

'Brian Bradford?' Jack pondered a moment.

He'd been rumbled with that feeble, bungling attempt at a made-up name thought Alex as he hung on with teeth clenched in a broad hysterical grin.

'I knew a chap in Kendal called Jim Bradford, chairman of the Fell Farers. You're no relation, are you?'

Alex breathed an audible sigh of relief and clamped a finger to his lips as he composed himself. 'No I'm not I'm afraid. Kendal is a lovely place though isn't it?' He recovered.

'Beautiful surroundings Brian…'

Who's Brian, Alex thought? Oh it's me, you daft sod, he remembered tapping his temple with his finger.

'…but I wouldn't live there these days, that bloody one-way system is a nightmare. I never know which way to go in, either from the north junction of the bypass down the Windermere road or from the south but then you get stuck in the traffic around that daft narrow one way bit in the town centre. Anyway, Arnold, yes he lives in Longnor…'

Thank fuck thought Alex, here we go.

'...You can't miss it Brian. It's the little house in the row as you go out on the Leek road. Just a door and two windows on the front, looks a bit odd, like it's got windows missing. Has a narrow ginnel down the right-hand side and one of them terrible wood effect plastic doors that his son fitted for him a few years back. He's a fine runner himself you know and maybe someone else you should meet. Wouldn't buy plastic windows off of him though, you just can't beat proper wood, can you? How about I get you a spot at one of the club meets to come along and meet some of the old boys and you could bring your camera?'

Alex scribbled down the address details on the back of the post it note he'd used earlier.

'Well thanks Jack that would be brilliant.'

He went to swap his phone into his right hand but realised he had the post it stuck on his hand so grabbed it between his lips. It was now stuck firmly to his bottom lip.

'I'll give you a call on that Jack. Thanks for your help with this it's been a real pleasure talking with you.'

'You are welcome Brian. A pleasure talking with you too. It's always nice to talk about the old days and those characters; you just don't get them in the sport these days—'

'You certainly don't, do you Jack? Good bye then, thanks, bye.' Brian, sorry, Alex hung up and sighed with relief. Nice bloke though he pondered, maybe I should do a photo study of the old boys before they disappear but I'd have to pretend to be Brian bloody Bradford and that would be a bit awkward wouldn't it...

'Well we've found you Arnold Pinkston,' he muttered taking the post it from his mouth and wincing as he took a bit of his lip with it. 'Ouch! You bugger! That really hurt,' he licked it madly trying to ease the pain.

Looking over at the empty cereal packet on the kitchen table Alex decided it was maybe time for a big shop. Rubbing his face firmly with both hands he opened his eyes and mouth as wide as he could in a vague attempt to feel more alive. Walking out to the car still feeling a bit vague he wondered how long it would be before mother swooped in for a surprise inspection and obligatory condemning of his pathetic, underachieving life. He kicked the head off a Dahlia as he passed the pristine border, regretting it immediately, chiding his petty attitude.

Alex surfed the cereal aisle in Morrisons, half collapsed over his trolley. He was pondering his usual breakfast conundrum of which low sugar muesli product could he mix with a more yummy sugary crunchy nutty one when a surprise text alert vibration reminded him where his phone was, in his jeans pocket. It was a text from Ammon.

'Been 2 police station was closed wtf! Newspaper office not much to add. Spoke to reporter who says he is interested if we find anything. Gave me address where Anna was staying but think M knows that. Are we meeting later, where? Ammon'

Alex punched the message in his phone app and chose the call option. The ring tone carried on for some time, time in which he was getting more and more worked up about the contents of the message. Ammon answered with a casual 'Hello'.

'Ammon! What the fuck are you doing going to the police?'

He clashed trolleys with an elderly woman who looked at him startled, presumably by his language and the mention of the police. He composed himself and opened his mouth to continue but Ammon replied.

'I did not see them, they were not there, the place was locked up my friend.'

'Well, good!' Alex scorned back at him. 'We don't want to catch the attention of the police right now do we? They'll be asking all sorts of questions.'

'Do not panic my friend I will not go back to them. Where are you now?'

'I'm in Morrisons in Buxton doing a shop. Where are you?'

'I am in Buxton too. I am going to buy some walking boots if we are to go into the mountains my friend.'

'There are no mountains where we are going, but yes, a decent pair of walking boots would be a good idea. Come meet me in the café here in Morrisons and I'll take you to a good outdoor shop I know.'

'Oh, that would be great, thank you. I am on my way after I get rid of this dog.'

'Dog! What dog?'

'A dog has been following me since I got out of my car. I think I ran over its bone.'

'What! How, do you, why? Oooh, you crazy dude, I'll see you shortly.' Alex shook his head, looked to the heavens and blew his lips out with sheer desperation.

Unloading his shopping onto the belt of the checkout, he looked up to see Ammon walking towards him. Noticing Alex had seen him he waved and smiled, pointing outside through the glass of the supermarket wall. Running alongside Ammon on the other side of the glass was a dog; a dopey looking, loppy footed Spaniel, with its tongue out to one side, glancing intermittently at Ammon as it negotiated people, trolleys and bollards in a quest to follow his every move.

'The dog,' Ammon mouthed, shrugging his shoulders.

Alex shook his head almost imperceptibly in an attempt not to draw any more attention to himself.

'I will go get us some coffee,' said Ammon.

Alex replied, half mouthed and half whispered, 'Yeah, get a table and I'll be with you shortly, cheers,' followed by a quick self-conscious thumbs up.

They sat face to face sipping their coffees in silence for an almost awkward amount of time. Ammon could sense Alex was not in the best of moods, he broke the silence tentatively.

'Have you heard from Maddie today my friend?'

'Yeah, she woke me this morning, from a really disturbing dream actually.'

'Aah dreams my friend, messages from the subconscious. You

should listen to them but consider their meaning with great care.'

'So, being locked up in a dark evil prison and then falling down a deep hole onto a decomposing body. What do you make of that little beauty?'

'Not sure about the prison, but do you have a fear of dead bodies?'

'No more than the next sane, zombie movie loving guy I don't suppose.'

'Aah yes, your culture has sanitized the whole death process for you. Like all the products here, everything is better when it is packaged nice and neat and tidy and the nasty stuff is out of sight.'

'I'd not really thought of it like that, I'd not really thought about it much at all, before my father…' Alex paused.

Seeing a distance appear in his eyes Ammon waited for him to return.

Alex snapped back to the now and replied to Ammon's earlier question.

'Maddie said she'd contacted Anna's mother through Facebook this morning and she's waiting for a reply. She's hoping to find out more about what was going on before Anna disappeared.'

'That is good. Everything we can find out will help build a picture of those final days.'

'I think I probably pissed Maddie off this morning mate. I'm sure she just sees me as some sort of wuss.'

'You two attract and repel each other like spinning magnets my friend. Maybe one day you will learn to spin together.'

'Very deep mate. I don't think spinning is my thing and anyway magnets attract all sorts of scrap metal as well don't they?'

'What do you mean my friend?'

'Erm, I don't know.'

'Ammon. Do you think she's dead and that is her body down that hole and we're going to find it, her?'

Alex and the potential reality of it all had collided somewhere between his ears, in a part of his brain where fear and his spirit of adventure wrestled for supremacy.

'I do not know my friend. If the only thing we do find is the truth then that is something we can give to her family and those who knew her.'

'You're right, we do need to do this don't we?'

'I think we do. It is the right thing to do, for the right reasons.'

'Ok mate drink up, let's go get you a sturdy pair of walking boots.'

5 A STURDY PAIR OF WALKING BOOTS

Ammon left the shop bouncing like a kid in his new boots.

'These are great boots Alex, thank you. You are very knowledgeable about such things.'

'Yeah, bit of an outdoor gear freak I'm afraid. That's a good shop though and they are a bargain at that price, just a shame about the colour.'

'I like green my friend,' Ammon declared marching off in front.

'Yeah, but I've never seen a green like that before. It's the kind of green you'd expect to see in the vomit of someone who's just eaten a cheap artificial Christmas tree. Still, once they're mucked up and worn in they'll be fine.'

Ammon laughed. 'You do say such funny things my friend.'

They walked on in silence for a few moments until Ammon decided to broach what he suspected might be a touchy subject.

'Alex?'

'Yes mate.'

'I am going to call Maddie and see how she is getting on, is that ok?'

'Of course it is, go ahead.'

Ammon put his phone to his ear and waited a few rings before there was an answer. 'Hello Maddie... Yes... Oh right... good... ok... so nothing out of the ordinary then?... No... I will ask him, hold on.'

Alex looked at Ammon anticipating a question.

'Maddie wants to know if we are meeting up today?'

'Erm, yeah, tell her we'll meet at mine at, what time is it now, erm, five-ish?'

'Yes Maddie.... Can you meet us at Alex's place... yeah, you heard that then... yes at about five-ish?... Yes.... Ok see you then, bye... bye. She says she has had a reply from Anna's mother and they could tell her no more than that she stopped contacting them at the time she disappeared. They have been over here and talked with police but have been unable to do anything. Must be so worrying for them my friend.'

'Well I have some good news for both of you. Haven't told you yet have I? I have an address for Arnold Pinkston.'

'Wow! That is great Alex. When are we going to see him?' Ammon was showing his obvious excitement as they approached their cars back on the supermarket car park.

Alex opened his car door. 'Let's talk about that later eh? See you back at mine.' He started into the car but hesitated and climbed back out again.

'Ammon!'

'Yes, my friend.'

'Where's the dog?'

Ammon looked around, relieved but slightly puzzled. 'I do not know. It must have found another bone my friend.'

Alex laughed and pointed homeward. 'See you at mine. Follow me.'

Maddie was already there when they both pulled up outside the cottage; she was leant against the door and looking a little impatient.

'What you boys been up to then?' she quizzed casually. 'That's a lovely sturdy pair of boots you're wearing there Ammon.'

'Yes, thank you. Alex found them for me, at a good price too. Alex has the address for the crazy man who saw the body Maddie.'

'Well we don't know what he saw yet do we?' Alex interjected.

'That's good though. When're we going to see him,' asked Maddie following Alex into the cottage.

'Let's have a brew and talk about that guys,' Alex suggested, grabbing the kettle and filling it under the kitchen tap.

'Have you got some biccies Alex?' enquired Maddie looking around for signs of food storage.

'Er, I have yes. They're in the shopping in the back of the car. Could you make us all a brew while I unload the car, please Maddie?'

'Can do; who's for tea and who's fuckoffee?'

Maddie slammed the drinks down on the kitchen table in front of the boys, sat down and opened the discussion. 'Do we all need to go see Arnold then? That's what I'm thinking to start with.'

Alex nodded in agreement. 'I thought that too, we don't want to overwhelm him do we?'

'I am not sure you know,' started Ammon, 'there is a chance that one of us could get through to him in our own different way.'

'That's a fair point,' conceded Alex.

Maddie shrugged her shoulders. 'Yeah maybe.'

'I'm going to go in my running gear,' Alex announced. 'That just might reassure him and help gain some rapport.'

Ammon and Maddie looked at Alex and then each other with the same "really!" mask they had both ordered and had delivered instantly from masks r us dot com; Maddie broke the silence.

'Let's just all go then. We have no idea what we are up against do we? The guy is nuts by all accounts so we might have to hold him down and beat it out of him.'

'Yeah, ok,' agreed Alex. 'Apart from the beating it out of him bit; shouldn't need to come to that, should it?'

'I think that is the right approach,' Ammon added making it a unanimous decision.

'Ok!' Alex clapped his hands together. 'When - morning, noon or evening?'

'We might have to stake his house out all day to catch him home,' Maddie pointed out.

The guys agreed and a plan was hatched to meet in the morning and drive out to Longnor. They would park up as if they were going for a walk and stake out Arnold's place until they were sure he was home.

Maddie laughed pointing to Ammon's feet. 'You've still got your new boots on Ammon. Are you going to sleep in them?'

'I might do that. I love my new boots, they are so comfortable.'

'Horrible colour though eh?' Alex grimaced.

'Not the best green I've ever seen,' Maddie knowingly rhymed.

This set Alex off into something of a spontaneous rap. 'Well making a rhyme that ain't a crime. But this is a green that's so obscene, if you gave it to a queen she'd scream, and probably dream a dream worse than my dream. Which reminds me… Not told you about my dream have I Maddie? My dream of falling down a hole onto a dead, manky, decomposing body—'

Maddie's face changed in a moment. Alex realised he was probably going to regret, something.

'That body could be Anna. Her parents are beside themselves with worry. Every day that goes by is another day without news. They're torn apart and you, you insensitive bastard!'

'Come on Maddie I was just pratting about. I had a real dream.'

'Fuck your dream you selfish tosser!' Maddie forced her way up from her chair pushing the table towards Alex and trapping him against it. Grabbing her coat she launched out the door and away.

'Oops!' exclaimed Alex in exaggerated wide-eyed surprise.

The guys sat in silence for a few moments.

'That probably was, a bit insensitive wasn't it, thinking about it?' admitted Alex.

'We do have to keep in mind the reality Alex, yes. That body out there could be Anna and that is bad. If it is not her we might never know what happened to her and worse than that her family will never know. And that is bad too. However, I do think Maddie overreacted a little. I think she has some issues that are unresolved for her.'

'We've all got fucked up lives one way or another haven't we,' proffered Alex.

'Life is no more than a series of problems my friend, some small some large. It is how we face them that is the mark of us as a man, or woman. Fucked up you say Alex. There is always a way to overcome the difficult times we find ourselves in. It may be that you do not have either the strength or insight at this time. May you find it my friend, as I know I will find mine'

'Thanks Ammon, wise words. You know, I've got a spare room

here. If you want to move in for a few days and save on your room at the pub?'

'That is very generous Alex but I feel I would be intruding.'

'No you wouldn't. This is a big enough place, there's ensuite bathrooms. As long as we keep the place tidy and clear up before we leave then mother will be none the wiser.'

'Ok Alex, thanks. I shall think very seriously about it. I have paid for the room for tonight so I will let you know tomorrow if that is alright. Thank you, it is very generous of you.'

'You're welcome mate. Another brew? And I'll text Maddie and apologise.'

'Yes, thank you. I would like another tea. Maddie gave me no choice, I would have had coffee, but I am actually liking your Yorkshire tea.'

'Yes I think that was Maddie's way of saying it's tea or nothing mate; fuckoffee indeed eh? Crazy broad.'

'She is a good person though. She has a very good heart'

'She probably is, and does. It's just not been my experience, with her.'

'Are you talking about school days? C'mon let all that go my friend, that is in the past.'

Alex held his arms up in protest. 'Yeah but it's recently as well.'

'That is just her way. It's her way of connecting with you without getting too close, close enough to get hurt again, do you not think?'

'Maybe I don't want to get close to her, she's bonkers mate.'

'That is your choice, while you still have one.'

'What do you mean by that you freaky dude? Anyway, I don't see you being a big hot shot with the ladies. You bumbled over pulling Evelyn, didn't you?'

'Cannot be good at everything, can I? Not everyone in this country sees me as equal my friend.'

'Ok, yeah, that's the world we live in isn't it? My own family don't even see me as an equal.'

'Touché my friend, touché.'

Later, after Ammon had left, Alex slouched back into the sofa, stared at the screen of his mobile phone and started to compose a message to Maddie. He composed and edited and re-composed and re-edited until he had something that he felt did the job.

'Hi Maddie, sorry, was insensitive of me, was just having a laugh. If we are going to get on in this thing we need to be a little more tolerant. Cheers A'. He pressed send and relaxed. Then thought again about the text; was it provocative in any way? Was he going to get screamed at again from a CAPITALISED retort barked out of the phone screen? He didn't have to wait long before his phone chattered and buzzed across the table in silent vibrate mode.

'No laughing matter. Tolerance is 2-way thing'

Well could be worse, he thought. Was it just learnt behaviour from his relationship with Michelle that he was constantly on the defensive? How was he going to respond to Maddie now?

The phone buzzed again in his hand.

'Pick me up tomorrow on the way. Text when setting off'

Alex quickly composed a reply. 'Ok will do. See u then' That was a cop out, he thought. Why bother getting too involved in her head stuff though. He picked up the phone again and looked at the messages.

'Time for bed,' he announced to himself. 'Could be a tough day tomorrow if this crazy dude fell runner ends up giving us the runaround.'

6 THE RUNAROUND

Alex threw his rucksack in the boot of Ammon's car and jumped into the front passenger seat.

'I just texted Maddie to let her know we're on our way. So, back down the lane to the main street and take a left.'

'Ok, hold on tight while I find the right automatic gear my friend'

'Ooooh shit! I forgot about your dodgy driving.'

'Only joking, I have mastered this beast now, I think ha ha.'

Alex laughed but wasn't wholly convinced so adopted a position that was cool yet poised ready to brace at any given moment.

As they arrived at Maddie's place she was walking down the driveway of her not insignificant property towards them. Ammon gasped with surprise.

'Oh my goodness Alex, this place is amazing!'

'Yeah, sorry, forgot to warn you, it's a pretty impressive place isn't it? And the crazy thing is it's all hers now.'

'What! This is all Maddie's home?'

'Yep, her mother died not long back, she's no siblings so all this is hers.'

'No wonder she is going through difficult times.'

'Why's that mate, because she's been left a fortune?'

'You don't get it do you?'

Alex climbed out of the car and dropped the seat forward to allow Maddie into the back of the black, two door, Alfa Romeo Mito. She looked at him with a sheepish smile as she entered the car. He wasn't sure what that was about and decided not to pursue it there and then.

'Your house is amazing Maddie, it is huge,' Ammon declared.

'Yeah, it's too big, in the wrong place and I just don't know what to do with it,' Maddie pleaded.

To which Alex bit his lip, managing to hold back a derogatory comment.

Ammon continued with his show of interest as they pulled away down the lane. 'Do you live in that mansion on your own?'

'It's not quite a mansion thank you Ammon. The housekeeper and her husband live in the cottage on the driveway back there. They're such lovely people. They look after the place and looked after my mother before I came back. The guy, Eric, does everything around the grounds, as well as taking care of the horses, well horse, I've kept one of the horses; he's a real beauty.'

'You were quite a rider at one time, weren't you?' Alex chirped in with a quick glance back over his shoulder.

'Well remembered Alexi-poos. I did pretty well when I was younger yes. Won a few shows here and there. Clyde, my horse, he's an ex hunter, he's just wonderful, I can make him jump anything. What my mother was doing with him I don't know.'

Arriving in Longnor Alex directed Ammon around the village until he recognized the house described to him by Jack Rydalsh.

'Jack was right,' Alex affirmed. 'The house looks like it's got a couple of windows missing. Odd little place crammed in there isn't it?'

'That house would fit in your living room I think Maddie?' Ammon couldn't help but boast.

'Pack it in about my bloody house Ammon and let's get parked up and see if the crazy guy's home,' despaired Maddie impatiently.

Ammon pulled up in a small layby just outside the village and immediately jumped out of the car.

'I am thinking we could probably see the back of the house from over this wall here. Hold on.' He went into the boot of the car and came back with an impressive pair of binoculars that Alex couldn't help but gush over. 'Wow! They're the business. Leica aren't they? Must be at least a couple of grands worth?'

'My father bought them for when we went to the dog racing. I know, a bit overkill but very, very clear image.'

'Did he make enough money at the dogs to warrant buying a pair like that?' Alex enquired.

'I am afraid not my friend, something else we disagreed on.'

Ammon rested his elbow on the wall and brought the binoculars up to his eyes. Maddie impatiently jumped up and down in an attempt to see over the wall that was a little too high for her shorter stature.

'See anything Ammon?'

Ammon fumbled with the binoculars while Alex strained his eyes, shading them with his hands in an attempt to make out any detail.

'Just let me focus and erm... I can see the back of the house very clearly. There is a window; I think it is the kitchen. No movement, no, nothing.'

He surveyed the scene for a few minutes looking for signs of anyone home while Alex continued straining his shaded eyes in anticipation.

'Someone has just walked around the back of the house!' announced Ammon excitedly. 'It is, Maddie!' he exclaimed even more excited.

'What the hell's she playing at?' Alex shrilled in frustration.

'She is waving and shaking her head, I think she means there is no one home. You have got to admire her getting stuck in. She is one who grabs the bull by the horns.'

'Yes, but, I wish she'd let us bloody know which bull's horns she was going to grab and when, instead of making us look like fools.'

'You can only be a fool if you let yourself—'

'Not now thanks mate,' Alex interrupted.

Alex and Ammon gave up their surveillance position and walked back towards the village meeting Maddie on her way back to them.

'Don't start!' Maddie launched into Alex seeing his apparent frustration. 'I'm not pussy-footing around when we can just knock on the bloody door. He's not home so that's that.'

Alex stood open mouthed in despair for an indecisive moment but slapped his hands to his sides restraining an initial reaction.

'Ok, ok, what do we do now then Miss Marple?' jibbed Alex holding his hands up in a symbolic gesture of surrender.

'Tea and cakes anyone? suggested Maddie smugly. There's a little tea shop in the middle of the village.'

'Oh yes Maddie that sounds like a good idea,' agreed Ammon walking off to follow Maddie into the village.

Alex followed on almost reluctantly, feeling a little usurped. She was such a loose cannon, he thought, but, he was going to make an effort today, to keep the peace if nothing else.

They sat around in the tea shop for a while discussing how they could best approach Arnold over a pot of tea and selection of cakes, which Ammon in particular was enjoying.

'Oh, this vanilla slice is so wonderful my friends, mmmm mmmm,' he smacked his lips and licked every morsel from his fingers with moans of pleasure.

Maddie chuckled at him with mild amusement. 'I'm glad your hands are above the table Ammon or I'd be worried by all that noise you're making. I'll go get some more water for the tea boys.'

She wandered off to the counter where it was obvious she had quickly established a connection with the middle-aged woman who had served them earlier. Alex couldn't quite make out what was being said but the woman was gesturing and pointing across the road in the direction of Arnold's house. As Maddie returned to the boys she pointed with both hands at the door and mouthed let's go.

'Arnold has walked passed while we've been in here guys. The lady behind the counter saw him passing with his shopping trolley full of fire wood.'

The boys scurried to their feet and followed Maddie out the door. Alex once again feeling his leadership in this campaign had been undermined by Maddie's intentionally humiliating tactics.

'Ok!' said Alex taking back the reigns. 'I'll make first contact and then we'll see how he responds.'

'First contact?' scoffed Maddie behind her hand. 'Is he an extra-testicle from the planet Ballbag Alex?'

'For Christ's sake Maddie give it up will you? We need to be serious about this and work together, not go firing broadsides when we're alongside each other. You were on at me for making light of stuff last night,' Alex scolded, trying not to allow her to wind him up.

'Ooooo get you Admiral Lord Nelson, kissed any Hardys recently?' Maddie couldn't resist pouring a little more fuel on his fire.

Alex seethed a little inside, although a part of him did want to laugh along with them. Ammon in particular, on the outside was enjoying every minute of it. As they approached Arnold's front door Alex tried to focus his comrades.

'Ok guys let's get it together.' He knocked three times firmly on the door. 'We need to show him we are serious about this,' he continued in a whisper.

'Ok, sorry Alex,' whispered Maddie, so unexpectedly for Alex that he turned to her as the door was opened.

'Ey up mi ducks, what yer after?' A gaunt wild looking character was in their faces no sooner than the door was opened.

Alex turned and flinched at the presence of the man he recognised as Arnold Pinkston, even though he was the best part of 30 years older than any of the images he had seen.

'Hi Mr Pinkston,' Alex started. 'It's a great pleasure to meet you.'

'What is it? Are yer witnesses eh?' probed Arnold raising a dark bushy eyebrow.

'Sorry?' replied Alex puzzled and surprised.

'Are you witnesses, you know, witnesses?' he repeated wrestling his poorly fitting false teeth back into his mouth. 'Witnesses of that Jehovah or some other nutter?' he continued raising his voice to a half-muted shout.

'Oh no Mr Pinkston, we just wanted to, erm, talk to you really.'

'Oh, well that's ok. Call me Arnold then eh?' His tone moderated to a raised whisper.

'What's it you want to talk to me about? That's a sturdy pair of boots lad!' He turned his attention to Ammon on seeing his new boot.

'What colour do you call that then? You're from Egypt, aren't you?' He looked quizzically and waited for an answer.

'I am, yes Mr Arnold—'

'Served over there during my national service boy.' He then followed with a few words in Egyptian Arabic with what sounded to be a convincing accent.

Ammon replied in English, 'My goats are fine thank you Mr Arnold but I have no cigarettes.'

'Good job gave up years ago ha ha,' he cackled then stopped suddenly.

He really is as mad as a bare arsed jockey at a hedgehog rodeo, thought Alex.

'Come through,' Arnold gestured to them to follow him into the house. 'You look like you're all off for walking? You're togged up for a run though aren't you boy?' he quizzed Alex pointing a finger at him.

'I love running, yes. I've read about you and your exploits and I'd love to talk to you more about that, but we're actually here to find out about what we hear you saw out in the Peak recently, if that's alright?'

Arnold paused with a faraway look before launching into a panicked and evasive response, 'Oh you don't want to know about that. They didn't believe me, they never do. They think I'm mad you know. They told me I didn't see anything so I'm not going back there cos I don't want to see what they told me I didn't see. I'm not going back and that's that. Much easier that way isn't it ha ha,' he cackled hysterically for a moment then turned to Alex.

'Do you want to run lad, we could go now if you like?'

At this point Maddie thought she would have a go. 'Sorry Arnold but the girl that went missing, Anna, was a friend of mine and I'd like to know if it was her you saw. It's breaking her mother's heart not knowing.'

'Oh sad it is, so sad missy, I can't say. I can't go back there to see what they say I didn't see though, you see. I know most of round here by the inch but this was off the route in the fog it was. I can't go back there!'

'You don't need to go back Arnold just tell us where and we'll go.' pleaded Maddie.

'Looks grand out there lad. I need a run, are you coming?' Arnold was heading for the door and out of it before they could get another word in. The three of them followed, calling after him.

Arnold turned and shouted over his shoulder, 'There's kettle on't fire and biscuits in't tin for those who don't want to run. Come on let's get up there lad!'

He was off out of the back gate and across the field to a stile over a dry-stone wall, with Alex close on his heels. Ammon and Maddie following an increasing number of paces behind.

Arnold, who Alex thought must be at least in his early seventies, was built like a Whippet. There was still a formidable amount of power there and his effortless style belied a man of his years. Alex was just managing to keep up with him but the others were left way behind and could only stand and watch as the pair galloped off up the fields to the open hillside beyond. Alex was well equipped wearing his trail running shoes but the others with heavy stiff boots were finding the going much harder. Arnold, however, was wearing an old pair of tanned leather work boots. Alex imagined he'd be just as uncatchable in clown shoes. He shouted after him between the deep breaths he needed to keep the oxygen flowing around his body.

'Arnold! You don't have to go back there. We will go, and we'll let you know what we find. I know this troubles you—'

At this Arnold stopped suddenly and turned back towards Alex who careered to a halt just short of him.

'It has boy! It has troubled me. You need to leave it alone though. They say there's nothing there so you won't find anything. What I saw wasn't really there was it?'

'But it was Arnold,' Alex shrieked back, 'You saw it and I believe you.'

Arnold turned and continued running up onto the high moorland. 'Why would you believe me? And if you do, why would you want to go back there and let them tell you there's nothing there?'

Alex struggled hard to catch up and carry on with his plea. 'I'll go back there, because I believe you Arnold, not them, there is a body there,

and someone, loved ones, are missing that person, and they need to know
—'

Arnold stopped and turned again. This time Alex stumbled to a halt
nose to nose with the evidently tormented man.

'I'm not going back there—'

'You don't have to—'

'But I'll tell you where it is boy, I'll tell you where I saw what I
saw,' panted Arnold between his relatively shallow breaths after his jaunt
up the hill.

'Thank you Arnold; you're a good man,' Alex fought to get his
breath back and compose himself.

'You will tell me what you find, won't you boy?' His expression
now sober and lucid.

'I will Arnold, I promise I will.'

Arnold stared into Alex for a few moments and then smiled a warm
crooked smile.

'Right boy!' Arnold postured his race starting position. 'Let's see
how you do on the downhill,' and he was off.

Alex, so pumped from the experience let fly after him, leaping
forward with total focus. Every step felt on the knife edge of a twist or fall.
Flailing arms fought to maintain balance in an ecstatic, exquisite fight for
faultless mastery. In every millisecond his body adapted and adjusted
countless times as if each limb had a mind of its own. Every rapid breath

hit the beat of a footfall. He was flying and the fear he had left behind was never going to catch him now. In fleeting moments, he caught sight of the majestic downhillsman pulling away from him with a beguiling yet comical grace. As Alex crossed the last field towards the rear of Arnold's house the others came into view. With full reverse thrust Alex came to a halt amongst them and immediately dropped to his knees gasping for air.

'Not bad boy,' said Arnold, hands on hips, showing far less signs of his exertion.

Alex could do nothing but roar with adrenaline fuelled fits of laughter as the others joined Arnold in delirious applause.

'Ok guys, you'll be pleased to hear Arnold's going to help us, so, we've got a job to do.'

7 A JOB TO DO

The three friends climbed back into Ammon's car, buzzing from the crazy experience they had just shared. Having parted company with Arnold on the best possible terms, all agreed they had somehow made a connection and most probably a friend.

'So, when are we going to go do this thing then guys?' Maddie asked ominously.

'Right now!' Alex announced with a palpable sense of certainty. 'We're kitted up, there's a reasonable break in the weather, at least for the next few hours, so, let's go.'

Alex gave Ammon directions out of the village and towards the main 'A' road south. 'I'm pretty sure I know the area Arnold was running. Like he says, there's a scattering of shake holes across a hill side off the main footpath. Some of the holes are pretty deep but they're surrounded by bushes and gorse, so unless you know they're there you could walk right past them. That's why it's not been found, I reckon. It was only when Arnold slipped down that slope that he saw into the hole and, well, whatever he saw.'

'He'd have been down there too if he'd not managed to grab that branch,' added Maddie, recounting Arnold's story.

'It sounds, a little unsafe this place Alex?' Ammon questioned sounding slightly nervous.

'We'll be fine. I've brought a short rope just in case.'

Ammon looked puzzled. 'A short rope, what if we need a long rope?'

'It's an outdoor term Ammon, a short rope is a rope you take just to be safe when you venture onto steep ground,' reassured Alex.

'I will tell you now my friends, I am not good with height,' Ammon admitted, raising his hands openly.

Alex frowned with surprise. 'I thought some of your family were circus performers?'

'Not everything in the circus involves swinging from a trapeze! As I say, I cannot be good at everything. I will do what I can, I promise you that.'

'Ok, sorry. Just thought with all your martial arts stuff you'd be—'

'A world class sky diver?' Maddie chirped in. 'He's wearing his winged flying suit under his long johns as we speak aren't you Ammon?

'Winged suit! I can think of nothing more terrifying,' Ammon laughed fearfully. 'Not my idea of fun at all.'

'We are not going to put ourselves in any danger Ammon, I bloody hope not anyway,' said Alex in a final attempt to reassure.

Checking the mapping software on his smart phone Alex guided Ammon to a layby close to the footpath that would take them up onto the hill. The three secured boots, packed rucksacks and readied themselves with a silent sense of foreboding under the already dulling autumn sky. A layer of threatening dark cloud sat thick and heavy on the horizon over which the sun gave a brief but barely warming appearance.

'It'll take us about an hour or so to get there I reckon, so, let's get going. If we don't beat this weather it could be days before we get another chance to put this thing to rest,' said Alex recognising the mood surrounding them.

Marching off along the footpath they snaked their way across the landscape before them, gaining height between trees and rocky outcrops. Once out onto the open hillside the landscape seemed to envelop them in its wildness. From here you could see little sign of habitation even though they knew it was down there, hidden from sight in the dales around them. The terrain became rocky, rough and undulating as they neared the small plateau of high ground where Alex was sure the shake holes could be found.

'Shouldn't be far now. They'll be around here somewhere,' Alex sounded unsure and the others sensed that.

'We could do with finding them soon!' protested Maddie, 'That weather is getting closer and there's a mist building up below us in the dale.'

'We'll be fine, it'll be nowt but a bit of a shower if anything,' said

Alex attempting to laugh off their concerns. 'Let's head off the path here, looks promising over there. Arnold sure likes his challenging terrain eh?'

They carried on through a gap in some gorse bushes where Alex stopped on the edge of a sizable hole and pointed down.

'What! Is it down there?' squeaked Ammon.

'No! Well I can't see anything down this one anyway. Come and have a look. These things are formed when the roof of an ancient underground river collapses, so some are really deep with steep sides. This one isn't very deep.'

After convincing themselves that there was nothing to be seen below, they followed Alex onwards through the undergrowth. A slight breeze roused the still air and began lifting the low cloud up out of the dales, fanning it in wispy clumps across the hill top. The darkening sky was becoming as big a threat as the certainty of seeing the body lying in the bottom of one of these holes but Alex pushed them on.

'We have got to find something guys, we can't leave now. We have to know one way or the other. Are you two ok?'

'How many more of these holes are there Alex?' Maddie's tone was edged with apprehension.

'There's a couple more but—' Alex stopped and pointed down a slight bank to a hawthorn lined edge. 'Look, someone's slipped down here.'

There was an obvious mark were a booted foot had slid down the slope gouging an arc into the soft clay surface. Three knowing gazes met realising the fear, shock and excitement of the moment.

'This is just what Arnold described Alex!' Ammon voiced low, resonating a deep felt dread.

Alex made a careful way down the slope, keeping a firm grasp on the thickest branches of the scrub. Finding a solid stance near the edge of the drop off Alex looked back at his friends with glazed trepidation in his eyes. The gathering cloud and dark skies gave the scene a far more sinister atmosphere than Alex had anticipated. Would this be easier on a bright sunny day? he mused to himself. This place had a presence that would probably always conjure up an uncertain ambience but today their heightened senses tingled with fear of the unknown. Slowly Alex turned to look down into the depths of the hole some sixty feet or so. He strained his eyes to see through the damp swirling mist and waited a few moments for a clear view of the void below.

'Shit, shit, shit!' came his stifled squawk. 'There's something down there and it's a body. It is a freaking body, oh shit!'

Maddie and Ammon could only look on, gripped with shock.

'We've got to be sure, we've got to be sure,' repeated Maddie. 'We need to know if it's Anna.'

She edged forward to where Alex was braced. He offered her his hand and helped her to a position on the edge where she too could safely look down. He grasped her jacket firmly and turned to Ammon with a fearful grin. Maddie peered down nervously for a few seconds trying to make sense of the scene below.

'What can you see Maddie? Is it a woman? Could it be Anna?'

74

probed Ammon.

'It's difficult to make out from here. The body looks to be jammed down between some fallen rocks. I can't make out the head. That's slumped down below the body. It's dressed in outdoor gear, a light blue windproof top, I think it is, with grey pants.'

'Did Anna have those clothes Maddie?' asked Ammon.

Maddie did not answer just looking back; eyes filling with fear and dread.

'Ok, we need to get down there,' announced Alex in a reluctant tone. 'Let's have a look around this hole and see if there is an easy way down. You two go that way and I'll go this—'

'No! We stick together,' Maddie cut in firmly disagreeing.

'Ok,' conceded Alex. 'Let's go this way. Take care over these slippery rocks guys.'

They navigated around the feature which was mostly obscured by masses of thick hawthorn and gorse, until they were nearly opposite their previous position. Here the edge was more exposed with fewer plants and just rock underfoot. Alex edged forward on his hands and knees to get a view downwards.

'We're actually on an overhanging section here,' he reported. 'The ground falls away under us. I can see a possible bit over to the right where it's lower down; looks like we might be able to climb down there. Can't make anything out from here at all, it's hidden behind rocks.'

The swirling mist had thickened as the breeze picked up over the high ground. Dark clouds had now moved overhead and drops of rain began to fall with the odd thud on their jackets. As they fought their way through the thick gorse and undergrowth to get to the spot Alex had identified, a rumble of distant thunder ridiculously added to the already building tension.

Ammon looked up at the sky and over to the horizon in the direction of the crash. 'I do not believe it, we are going to get caught in a raging thunder storm now my friends.'

'It's ok mate; we are prepared, aren't we? You've both got good waterproofs haven't you?' asked Alex checking them both head to toe.

'Let's get this done,' rallied Maddie. 'I don't want to leave until we know if that is Anna. Please let it not be.'

Alex and Ammon agreed turning and nodding to each other. Wading on, parting the bushes around them, they made their way to the lower ground at the southern edge of the hole. The foliage, now wet and cold with the rain, spattering them as they passed. Ahead, Alex pushed through a gap into a small clearing. The others followed through and they stood together scanning the precipitous chasm before them. From here they could just see the body lying between two fractured rock sections. Alex beckoned to Ammon for the binoculars and surveyed the scene.

'I can't see much more from here. We are going to have to get closer'. Alex shrugged off his rucksack and dropped it in front of him. Pulling out a rope he began to coil it onto the ground.

'I can climb down this bit in front of us, it looks pretty easy, but I'll fix the rope then I can be sure of getting back up safely. Who's coming with me?'

Ammon and Maddie looked down at the route Alex pointed out. It was a pretty easy down climb of about thirty feet with a reassuring twisted tree root handrail about halfway down.

'If you're ok Ammon I think we should all go down there,' suggested Maddie.

'No, you two go down, I will stay here, that is the most sensible thing to do I think.'

Alex and Maddie exchanged a nodding glance and agreed it would be sensible to have someone stay up top. Fixing the rope to two well rooted hawthorns Alex threw the rope over the edge. The rain was getting squally and heavier now as the wind began to whistle amongst the undergrowth, whipping smaller branches to and fro almost urging them onwards with its irregular thrashing rhythm. Alex made his way down the rocky wall with reasonable ease and waited at the bottom looking up to guide Maddie down.

'Take care Maddie; it's a bit slippery on some of the wet limestone.'

As she neared him he held up a hand to steady her down the last tricky few steps. She paused uncertain of where to place a foot next. Before Alex could stop her, she dropped a foot down towards a loose rock which gave way, her foot slid down as she desperately sought to find grip. Losing her balance, she teetered backwards violently. Alex stood firm and thrust his hand up to push her into the rock. His hand connected with her behind as she managed to grab a good hold and regain her balance. She looked down at Alex, sighed with relief and grinned.

'You can remove your hand from my butt now if you like, thanks.'

Alex looked away self-consciously, 'Erm, sorry, yes. Are you ok now?'

Maddie found her footing and continued to the rock-strewn floor of the hole as Alex started to make his way towards the body looking back to be reassured Maddie was following him. The body was slightly above them now with the floor dropping away to the centre of the hole. It was clear that they would only get full sight after they were able to see over the rock section that stood between them and it. Alex waited for Maddie to catch up with him before venturing further. Stood side by side they looked at each other knowing the possible horror that was just a few feet away. Maddie grasped Alex's arm as they shuffled forward both trembling with fear. Maddie covered her face breathing heavily.

'I pray it's not her, Alex,' she whispered cutting through the paralysing fear they shared.

Alex looked back at her and said nothing.

They edged forward and peered horror stuck into the void. The death ridden body was twisted in its rocky tomb. It was obvious from the skin visible that decomposition was well advanced. A sweet smell of decay hit their nostrils but thankfully the gusting wind diluted its intensity. The right arm and a left leg were obviously broken and long dried blood stains covered the clothing. A gaping wound on the back of the head was deep and empty. Something had been feeding from the remains of this wretched corpse as nature took its course.

'It's not her Alex, it's not Anna.'

'No, it's a guy isn't it, I think.'

'I'd say so yes. Can you see the face?'

Alex slowly moved along towards the head to get into a position to better see the face. Looking back at Maddie, his expression gave away his fear and anticipation. He ducked down to take a look, rearing back immediately before turned away to retch.

'Oh God, it's horrible. Oh my God Maddie, don't look please. It's a guy, yes, middle-aged maybe. I think he's been here for a good while.'

He stood arms wrapped around himself, shaking with the horrific sight seared in his mind. The face was that of a man, his facial hair matted in dried blood, skin torn and dry and the eyes pecked out as if by a feeding bird. Hearing Ammon shouting he looked up, his face pale and horror filled.

'Is it her Alex? Is it Anna?'

Alex raised his hands to his face in an attempt to project his reply. 'No, It's not her. It's not Anna. It's a guy Ammon, it's a guy.'

Maddie grabbed Alex's arm and ushered for them to go. 'Come on Alex, let's get out of here and call the police. Come on.'

Suddenly a flash of lightning forked across the sky overhead, accompanied by a thunderous crash that shook them both to the core. Alex raised his eyes to the heavens as a torrential downpour followed.

'Oh come on!' he screamed skywards. 'How much more fucking

dramatic do you want to make this scene, you bastards.'

Maddie laughed in hysterical agreement gripping his sleeve tightly for support.

'Photographs!' shouted Alex stumbling back to the body while grappling his phone from his pocket. He hastily took a few shots from different angles before making his way back to Maddie.

'The police have got to believe us now, and Arnold. They owe him some sort of an apology, I reckon.'

On returning to the rock face Maddie grabbed the rope and with Alex's help made her way back up to Ammon. It was hard going in the pouring rain with the smooth limestone now treacherously slippery. They were glad of the rope, without which the climb back up could have been a very different task. Both back up and safe, Ammon pulled the friends together in a group hug. There wasn't much to say now, Alex's face said everything until Ammon looked out from under his hood, shivering.

'My waterproof jacket is not waterproof,' he complained. 'There is a waterfall flowing down my back. Not very pleasant my friends.'

Alex shook his head and smiled briefly, 'Let's get going then mate. We'll phone the police when we get back to the car.' He stooped forward, hands on knees, trying desperately to spit out the taste of vomit from his mouth. 'Come on,' he repeated, dragging himself up and onwards.

Ammon and Maddie followed Alex in a short procession back to the main path and away down the hillside to easier ground. The rain didn't cease as the cool autumn evening closed in around them. It was almost dark when they reached the car; they quickly scrambled in, thankful to get out of the weather.

'Anyone fuckoffee?' offered Maddie tearfully producing a metal flask from her bag.

'So that is actually coffee then is it Maddie,' enquired Ammon.

'It is actually coffee yes, but it's decaf, with full fat milk and demerara sugar, so if you don't like that you're stuffed,' asserted Maddie as she produced two more cups whilst choking back more tears.

'Thanks, that was very thoughtful of you,' said Alex. 'Are you ok?'

'Yes, thank you Maddie, that is much appreciated,' agreed Ammon. 'I'm so sorry you had to see that, but at least now we know.'

Alex sighed deeply, covering his eyes in shivering recall, 'That poor guy, Jesus. We need to get this reported to the police as soon as possible. I suggest we go to the nearest police station, now, and report it in person. They're probably gonna have loads of questions. So, let's get it done and over with.'

They all agreed that Alex's suggestion would be the best course of action, hopefully allowing them to put this episode behind them.

Ammon whacked the heater on full blast, directed the ventilation to the mist covered windscreen and revved the engine as he waited for the screen to clear. Maddie pulled herself up forward between the front seats and sniffled back her obvious emotions.

'We still have a big question to answer, where the hell is Anna?'

Alex took a last gulp of coffee and handed the cup back to Maddie. 'I'm afraid, that, might now, be a matter for the police.'

8 A MATTER FOR THE POLICE

Alex pushed open the door of the police station. It had a particularly heavy
return mechanism, so, what had started as a one-handed push became an
unexpectedly awkward one hand and a shoulder.

'Bloody stupid thing,' he muttered under his breath, holding the
door open for Ammon and Maddie, who both entered silently and headed
for the reception desk. Leant on the counter was what Alex suspected to be
a desk sergeant, wearing a vague smirk on his face; as though one of his
only pleasures in life was to watch people struggle through that ridiculous
door.

'And what can I do for you this evening madam?' he enquired with
a quiet, questioning policeman's tone.

'We've come to report that we've found a body, of a man, at the
top of a hill, in the Peak.'

They had agreed that it would be Maddie who fronted the initial
interaction at the police station; from there they would play it by ear.

'Ok madam, and who found this body and when?' he replied,

turning a page in his report book.

'We did, all three of us were there when we found the body, about an hour ago.'

'About an hour ago,' reflected the officer. 'So, four thirty then. Can I have all your names and addresses please?'

They each gave the officer their details in turn before he returned to questioning.

'Has life extinct been declared on this body madam?'

Maddie screwed up her face looking puzzled. 'Erm what do you mean, sorry?'

'Can we confirm that the gentlemen in question was indeed deceased madam?'

At this point Alex saw fit to intervene. 'I'd hope so. His eyes had been pecked out and his face was hanging off.' Alex recognized his attitude could have been seen to be a little confrontational so he took a breath and attempted to rein it in. 'Sorry, yes, he was definitely dead and has been for some time.'

'Can you be certain of that sir?' challenged the officer dryly with a deep analytical stare.

Alex lost it this time. 'Yes, I'd say so. His deodorant had definitely stopped working some time ago and he's got a big hole in the back of his head. So I'd say that's pretty dead wouldn't you?'

'Can I remind you sir where you are and the seriousness of this incident, there is no place for insolence sir—'

Alex jumped in looking increasingly stressed. 'Look, I'm not a bloody doctor but I think I can tell a dead body when I see one and this guy is definitely dead!'

'Now sir I appreciate you have just had a very nasty experience, and we will be able to help you with that, we can organize some counselling for you, but, can we try to stay calm here sir?'

'Yes, sorry, it was pretty horrific actually, yes, I'm just a bit stressed I suppose. Sorry.' said Alex taking a few more deep breaths and trying to compose himself.

'Thank you sir. Now, how and where did you come upon the body of the deceased gentlemen?'

All three launched into answering the question at the same time; emptying their heads at different tangents and caring not if they were speaking over each other and fighting to make their version heard. That was until Alex stopped them with an exclaiming and challenging,

'What the…?'

The officer looked quizzically at each of them in turn. In those moments they all recognised their little team had become a sum less than its parts, with the testing time bringing out the worst in them.

'Arnold Pinkston and Anna, I heard from that cacophony,' summed up the officer calmly.

Alex's heart dropped into his shoes. He had told them not to mention Anna for fear of being accused of interfering in an ongoing police inquiry with the undoubted repercussions that could have.

'I assume you are referring to Anna Bartosz, the girl who went missing a couple of months ago? Am I right?' the officer continued.

Maddie answered indignantly. 'Yes, we heard about the body and thought it might be her.'

The officer braced himself with both hands against the counter. 'You do understand that this missing person enquiry is ongoing and a matter for the police—'

'So why haven't you investigated the sighting of a body by Arnold Pinkston then?' snapped Maddie rubbed by his condescending tone.

'I'm sure that that line of enquiry is being followed up madam,' started the officer somewhat taken aback.

'So why is the body still there and Arnold left feeling like a gibbering idiot, Mr Policeman?' relaunched Maddie.

The officer took a moment before replying in a calm but officious tone. 'I'll thank you not to take that tone madam. I cannot comment regarding an ongoing enquiry. Now, let me take some more details regarding the finding of the deceased gentleman and we'll see if the Detective Inspector would like a word with you regarding Anna.'

'So, your Detective Inspector's going to give us a good telling off is he, for interfering? When you plods haven't got any hope of finding Anna cos you're too busy leaving bodies lying around the Peak for others to find!'

'Maddie! Give it up,' Alex interrupted forcefully through gritted teeth. 'We're probably in enough trouble as it is.'

'Thank you sir. I would be grateful if you took the advice of your friend here madam. Again, I accept that you've had a deeply unpleasant experience, so, I will overlook your outburst this time.'

Alex's head was now throwing all sorts of outcomes into his overheated and near exploding melting pot. Anna's disappearance, following up on Arnold's sighting, getting involved in an ongoing police investigation, finding the hideous corpse and now Maddie blabbing her way into who knows how much trouble. Why had he gone along with all this?

The officer continued the questioning, taking down all the relevant information as well as Alex's description of the location and the grid reference he had taken from his GPS enabled sports watch. Maddie said nothing more throughout the proceedings, but Alex could almost feel her lining up the big guns ready to drop some serious ordinance down onto him. He didn't care, after this escapade he was done with her and all this nonsense she'd dragged him into.

They all looked on as the officer finished up his notes, collating and aligning them with a double tap down on the counter top. 'Take a seat please, while I see if the DI is free to see you,' he said picking up a phone and dialling a short internal number. He spoke at some length before putting the phone down and continued with his paperwork.

Alex, Ammon and Maddie sat silently on purple vinyl bench seating, staring forward, each conscious not to catch the eye of the others. Moments later a door opened and in walked a portly, shabbily suited, middle aged man with a thick black 'tash. He looked over at the three sorry states sat side by side and breathed a deep audible breath.

'I'm Detective Inspector Andy Fell, would you follow me please?' His voice was low with a rising inflection. This wasn't a question it was an order. He led them to a small grey room a short distance down the corridor from the front desk. Holding the door, he beckoned them in with a nod. The room was empty except for a table and four chairs. Instructing them to take a seat he sat down behind the desk placing a report sheet in front of him.

Alex had never really been in trouble with the police before, certainly not since he was a youngster and then it was a stern telling off by the local bobby for scrumping apples or drinking with mates in the local meeting places, so this was an unknown and concerning situation.

The D.I. sat eyeing them for a few moments with his hands clenched on the desk in front of him. 'So, what questions do you have for me?' he started.

Maddie looked at the others before venting her displeasure, arms folded across her body. 'What are we in here for would be a good one to start with?'

A tiny smirk appeared on one side of the D.I.'s rubbery pot marked face. 'Potentially, Ms Gresham, there is a case to answer for interfering in an ongoing police investigation. Now, personally at this time I don't think I have any cause for concern, but if you persist in this private investigation of yours at some point you could land yourselves in some trouble. Am I making myself clear?'

They all nodded in agreement recognising this was probably getting off lightly.

'I appreciate you reporting the finding of the body. That must have been a pretty shocking experience for you all.'

'I did not get close to the body sir,' offered Ammon, 'Maddie and Alex saw the horror up close.'

'Thank you, Ammon, is it?' the D.I. replied looking down at the report.

Ammon nodded.

'There are counselling services available if you feel you need any help there?' he glanced at each of them in turn, seeing no reaction. 'I'll take that as a no for now then?'

Maddie cleared her throat. 'Can you just answer for me why you didn't take Arnold Pinkston's reported sighting of a dead body seriously?'

'I'm not aware of the full story surrounding that issue Ms. Gresham, but, Arnold has reported many bizarre things over recent years and I guess it was fobbed off as another of his eccentric ramblings. As it transpires in this instance it would appear there was some truth in his sighting, an issue I will ensure is looked into.'

'And what progress have you made finding Anna?' Maddie continued now with Alex's growing approval.

'Off the record Madeline,' he leant forward to emphasize his candid intention, 'as we say in these situations, we have very little to go on at this time. Forensics found no obvious leads and any evidence trail has gone cold. This often happens with a missing person case, but, to me, I'll admit, this feels a little more sinister, with all her possessions being left behind in her lodgings. What I don't want is you lot doing a Scooby Doo on me and compromising a police investigation. If you know anything or find anything you come to me straight away, is that clear?'

They all nodded in unison.

'Ok, I've nothing more to say about this episode, so, if you have no more questions get out of my sight and behave yourselves. Somehow I don't think I've seen the last of you lot.'

As they stood to a symphony of scraping chair legs Alex took up the offer of more questions. 'I think we would like to know what you find out about the guy we found today, if that's possible?'

'I will make sure that happens Alex, as soon as we have an identity we'll let you know. Rest assured there will be a recovery team out there at first light to collect the remains of this poor soul.'

The D.I. led them out into the station foyer and nodded a goodbye as he walked off down the corridor.

The three wandered back out to the carpark and into the still darkness of the enveloping night. It had stopped raining and the clear, damp air demanded you fill your lungs, especially after being cooped up in the stuffy police station. The relief of getting through the proceedings without any significant consequences had brought them back together somewhat; although they walked back to the car in silence.

Ammon slammed his door and turned to the others. 'Well that was not too bad was it my friends?'

'Could have been worse,' assessed Alex.

'Could have been much worse,' acknowledged Ammon starting the car and manoeuvring out of the car park.

'Did you get that guy's name?' Maddie giggling hysterically from the back seat before launching into a comedic routine with the addition of a gruff manly voice. 'What do you think happened to this poor soul then sergeant?' Her voice changing to play another character. 'Well sir, I think he was walking along the cliff edge, got too close, Andy Fell. How ridiculous is that?' She continued in fits of laughter. 'And he fell, do you get it?'

The guys couldn't help but join in, Alex feeling more relaxed now and questioning his reluctance not to be more assertive in the interview situation. They had done a good thing, but now it had to end before they got into serious bother. He was still annoyed with Maddie after her revealing everything he had told them not to mention but was not wanting a confrontation right now. Maddie had also withdrawn the big guns, feeling she'd got something of a result with the D.I..

'Chippy tea!' shouted Ammon braking hard and pulling up alongside the pavement. 'Anyone for chippy tea? I am starving.'

Alex simulated peeling himself off the windscreen and shook his head. 'You could have given us a bit of warning mate.'

'Yeah you twonk,' Maddie concurred. 'I think the G-force has detached my boob implants.'

Ammon's face contorted showing fear and surprise. 'Oh, my God Maddie I am so sorry, you really have —'

'No! I was pulling your big fat stupid leg,' Maddie cut in with deflating vex. 'Now go get me fish-cake, chips and peas, this place does brilliant fishcakes.'

Alex laboured his way out of the car in fits of laughter before flipping the seat up to let Maddie out of the back.

Ammon stood in the queue at the counter of the fish and chip shop, while Alex and Maddie stood outside gazing in through the large glass window. It was obvious that Ammon was feeling a little self-conscious being spectated on by the pair outside, who were apparently sharing a humorous exchange at his expense. In reality their joke was purely to make him think just that, as they giggled at his cute sideways glances.

Sitting on the wall outside the shop they opened their individual packages of take-away food.

Alex took a big sniff of the steam rising from his meal. 'Mmm wonderful, fish and chips out of a paper wrapper, a treat indeed eh?'

'Never taste as good as they smell though, do they?' reported a mildly disappointed Maddie.

'It is not a fine Hawawshi or a Kushari but it is very good my friends,' Ammon lamented gazing up and left at a past food memory.

'Don't even start telling us what's in those concoctions mate,' squirmed Alex. 'Camel's eye balls perhaps, or maybe Lizard's gizzards and goats' bollocks?

'Not at all my friend,' chuckled Ammon. 'I would love to take you to my home land, the food is wonderful, we should do that one day yes?'

They all agreed that would be a great thing to do at some time in the future. Alex pondered a moment, struggling to see that scenario played out before shrugging it off and changing the subject.

'When are we going to see Arnold then, to put him right about the nonsense with the police?

'No time like the present,' suggested Maddie.

Alex tutted loudly. 'Not now Maddie, it's been a long enough day hasn't it?'

'If we do not do it now my friend, we may never find the right time, and his house is on the way back is it not?' proposed Ammon logically.

'Out-voted again,' despaired Alex hanging his head.

'Out voted, out gunned and outed as a closet... banana,' laughed Maddie not quite able to finish with a fitting punchline.

Alex retorted in an indignant posture. 'If you are inferring I am yellow and bent madam, then look no further than my gay Chinese friend Chui mi Wang.'

Ammon looked on confused as Maddie seeing the joke giggled furiously. 'That is awful and homophobic, you cretin.'

'As though you could forget Maddie, one of my best mates at school, Adam, was gay and he had the wickedest gay jokes I have ever heard.' regaled Alex in his defence.

At that Maddie jumped up and headed for the car. 'Come on gents, let's go see Arnold before I say something I will probably not regret.'

Alex recognised her sarcasm. 'Questioning my sexuality, no doubt Ms Gresham?'

'I can tell you that if you were hermaphrodite it would be much easier for you to go do what I'm going to suggest you do next, so come on get in the car,' scolded Maddie.

'Both sex organs eh, now that would be novel wouldn't it Ammon?' posed Alex.

Ammon flinched and shuddered. 'That is just so weird my friend, what if your thingy was not long enough?'

'Just get in the car!' shouted Maddie.

It wasn't long before they arrived outside Arnold's odd little house in Longnor. Through the downstairs window, fire light flickered around the small living room, the undrawn curtains exposed little in the otherwise darkened interior. Approaching the front door, the three friends paused, waiting for each other to take on the job of knocking. Alex finally stepped forward proffering three sharp raps on the questionable wood effect plastic door. A vague cursing voice could be heard, probably expressing displeasure at the interruption. This was followed by the clomp of footsteps on wooden floorboards as the protestor approached. Looking at each other a little puzzled, the three callers stepped back in anticipation of some potential fireworks. The surprise came as the door was tentatively opened by not Arnold but a stout grey-haired lady whom both Alex and Maddie immediately recognised. It was the landlady of a pub they used to frequent in their early drinking days, a larger than life character known locally and fondly as Crazy Claire.

9 CRAZY CLAIRE

'Claire!' exclaimed Alex and Maddie almost simultaneously.

The bewildered lady peered out at the seemingly unfamiliar shadowy faces. 'Oh, hello, I recognise the both of you, bit more grown up but you know me, I never forget a face. Are you after Arnold? He's just helping me pickle some garlic from the allotment. Come on in and check out the old hunk in his Great British Bake Off pinny.'

Alex had to chuckle after noting Ammon's expression of surprise, his eyebrows locked at the upmost extreme. His mind flitted back to the first time he'd been out to the Red Well Inn where Claire, at that time, was the landlady. She had always been loud and jolly and Alex remembered at first exposure a bit annoying. It hadn't taken long for him to warm to her as almost everyone ultimately did. A lot of the girls saw her as a mother figure, always there with her down to earth and more often than not amusing agony aunt advice. When serving behind the bar she never stopped talking to someone or anyone, with her crazy observations and playful ribbing.

The gang followed Claire into the narrow hallway and onwards towards the kitchen.

'Are you still at the Red Well Claire?' asked Maddie.

'Oh no, not been there for a few years now my dear. It's a Beefeater or one of those damned awful places now you know, bits of shoe leather masqueraded as steak in a swamp of watery gravy and frozen packet veg. Bloody rubbish if you ask me.'

Stepping into the kitchen, there as promised was Arnold, pinny and all, intently gazing at an array of jars as he carefully filled each of them with pickling vinegar.

'Be with you in a mo,' he said from the depths of concentration. 'Just one more jar to do.'

'Look at him,' chuckled Claire. 'The Albert Einstein of the pickling world. He'll solve some of the unexplained mysteries of the universe one day he will, string theory; more like string vestigations, if the moths don't get there first that is.'

That's why she's called Crazy Claire, Alex reflected to himself unable to stop laughing, along with the others.

'You crazy woman,' poked Arnold surfacing from his absorbing task.

'That makes a matching pair then don't it my love,' jibbed Claire grabbing Arnold and kissing him on the top of his head. 'Now do these people want some tea and cake? It's experimental is the cake, prune and custard Bakewell tarts. You won't find them in Mr Hollywood's cookery books I'll tell you that for sure.'

All agreeing to tea Claire shuffled over to the sink to put the kettle on, creating a gap in the conversation that Alex thought he'd better grasp while he could.

'Arnold, I said I'd come back when we had some news. So, I'm here to let you know that you did see something in that hole, it was a body, but it wasn't the missing girl we thought it might be.'

'Oh, dear Lord,' burst in Claire. 'It was you three who've been to check out the sighting then was it?'

Arnold clasped his hands to his head. 'I knew I'd seen something down there and they said I hadn't, I wish I hadn't though. Who was it young fella, do they know?'

Alex shook his head. 'No, they don't, not yet, they did say they would let me know when they do. It was a middle-aged man, he'd been there for quite a while too.'

'Oh, you poor souls having to see that sort of thing, how horrible,' consoled Claire putting her arms around Maddie and Alex and gesturing Ammon to join them.

Arnold looked dejected but ratified. 'They'll maybe think on and listen to me next time then eh?'

'Yes, my love,' began Claire softly. 'But not if it's on one of your major fruitcake days though eh? I wouldn't trust you with a damp flannel in a hall of mirrors on one of them days, love you as I do you crazy old cockerel.'

'I've been better since we hooked up though, haven't I love?' said

Arnold with a huge grin on his face.

'Yeah, good food and a drug cocktail sees you right most days doesn't it my love, when you remember to take the bloody things that is,' she confessed rolling her eyes at him.

Maddie was clearly appreciating Claire's sense of humour. 'How long have you been together?' she asked.

'Oooh, about six years now I'd say,' replied Claire rocking back on her heels to do the maths. 'Don't live under the same roof as the old codger most of the time though. I've been living above the Pack Horse Inn down the road in Crowdecote since I left the Well, you'll find me behind the bar there most days. Actually, I've been looking for a pub for me and him to run but the brewery hasn't come up with anything yet. Anyway, what have you kids been up to since I last saw you?'

Alex and Maddie recounted their potted histories to Claire's ever probing questions, revealing as much to each other as they did to her. During the process Alex came to the rather depressing conclusion that his autobiography would make pretty dull reading. University, freelance photographer, failed relationship and back here, not the windswept and interesting profile he'd dreamt of as a teenager drinking with his mates down at the Red Well Inn. He had travelled for work and there had been several foreign holidays but nothing he considered as a real adventure. Tuning back in to Maddie's story he began to consider where his safe little existence had actually taken him. Maddie's life on the cutting edge of software development with regular trips to Japan and America made him feel even more inadequate.

'…I just loved Japan, It's the most amazing place. We made some great friends there and they introduced us to the culture and ceremony around food and hospitality, it's just so cool…'

To be fair Maddie's stories and enthusiasm made interesting and entertaining listening, with Claire being more than willing to absorb her experiences. Note to self, thought Alex, make the rest of my life more interesting than what has gone before, travel more, do more – stuff, maybe even try sushi. How had Maddie come to this modest here and now after the glamour of her past life he questioned? It was then he began to see the similarities between them, two drops of rain landing on the same window pane before running down side by side with the possibility they may collide and become one. Where did that come from? Joining up as one with that crazy mare, really? Anyway, he consoled himself, we all end up in the puddle at the bottom that evaporates back into the atmosphere to fall again as another life of limitless potential and missed opportunities. Note to self, try to be a little more optimistic. Baggage came to mind, he'd actually lived long enough to collect baggage in his risk averse, responsibility shy existence. A sequence of personal life traumas combined with unresolved issues from his unstable youth stacked high like suitcases on a wobbly airport trolley. Where one significant bump on the precarious tiled floor of life could bring the whole lot down on top of him. He huffed loudly into the midst of the ongoing conversation and noticed it. He looked around the room where everyone had stopped to stare at his apparent ignorance.

'Oh sorry, I was miles away, do carry on Maddie, sorry.' He shrunk away embarrassed but seemed to have got away with it. He'd been so proud of his splurge of analogies that he'd drifted off into his own little world. He was nodding, acknowledging and reflecting now as he followed the conversation. From Maddie's scowl it appeared he'd swung too far the other way and was overcompensating, he needed to reset.

'Sorry, can I use your bathroom please Arnold?'

'Upstairs or out in the yard lad. Light for the outside is on the left side of the back door there,' said Arnold pointing towards the back door.

Out in the yard sounded like the way to go thought Alex, a breath of fresh air would help get his head straight. The outside toilet door creaked open loudly for its diminutive size, revealing a small room adorned with fell running photographs crammed in around the walls. Pointing his manhood to the porcelain, Alex browsed the array of fading images all featuring a youthful Arnold leaping down hillsides, breaking through tapes and holding trophies. Captured moments from times gone by, etched by light bounced from every surface in a scene onto celluloid film behind the all-seeing eye of a camera lens. A strict chemical process to follow, modestly reproduced the spectrum of black to white in every grain of information. Ephemeral, frozen reality in little windows to the past. Images like this always held Alex spellbound, it was what had drawn him so magnetically into photography. He was good but he knew what brilliant looked like, he skirted it on occasions, although top level consistency and the eye of a real master eluding him in his quest for true recognition.

When Alex returned to the others, they had retreated to the living room, basking in the light of a huge wood burning stove set back into a stone-built inglenook fireplace.

'Lovely stove Arnold.'

'It's a beauty isn't it lad?' was Arnold proud response. 'I got my way on that one didn't I love?'

Claire frowned and shook her head, 'He did as well you know. I'd seen this smashing modern looking thing with one big door, he said I'm not having that monstrosity, didn't you love?'

'I bloody did an' all. I like to have the doors open like it is now,' he pointed at the stove, doors flung back exposing the heart of the warming fire. 'Imagine it with one door, pig ugly is what I say, like a sow with one ear. What do you reckon lad?'

Alex sniggered uncontrollably. 'I totally agree Arnold, brilliant. How could I ever buy a stove with one door after that.'

Claire obviously tickled by the recollection, burst into uncontrollable fits of laughter, shrieking out repeated snippets of a sentence she strove to put together. A contagion took hold with everyone, as laughter filled the room, subsiding then building again out of nowhere, sparked by another shriek from Claire as she tried desperately to compose herself. A snigger from Arnold was enough to set her off again or his gurning face peering around the wing of his chair. In the silent recuperative time after the storm of laughter, Alex sat back feeling incredibly relaxed. It wasn't just the warmth from the fire he felt but the warmth of the good people they were sharing time with, unusual but special. Few things can have more impact on your soul than the simple company of friends he conceded. It occurred to him that he missed few relationships back in Manchester; it was already feeling like a world and another life away.

'The prune and custard Bakewells are stunning Claire, thank you,' said Alex as they got up to go.

'You are very welcome,' acknowledged Claire. 'Thank you for coming and setting the record straight for the daft old bag of bones.'

'Yes lad, and call in if you want to go for a run, won't you?' added Arnold springing to his feet, race ready with arms pumping.

They said their good byes and left the unlikely couple on the doorstep waving them off. Back in the car Ammon giggled. 'That is one great lady my friends, you don't meet people like that everyday do you?'

'You certainly don't, a real gem,' agreed Maddie.

After a few dark, silent miles Alex turned to Ammon remembering his offer of a room at the cottage, 'Are you coming to stay back at the cottage tonight Ammon?'

'Oh, erm, no Alex, erm, Maddie has offered me a room and I think it will be better that we are not on top of each other. She has so much more space my friend.'

His uncomfortable reply forced Alex to hide his disappointment. 'That's ok mate, no problem. As long as you've got somewhere cheaper and out of the pub.'

'I am thinking of going back to Manchester in the next couple of days my friend. I must see if I can patch things with my father. If he will not change then it is me that will have to be the adult and make something happen.'

'Ok mate, well, all the best with that. You will keep in touch won't you?'

'I will, I will my friend. We could meet when you are back yourself, could we not?'

'Yes mate, of course, I'll call you when I'm back,' Alex

maintained his upbeat cover, hastily cloaking a sudden feeling of loneliness. This adventure's unintended outcome had been to unite this unlikely team and be a distraction from an unresolved baggage ridden reality that was looking more and more worthy of running away from.

Alex stood in darkness at the cottage door as Ammon's car headlights disappeared down the lane, decaying with the sound of the engine into the night. A growing fear came over him as his mind revisited the gruesome image of the dead man's face. He rushed the key into the lock, feeling it's every engagement with the mechanism, twisting it and forcing down hard on the handle he flung open the door and leapt in, fumbled frantically for the light switch and; safety. That was a bit excessive he thought, but then it's not every day you find a decomposing corpse in the midst of a demonic storm. Did he need that counselling? Nah he'd be fine…

Lying awake in bed staring up at the ceiling, he playfully allowed his eyes to find patterns in the textured wallpaper. Meanwhile his tired mind hopped around from one thought to another, crossing an ocean of grey normality on a maze of brightly coloured stepping stones. The last few days had been full on, and processing it all along with the accompanying feast of emotions had left him in an elevated state of anxiety. His new mate Ammon, the missing Anna, the crazy Arnold and Claire, the body, the police, and the fiery warrior Maddie all fought for his attention. An evolving image of a Boadicean Maddie, complete with speeding horse drawn chariot and brass chest plate was suddenly interrupted, by a text notification tone. Alex grabbed his phone and strained his tired eyes to focus on the screen.

Maddie - 'Hi A, not sleeping, are you awake? M'

Alex sat up and began typing his reply, 'Same, not sleeping, crazy day eh?'

Maddie - 'Can't stop thinking about that guy, wasn't Anna but was someone's loved one'

Alex - 'I know, can't get the image of his face out of my mind'

Maddie - 'That wasn't him, just his remains, you must try to think of it like that'

Alex - 'I know, I'm trying, not sure looking forward to find out who he was, that will make it more real'

Maddie - 'Yes me too. Great evening with Arnold and Claire though eh?

Alex - 'Yeah they're a great couple, made me feel better.

Maddie - 'Hope you didn't mind me offering a room to Ammon?'

Alex - 'That's ok. He's off back soon, shall miss him, he's got great wisdom in his madness'

Maddie - 'He does make a lot of sense at times alright'

Alex had no reply and not much more to say in his head. These few exchanges had helped and he hoped it had helped Maddie too.

Maddie - 'btw I'm not stopping looking for Anna'

Alex - 'That's risky! I don't know what to do now'

Maddie - 'Help me'

Alex - 'Why have you just been attacked by a giant stuffed fox?'

Maddie - 'lol no! my bed is plummeting towards the centre of the earth on a crazy rollercoaster'

Alex - 'You're ok as long as there isn't a scary clown with shark teeth in the car behind you'

Maddie - 'Fuck there is! He's eating a massive bag of Hula Hoops though so he'll be ages'

Alex - 'BBQ flavour?'

Maddie - 'Salt & vinegar'

Alex - 'Are you sure big scary clowns don't normally like S&V'

Maddie - 'Good night crazy dude'

Alex - 'Good night fiery warrior queen'

Maddie - '???'

Alex - ':-p'

Maddie - 'Zzz zzz zzz'

Alex lay back and closed his eyes still grasping the phone in both hands. His mind was more settled now, a few things had resolved themselves for him and that was fine, but tomorrow was another day and back to square one.

10 BACK TO SQUARE ONE

Spreading his favourite lime marmalade on a slice of toast Alex sat looking out of the kitchen window onto a beautiful day. The early morning sun was helping to lift him after a bad night's sleep dominated by a dream he was still struggling to remember. Sipping his tea, he thought about how he would fill his day now all the excitement was over. He never ran on mornings when he felt he'd not slept well, but considered going out later and maybe taking his compact camera. Before that he decided he must go see if he could get some sense out of his mother and have another look at that guitar hidden away in his father's old workshop.

Heading up the driveway to his mother's front door he hesitated, right to front door or left to garden and see mother after? Left to garden won out as he lifted the latch of the ornate iron gate. Covertly he made his way down the path alongside the house, not wanting to attract the attention of his mother. Listening carefully, he thought he could hear his mother shouting and laughing. He scanned the windows as the plants thinned out in the deep border between him and the conservatory at the back of the house. Through the conservatory window he could make out his mother's face over the back of a chair. Edging forward he strained his eyes to make out what was going on inside. Having moved that few steps further he could now behold the full horror of the scene; well thankfully not the full horror, but enough to make sense of what was going on in there. His mother was knelt on a conservatory chair bracing herself on the backrest whilst George - he of the Horticultural Society and gall stone removal – was servicing her from behind and she was evidently being pleasured, not a sight for any son to see. Alex cringed violently and partially covered his face with a hand. Keeping low he scarpered off towards the workshop glancing back briefly to check if he had been seen. Grabbing the workshop key from where he'd left it, under a plant pot, he hurried inside and out of sight.

With the door firmly closed behind him he clamped his head in his hands. He wasn't sure if he could see a funny side to what he'd just witnessed, shaking his head to expel the recurring vision until he couldn't help but break down in fits of laughter. He stomped around the room hysterically until he'd rid himself of the initial shock.

Opening the cupboard at the far end of the workshop he gazed upon the guitar again. It really was a beauty, he thought, but whose was it? He took it out, sat down and laid it across his lap. Pulling his electronic tuner out of his jacket pocket he began to carefully tune the wonderful instrument. It came into tune easily and beautifully. Strumming a few chords, he hummed the melody of a simple song he'd written a lifetime ago. After familiarising himself with it again he began to sing the parts he remembered, humming the rest; that was until he found himself being discordantly accompanied by his mobile phone's ring tone. He grabbed it and checked the screen, it was Ammon.

'Hi Ammon mate, what you up to?'

'Alex, hi, how are you my friend? Where are you?'

'I'm at my mother's mate, what you up to?'

'I am going back today my friend. I am in the car and ready to leave. I thought I would come to see you first. Can you meet me now?'

Alex thought briefly before realizing getting back past the conservatory might not be easy or advisable.

'I can't get away from here for a while I'm sorry mate. Are you coming back, when are you coming back?'

'Erm, I do not know. I will be back some time, especially if I can keep the thing going with Evelyn. I have told her, she seems to understand. Just some things I need to do Alex, to try to connect with my father.'

'Wish you luck with that mate.'

'I will need it, I think. Well take care my friend and keep in touch with Maddie, she is a good lady you know. You two share some good things'

'Yeah, like mutual disrespect and hatred? She's like one of those wagons on the motorway that drops cones to shut down lanes. She seems to take great pleasure in shutting down my lane, and she's always got a smug look on her face while she does it.'

'That is some crazy analogy my friend. You do make me laugh. Let me try. A relationship can be like driving a car at night. You can never see beyond the headlights, but you can make the whole journey that way. Do you like that one my friend?'

'Rubbish mate. I don't know why you waste your time trying to get us closer. It's a match made in a Hadron collider.'

'Oh, I like that one my friend. And one day sparks will fly?'

'No, Ammon. One day we will collide and create a black hole.'

Ammon laughed. 'Anyway, I will miss you my friend. Let's keep in touch and I will see you soon.'

They said their goodbyes and Alex returned to the guitar. He was ok, he'd see Ammon again soon but right now he too had to start sorting his life out.

As he continued playing the guitar his thoughts were drawn to the house sign he had found a couple of days before. He repeated the inscription, Hidden Haven, over and over in his mind trying to make sense of it. There was no way that his mother would consider renaming the house. As far as he remembered she as good as bought the house for the name and the historical connections with a branch of her ancestry; Wheeldon Trees, he was sure it would stay. Maybe he should ask his mother, can't do any harm, can it?

The more he explored every nook and cranny of the workshop the more he discovered and the more he wanted to preserve its contents. This would have to be something else he discussed with his mother; after all she had not been in here, possibly ever. He had toyed in the past with the idea of making one off arty wooden picture frames for his photographs. There was everything he needed in here and it would also be an opportunity to reconnect with his father. He had some real issues to resolve there, this could be as therapeutic as it was opportunistic. That little spark of an idea sent a wave of excitement crashing on the shores of desert island Alex. He took a moment to rest his mind in the shady hammock on that serene tropical beach. The next wave that crashed upon his shores wasn't so welcome. A wave of paranoia woke him to how protective he had become of this space and in particular its cherished contents. Would his mother's spite see her decide to empty it or knock it down and make it into a horticultural habitat for rare orchids? He couldn't take that chance; he had to make his intentions clear right now.

On leaving he tucked the key away in his pocket. The door was reasonably sturdy so it would take someone other than her to gain entry without the key.

How to approach mother, he thought, as he headed for the back door. The unwelcome realisation that his mother and George might still be in the conservatory drew him to carefully glance in. Mother wasn't there but George was, dead to the world sprawled out on the wicker sofa and snoring, which Alex could hear even through the double-glazed windows. Having knocked loudly on the back door he entered the house hailing his mother with an inquiring voice.

'Alex, is that you? What are you doing here?' was the not so welcoming response from his mother.

'Just come to see you mother, don't sound so excited will you eh?'

'Sorry dear, been a stressful time recently, what with George coming out of hospital and needing somewhere to convalesce, I've become his flipping nursemaid.'

'Yes, I saw him in the conservatory snoring like a trouper on the sofa.'

'Oh, the man snores for England you know, but he does have his uses.'

'Mother, what do you mean by that?'

'Oh, you know. What did you want anyway? I've so much to do at the moment, Red Cross, WI and going away, yes, we've fixed a date for the Cervara trip I'm pleased to say.'

'I bet you are—'

Mother stopped him with a momentary freezing stare; perhaps he'd allowed a little too much sarcasm out in that serving.

'I'm sure you'll have a lovely time,' he added smiling as genuinely as he could muster. 'And let's face it, you deserve a good holiday.' He must have got away with that, he thought, along with a little buttering up for the coming conversation.

'Thank you, Alex. I'm sure I will,' Mother replied with a perceptible hint of suspicion.

The iron isn't exactly hot but time to strike, he thought. 'Dad's workshop; I've been looking around in there and there's a few things I'd like to have, if that's ok with you?'

'Never been in the confounded place, it's coming down as soon as George and I finish planning the new garden layout. Take what you want and be quick about it, that's in the calendar for when we get back from Italy.'

'Thanks Mother. You know there seems to be a few woodworking jobs in there that Dad never completed for people.'

'What sort of things Alex?' she looked quizzically.

'Well, there's a house sign for one. It's really beautifully made. I was wondering if you might know anything about it. The inscription is Hidden Haven?'

Alex caught a fleeting look on his mother's face that he had never seen before. He had touched a nerve and wasn't sure how to follow up.

'I have no idea about that Alex,' she replied with a tone that tweaked Alex's dormant paranoia. 'You can burn it all as far as I'm concerned.'

Alex took exception to this and consciously metered it out, 'That's not very nice mother is it? This was Dad's passion, what he loved to do—'

'Don't talk to me about your father's passion Alex. He spent more time with those bloody bits of wood than he did with me and that's not the half of it.'

'What the hell are you talking about mother? This is my Dad, your husband, you're talking about. You have no right to talk like that about him. You took the fucking piss with him for years, no wonder he escaped when he could.'

'Don't you swear at me you little bastard—'

'Bastard am I now Mother, is there more I should know?'

'My marriage hadn't worked for years, and it was not of my doing.

Your useless father just couldn't measure up.'

'Your marriage? A wonderful man like my Dad didn't measure up to your poncy standards. You're a fucking hypocrite Mother, how dare you?'

'You always were a nasty piece of work Alex Hidde, not like the others.'

'Oh, now don't get me started on that. Yeah, go on, make me feel like the shit you've always managed to knock me down to. There's nothing wrong with them two and there's nothing wrong with me. It's you that's got the problem and it's done a good job of fucking me up for most of my life you'll be pleased to hear.'

'Don't be ridiculous Alex. You've just never had it in you—'

'What? Just like my poor old Dad then, never had it in me, never fucking good enough, surprise, fucking surprise.'

'Yes! And I'll be glad to see the back of you too!'

'Back of me eh Mother? For fucks sake, you emptied this house of any sign my father was ever here within days of his death. I thought that might be some sort of mourning reaction, but no, you actually wanted rid of him and his memory, didn't you?'

'Yes, I did! And I wish I'd made it happen sooner.'

'I don't fucking believe you Mother. You are pure fucking evil.'

Obviously roused by the noise snoring George appeared on the scene. 'What the hell is going on here? How dare you speak to your mother like that young man?'

Alex paused and looked down at the little tubby man, whose eyes were flickering about nervously assessing a bigger, stronger, younger man.

Alex took a breath and addressed him calmly but firmly, 'Fuck off you flowery little tosser.'

George looked up at him, his twitching mouth giving away his brain's attempts to form a response, until Mother stepped in.

'Just go sit down George, I will sort this out, thank you.'

'As long as you are alright my dear,' checked George managing to muster a vaguely fearless expression behind the protection of the instructed retreat. Strutting off back towards the conservatory he left Alex and his mother face to face in their vitriolic exchange.

'I think you've said enough Alex.' Mother continued with the finality of a head mistress. 'You are no longer welcome here, do you hear me?'

'I hear you mother. I'll be back for the workshop stuff as soon as I can. Don't touch anything in there until I get chance to move it; at least give me that.'

Alex headed off out of the front door expecting a last word from his mother but she was uncharacteristically silent. Fumbling in his pocket for his car key he became aware he was shaking. He'd had some battles with his mother before but never hit a vein of such bitterness quite like that. She had just raised questions for him that seemed to undermine his entire existence. Rocked and emotional he returned to the cottage with a deep need to run away. Maybe that was what he needed a run out into the Peak to sort his head out. Yeah, how about a run out to the shake holes and see if he could exorcise some resting demons.

11 RESTING DEMONS

Changed into his running gear, Alex was back in the car and away in no time. He'd also grabbed his small compact camera, zipping it into his hydration belt pocket. Once out of the village he rammed his foot firmly to the floor shifting hard and fast through the gears. The hedgerows and drystone walls blurred as his focused, tunnelled vision picked out the entry point of the next rapidly approaching bend. Heavy braking threw the car into oversteer, requiring a rapid correction to control the twitching of the back end before he could feed in the power again. He fought furiously with the wheel to keep that power pulling him out of the corner and onto a short straight over a narrow bridge, where all four tyres left the ground. The car landed with a predictable thud before the bonnet dove down under more heavy braking, setting up for the next bend. He continued to speed on recklessly around the lanes, still struggling to digest the bitter argument with his mother. He knew these roads well but the way he was driving left no room for error, his, or some innocent soul coming in the other direction. Screeching the car around another bend he eased off; it wasn't far now. His heightened adrenaline fuelled senses tingled furiously with flight response. A good run would sort him out.

It was still the same glorious day he had woken to and he was determined to bring something positive into it. The ground under foot was damp but firm as he made his way up onto the open hillside while maintaining a comfortable pace that allowed him to take in the surrounding splendour. He was taking a different route across to the shake holes on a less direct path to the one they had taken the day before, with the idea of making it a circular route if he could pick up the right path back down. For him there was nothing more exhilarating than running out in the hills. The primitive sense of a human being belonging in the landscape, physical fitness, awareness of the topography and navigation skills scaled the surroundings to a manageable and masterable environment.

Was anything becoming clearer, pounding out these miles under this clear sky? Was anything making any more sense, surrounded by the beautiful predefined order of nature? He knew one thing for sure; he needed to get away from his mother. That was something he'd been practising for years with the consequential loss of the relationship with his father. There was no reason to make any contact with her now. She was proving to be even more rotten than he had ever imagined. Strange for someone who spent so much of her time allegedly doing good things for the community. He had long thought that was all a show, an ego stroking power play. It was all about her and her cronies looking after their self-interests and suppressing anyone who suspected them of the institutionalised brand of corruption they fostered and guardedly managed. Woah, he was sounding bitter, he admitted to himself. In reality he had known all this was going on but chose to keep away from its source rather than label it for what it was. The result being he had shown little support for his father, who had suffered for far too long. The emotional weight of that admission could have broken him in that moment but he pulled himself back shifting focus to the rough terrain under his feet. He screamed through gritted teeth pushing on harder towards the hill top and approaching shake holes.

Diverting from the track Alex leapt through the undergrowth towards the craggy edge where they had descended into the hole on the previous dark stormy evening. All was light and bright today. It could have been another place on another planet. Alex crouched down and sat on the hard, cold limestone edge looking across at where they had found the body. It was gone and from here there was no sign it had ever been there. Did he need to go and inspect the site further, he questioned. His curiosity was such that there was only one answer. Taking the drink bottle out of his belt he drank deeply, quenching a thirst he'd ignored for at least the last couple of miles. He was glad he'd come back here. The horror of the images he wanted so desperately to erase had become a little more sanitised wrapped in the new context he was busy weaving. In the drier conditions and wearing a grippy pair of trail running shoes, he made his way down into the hole with ease. Bounding across the boulder strewn floor and looking down into that void again brought him further relief. There was no trace of that poor man's broken body ever being there. Looking up to the top of the crag he could make out a rope wrapped with hazard tape strung across the slope from where he first looked down. It was a dangerous edge, that probably should be protected, but he still didn't think this guy had slipped. It was an obvious possibility but it didn't feel right to him. He sat back braced on his locked arms and threw his head back. Shutting his eyes to the glaring sun, he briefly felt some warmth from its autumn rays. He took a long deep breath, exhaled a little more of the tension built up within him and thought more about his father.

Sixty-five was no age to die, he thought. His father had taken early retirement so had not worked for a few years, but as far as Alex knew he was a fit healthy guy with many more years to look forward to. It had been quick, a heart attack out in the garden and within a few hours he was gone. No time to say goodbye, no time to just say those things you hope for the chance to be able to say; before it's too late. Scrunching his eyes up tightly he fought to suppress a scream from within. The tears and pain would last forever; he could see no end to it. There seemed to be no resolution or no way to forgive himself for those missed opportunities. He knew his father loved him; they had shared those unspoken moments. He searched his mind for one of those times to replay over and over again, hoping to see that recognition in his father's eyes just one more time. As a cloud passed across the sun a sudden shiver broke him from his inward spiral. Wearing only a thin running top soaked in cooling sweat, he was starting to feel a chill. It was time to go. Bounding to his feet he was off and away down the hill side, the undergrowth brushing his legs with flashes of autumn's umber withered sprigs. Plunging headlong down the broken trail he allowed his focus to be consumed by the technicalities of the descent. To close his open wounds, he knew he would have to share them, but for now to supress the pain would suffice.

As he walked the last few yards back to the car, he realised he hadn't taken a single photograph that day. He could always see a photograph in any situation; he prided himself on that ability. Today though he hadn't even thought about it. Maybe a sign of how troubled this time felt for him. Things were starting to stack up and he needed to clear some of the wood before he could see the trees. He thought about his current level of resilience and the formula his college tutor had once told him. Your resilience at any given time is a product of your ability to cope versus the weight of what you have to cope with. He felt his ability was pretty high at the moment so it was the weight of what was stacking up that was his likely his problem. He had to admit that the events of the previous days had actually given him strength. Ammon had become a good friend he could rely on and should be someone to keep in his life. Even Maddie had been good for him. She was always so strong; something he loved to hate about her perhaps. They always knew how to bring light and laughter into a dull place, he chuckled as he remembered the crazy text exchanges and the saga of the stuffed fox. He so needed to laugh more right now and give up all this feeling sorry for himself.

It was a much more sensible driver that took the return journey back to Sterndale. In the midst of all that was whirling around his head, he was feeling pretty chilled. An acceptance before the storm maybe. One hand on the wheel and the other toying with his mobile phone he coaxed the car through the bends with a fluid laziness. A sudden buzz from his phone caused him to recoil and drop it into the passenger foot well; swiftly grabbing it he returning his eyes to the road ahead. It was a call from a number he didn't recognise; he answered swapping hands on the steering wheel.

'Hello!' he greeted chirpily.

'Alex Hidde, D.I. Fell here. Can you talk Alex?'

'Oh, hi, I can talk yes, I'm driving but I'm on hands free.' He lied. Hopefully convincingly he thought. Talking to a police officer on a mobile phone whilst driving felt, dangerous.

'You'll be pleased to hear we've recovered the body of the deceased gentleman and managed to make a preliminary identification. It is subject to further procedural confirmation but I can let you know what we have at this point.'

Alex swung off the road into a layby, pulled up and killed the engine. 'Thanks for getting back to me Mr Fell. So you know who he is?'

'I do Alex. His name is Richard McGuire. He was a school teacher from the Newcastle area. From what we can initially ascertain, it looks as though he accidentally slipped and fell off that crag. Probably after losing his way in bad weather. The really sad thing is we think he was out looking for his daughter. She went missing in the area a few months ago. Very sad state of affairs. How are you Alex? How have you been coping after your experience?'

'Erm,' Alex stalled, considering the question and the unexpected concern the inspector shared. 'I'm ok I reckon. Different now knowing who he was.'

'Is there anything else I can help you with? Anything else you would like to know that might help?'

'I, err, I don't think so right now thanks.'

'Ok Alex, I'll let you know if anything more significant emerges. Good day Alex.'

'Thanks Mr Fell, good bye.'

Alex mulled over the conversation which was now posing some serious questions for him. Another girl missing? Wasn't that too much of a coincidence? All he could think was that this other missing girl and Anna could be linked. He set off towards home, in haste again. There, he would call Maddie and Ammon to get other perspectives on the news.

As he approached the village a sudden thought crossed his mind; to get the guitar out of the workshop and safely in his hands. Driving down the lane towards his mother's house he parked the car short of the driveway to be certain of getting in and out without being seen. Approaching the house, he noted there were no cars on the drive, thankfully no one was home. Walking down the pathway into the garden he checked each window as he passed. The house was empty, no lights on, no signs of life.

Opening the cupboard doors, he breathed a sigh of relieve. The guitar was still there. He had no reason to suspect it wouldn't be, but its value to him now seemed far beyond any price tag. Guitar in hand he turned to leave when something caught his attention that he'd not noticed before. It was only a small kettle, tea pot, tea caddy and a mug but it brought a smile to his face. It looked to be untouched since his father last used it over a year ago. There was still a carton of milk too; he wouldn't check out its contents right now but it did lend weight to the notion that his mother had never been in the workshop.

Back out at the car he carefully laid the guitar down on the back seat wrapping the centre seatbelt around it for added security. Sitting back and resting his head firmly against the restraint he thought about the house, the home and how little it meant to him. He had no connection with it other than the past. A feeling of loss and abandonment hollowed him. He felt truly alone, possibly for the first time ever. The security he found in his relationship with Michelle had been the foundations he had built himself from, his business and his social network. He knew he hadn't lost many, so called friends, in the split, no one that he thought counted anyway. He had lost touch though, and in his mind he'd moved on, he just didn't know where to yet.

Alex had to hold the phone away from his ear while Maddie vented her reaction to the news from D.I. Fell.

'That's bollox Alex. He's spinning you a line there for sure. He doesn't want us to start sniffing around the Anna inquiry again with the knowledge of another girl having gone missing.'

'I know Maddie, I'm thinking the same, and I'm also suspicious of the fall our guy supposedly took. I reckon he was pushed by someone who felt he was getting too close.'

'That's a little more of a leap Alex but you could be right.'

'Yeah, maybe, I know, but I really do think there is someone out there who needs stopping but where do we start.'

'I don't know Alex. I know of three girls now, all gone missing from the local area. Anna, Katy McGuire and a Kiwi backpacker, Keira Lightfoot, all reported missing in the local press over the last two years.'

'You have been busy, haven't you?'

'I told you I wasn't giving up Alex. Just don't know where to go next.' Maddie tailed off to a silent pause.

'Well Maddie it's like all the toilets have been robbed from the police station cos they have nothing to go on either.'

Maddie tutted, 'ha ha, the old ones are the best, don't give up the day job Alexi-poos.'

'It'll probably take another disappearance to shed some light on things,' continued Alex. 'By the way, I was going to call Ammon but thought he might be up to his neck in it right now so I'll wait until he gets in touch.'

'I agree Alex, he's having a hard time with his father right now, let's give him some space.'

'I think we need to get our heads together and see what we can come up with. What do you say Alex?'

'Yeah, you're right, let's do that.'

'Ok, I'm busy tomorrow but Thursday would be good for me. You ok with that Alex?'

'Yep! Let's talk tomorrow evening and make a plan.'

'Ok, see you Alex, bye.'

'Ok, bye Maddie.'

So that was that, a date set to get together with Maddie. Good idea or bad idea? Alex stewed over the possible consequences.

A quiet evening in trickled by, filled with a hunt for possible saleable Peak District prints he could mount in interestingly designed hand-crafted wooden frames. He'd got a few, and a few good ones at that. He was starting to get quite excited about the project. Sketching some ideas for frames, he considered each image and how it could be enhanced with the right shape, wood grain or texture. His phone began to ring but he left it, deep in creative thought. It rang again, this time he dragged it closer to him across the desk, it was Ammon.

'Hi Ammon mate how—'

'Alex, my friend, I'm coming back tomorrow. I've been trying to contact Evelyn and she has not got back to me. Alex, I think she has gone missing.'

12 MISSING

'What! What do you mean gone missing? How long have you been trying to contact her Ammon?' implored Alex.

'Since last night my friend. I called Bill Palmer at the pub. He says she has not been in for her shift last night or today and he is going to sack her because she has not called in sick or anything.'

Alex responded thoughtfully, 'There could be a perfectly logical innocent explanation. If it was only last night, she could be ill or have a problem with her phone or something eh?'

'Yes, it could be my friend but I cannot help but think the worst. If someone has got her I will make them pay, so help me God.' Ammon's voice was shaking with anger. Definitely a side of him Alex had not seen before. He suspected an angry Ammon could do someone some serious damage.

'Have you thought about calling the police?'

'I do not want to call the police yet. I want to check this out for myself and be sure I am not overreacting.'

'I think that is probably the best start mate.'

'I will see you in the morning Alex, I am going to call Maddie and then try to sleep.'

'Ok Ammon, you do that mate, and we'll be here for you tomorrow, alright?'

'Alright my friend, see you tomorrow.' Ammon hung up his voice fading into sadness.

If Ammon was right, thought Alex, and Evelyn had been taken, then the evil had been brought home into their very midst. This fateful prospect changed everything in Alex's mind. If there was a lead they could follow, it may be possible to expose some unguarded flank of this despicable adversary. The thought of confronting a person capable of such things evoked conflicting emotions within him. A real sense of fear and a tentative craving for the elation of redemption.

His next thoughts were ominous and disturbing. It now occurred to him that Anna was by now most probably dead. She'd been missing for a few months and within the last couple of days another victim had been taken. He lay awake for some time, his imagination conjuring with possible events and scenarios that may have befallen these missing girls. Was there a serial killer on the loose, and if so where was he? What horror befell his innocent victims? Could he be stopped? Could they be instrumental in stopping him? He badly needed to sleep; tomorrow was going to be a long day.

Alex was running towards the screams of a woman in certain peril. He was in a huge barn with stalls on either side that seemed to go on for ever. He was fighting hard to run, his limbs stiff and heavy. The floor under him was strewn with puddles of sullied water, a mixture of foul-smelling animal urine and diesel fuel. Above him chinks of light outlined roof windows opaque with dirt stained glass. He had to run fast but silent so as not to alert the scarecrows that inhabited the stalls on either side of him. They were there in the shadows; pitch forks in hand, ready to stop him dead in his tracks. The screams were becoming more regular and more bloodcurdling; was he too late. He was bruised and battered running as hard as he could, bare footed on the hard-cobbled floor. Ahead he could see two giant doors. A plane of light shone through the gap between them and someone was hammering on them hard and determined. Someone wanted to get in as badly as he wanted to get out. The hammering continued louder and louder until it permeated reality and the dream decayed into an awakening. The knocking continued accompanied by shouts of his name, though the rising veil of sleep. It was Ammon and Maddie at the front door and it was still very early, in fact the clock at his bedside, through blurry eyes, read five am.

Alex leapt out of bed and down the stairs to the front door grabbing his bath robe en-route. Hastily dressing, he flung open the door to the excited friends and stood back as they brought in their anguish.

'I am sorry for waking you so early my friend. I could not sleep so I have driven over during the night and called Maddie.' Ammon, clearly distressed, was trying to maintain some rational focus and calm.

Maddie had her arm around him offering comfort but her face showed worry.

'It's ok,' assured Alex filling the kettle under the kitchen tap. 'We need to act on this fast, don't we?'

'We checked out her lodgings on the way here. There's no sign of her, car's gone, curtains open, no one at home,' started Maddie taking out a laptop computer from its case. 'I'm going to have a go at hacking into her online accounts and see what we can find.'

'Ok, I'll make some coffee guys,' declared Alex. 'Are you ok Ammon? Need anything to eat?'

'If you have bread, I'll have some toast thank you my friend. I have not eaten for hours.'

Alex grabbed a loaf from the bread bin and chucked it across at Ammon while nodding towards the toaster.

'Help yourself mate, there's butter, cheese and jam in the fridge, knives in the top drawer there.'

Maddie worked diligently on her laptop, jumping from window to window, manipulating code and running apps. Armed with Evelyn's mobile phone number and the little that Ammon knew about her online profile, Maddie continued working, intensely focussed for some time. The boys began to consider the facts, their assumptions and discussed what they should do next.

After some discussion Alex summed up, '…so, no phone contact, car's gone, flat's empty, pub landlord hasn't seen her for two days, and all was well when you last spoke to her Ammon?'

'Yes, fine, as far as I know everything was fine.'

Alex sat back and sighed, 'We are going to have to go to the police with this if we don't come up with anything soon. Somebody else is going to miss her, and do that anyway at some point'

'Ok guys! I'm into her Facebook account,' announced Maddie, blowing her lips out with a big sigh of relief.

The guys scampered around her and checked out the screen, while Maddie scoured the page for signs of any recent activity.

'Well, nothing to report here, no updates for two days, but, that doesn't say much as she doesn't seem to be frequently active. I'll post a message asking her to get in touch because we are all worried about her. So, that's about as much as we can do there.'

'Anything else you can get into Maddie?' Alex enquired.

'I've checked her answer phone and there's nothing on there. She's got a WhatsApp account and I think I'm nearly into that, give me a minute.'

Maddie's fingers danced around the keyboard, screens opened and screens closed as the boys looked on in amazement, munching their toast in her ears.

'Will you fuck off with that toast you two? It's driving me crazy. I'm in guys! Into WhatsApp.'

All faces returned to the screen of the laptop.

'Ok Ammon, who do you recognise in this contacts list? Again, she hasn't used the app for a few days. Spoke to her sister last Sunday.'

'I do not think there is anything out of the ordinary there. I only spoke to her on the phone. If she has not contacted anybody for two days, I think something is not right.' Ammon spoke with a despondency that was obviously weighing heavily on him.

Maddie tried to console him. 'There's nothing conclusive Ammon. She doesn't use these accounts often anyway.' She slowly drummed the table with her fingers for a moment deep in thought. 'I do know someone who might be able to get us into the ANPR camera system so we can trace her last car journey.'

'The what?' quizzed Alex, 'Do you mean the number plate recognition cameras on the road sides?'

'I do indeed Alexi-poos. I'll just make a phone call to an old mate and see what we can do. What time is it? Seven thirty, not too early then.'

Maddie stood up stretched, tapped a contact in her phone and waited. Walking over to the window she looked out across the garden while the guys made more drinks and more toast. The ridiculously loud kettle drove Maddie to the front door and out onto the driveway. They could hear her going through some initial catching up ritual with an old friend. Followed by some technical jargon and a fair amount of laughter. She ended the conversation as she walked back into the room with a big thank you and we should catch up soon. Passing Alex, she swiped a piece of toast off the plate in his hand. He moaned something briefly through a mouthful and raised his hands in surrender.

'Any joy Maddie?'

'I reckon so Alexi-poos. Let's see what we can do here.' She settled into another round of keyboard bashing, punctuated by the occasional frustrated exclamation.

'Ok Ammon what's Evelyn's car reg?' Maddie proudly requested.

'Oh, sorry Maddie, I do not know that.'

'You are joking aren't you? Bollox! I'm in the system and we don't know her car reg. God help me.' Maddie showed no mercy for the oversight.

'Hold on,' shouted Ammon grabbing his phone from his pocket. 'I have a picture of her in front of her car, hold on, yes, here it is!'

'Brilliant Ammon, what's the reg?' perked up Maddie.

Ammon read out the registration plate number from the photograph on his phone while Maddie entered it checking each digit as it was given. She slammed in a few more key strokes and studied the results.

'Ok, her car was picked up yesterday. M1 southbound, M1 southbound. Ok, she's tracked down to the A405 North Orbital, St Albans Road. Then, nothing. So, she's somewhere in the London area, that narrows things down doesn't it?'

'But what is she doing in London?' Ammon looked puzzled but somewhat relieved.

'What does that mean?' Alex questioned. 'Does that mean she's not been taken by our local resident evil?'

'Who ever said he or indeed she was local?' Maddie threw in.

They all fell silent and thoughtful contemplating this unexpected revelation.

Ammon turned to and fro indecisively, stroking his chin to maximise the depth of his ponderings.

'I do not know what to think my friends. Has she just run off or, is there, still something, sinister, —'

'Afoot?' Alex finished off Ammon's straying sentence. 'We have to consider that is a possibility.' He looked around for some consensus. 'What do we do now guys? Do we still go to the police?'

'If she doesn't get in touch with anybody soon, someone else will report her missing and the police could come looking for us,' Maddie surmised with growing certainty.

'Bugger! What do we do then guys?' exclaimed Alex with dawning recognition of the apparent catch twenty-two situation they had found themselves in. 'We have to think about what is best for Evelyn. What do we need to do to make sure she is safe?'

'You're right Alex. We have to do what is best for Evelyn.' Maddie concurred firmly.

Ammon stared through both of them trying desperately to focus on some illusive truth. 'You think she has run out on me, don't you? And I think you might be right.'

'Come on Ammon,' Maddie reassured, 'We don't know anything for sure. There's still a lot here that doesn't stack up.'

Alex slammed another couple of slices of bread down into the toaster, 'I think we need to report this to the police before they come looking for us. Therefore, this time, we need to agree what we tell them, and stick to it.'

'Alright governor. Anyone grasses and we'll be measuring 'em up for a concrete cardigan,' croaked Maddie in a blokey, East End accent.

'Come on Maddie, seriously, what do we tell them? That you've hacked all her accounts and the bloody number plate recognition system? You'll probably get locked up for that?'

'Yeah, you're maybe right Alexi-poos. And this ass is far too cute for a women's prison,' laughed Maddie slapping her behind. 'Ok, sorry, all we need to tell them is the bare minimum. Just report her as missing and let the police do their work.'

At this point Ammon decided to share his thoughts, 'Yes, I think you are both right. It is best that I report this, and just tell them what I know. There is no reason to involve you my friends.'

Alex grabbed a note pad from the kitchen table and threw it over to Ammon, 'That's the number for our beloved Detective Andy Fell. Probably best to call his crew with this mate.'

'Thank you, Alex. I will make this call outside if you do not mind.' Ammon took his phone from his jacket pocket and headed for the front door.

Maddie and Alex looked across at each other both trying to work out what the other's facial expression was telling them. Maddie smiled pitifully in the direction of Ammon. Alex shook his head in agreement.

'He's such a lovely bloke. He doesn't deserve her running out on him. If that is what's happened here.' Maddie's sympathy was evident.

'It's looking like that isn't it,' Alex agreed. 'But he's right to report it isn't he? We've got to be sure she is safe.'

Ammon returned into the kitchen with a knowing grin on his face and the phone still at his ear.

'What is the address here Alex? Mr Fell would like to come and talk with us.'

Alex returned the grin followed by a comical exaggerated look of surprise.

'It's Willow Trees cottage, second left after the square then down Mires Lane and we are left opposite the entrance to Leagrove Farm.'

'You got that did you Mr Fell?... Ok... we will see you in about an hour... thank you, goodbye.' Ammon hung up the call, then checked again to ensure it had definitely disconnected before speaking.

'Someone else has reported Evelyn missing, this morning. He did not say who, but he wants to ask us a few questions.'

13 A FEW QUESTIONS

'I'd better go get dressed then.' Alex jogged off up the stairs still in his bath robe.

'I think I'll get my laptop out of the way before big old cheesy chops gets here,' announced Maddie, running a finger over the touchpad and bringing the screen back to life.

'Oh my God!' Maddie's shocked outcry was shrill but muted. 'Guys, I've got a message from Evelyn.'

Ammon jumped to his feet and joined Maddie at the screen. 'What does it say Maddie? Is she alright?'

Maddie read the message slow and deliberately. 'Hey guys I'm ok. Sorry but I had to get away. Tell Ammon I'm very sorry but it wasn't working for me. I'm visiting my ex and we are going to give it another go. Take care all, love Ev.'

Ammon slapped his head and resorted to his mother tongue to express his shock. '…I am sorry my friends. Why is this? I did not see that coming, not at all.' He stared into the screen with bewildered disbelief.

Maddie put an arm around him and said nothing.

Alex came back down the stairs into a situation he sensed needed some empathy and tact. 'Sorry Ammon. Are you ok? Don't know what you said then but I do hope it helped mate.'

'I am ok, yes, as long as Evelyn is ok. It was early days for our relationship anyway wasn't it?' He was doing his best to sound philosophical, hiding his evident hurt. 'What do we tell Mr Fell now my friends?'

'Exactly what we know,' affirmed Alex. 'We haven't done anything wrong have we? It's just a reply to a legitimate message.'

'I suppose so, yes, I will just say what I know... Do you think I could have some more toast please Alex?'

'We're into freezer bread mate, but no problem. Just push the defrost button on the toaster when you drop it in.'

Ammon opened the freezer door and rummaged around briefly before surfacing with a loaf of frozen sliced bread. Opening it he placed it down on the worktop and began dejectedly prizing the slices apart with a slightly inappropriate bendy butter knife.

Maddie continued tapping away at her laptop keyboard while Alex paced expectantly around the kitchen, stopping at the sink now and then to tap out an impatient tune with his fingernails. Ammon joined in with an occasional drum of the butter knife on the bread board. Maddie, infected by the beat, jammed along with her keyboard tapping. Alex tapped harder and faster. Ammon's butter knife percussion built with the addition of a rhythmic hand slap to the worktop. Maddie tapped along adding a melody line of improvised wordless vocal scat. The symphony of expectation built almost to a stress releasing crescendo but for the random offbeat interruption of a firm and official knock at the door.

Alex greeted D.I. Fell with a reserved hello.

'Can we come in please Mr Hidde?' Alex stepped back as the D.I. marched in followed by a woman officer.

'This is Detective Constable Charlotte Mason. She'll be helping me out with this enquiry.'

Maddie and Alex shared a tormented knowing glance. They both instantly recognised Mason from school where she was an unpopular, arrogant bully and a constant adversary of Maddie's.

'Alex. Maddie.' Mason nodded a grin at both of them before lifting her nose.

D.I. Fell scanned the three of them sensing the recognition. 'You know these two Mason?'

'School sir.'

'Really Mason, you went to school?' he questioned sarcastically.

Maddie and Alex shared a smirk which Mason picked up on with a telling pout.

'Certainly did sir. Best in the area it was too.'

'Good Mason, well done.' His reply held another wisp of sarcasm. 'Now then, an update for you firstly. We've just had a report that a

Facebook message was sent by Ms. Doyle today to a family member purporting to the effect that Ms Doyle is safe and well and with an ex-boyfriend. We've also traced the movements of her car and it was last seen in North West London.'

Alex, Maddie and Ammon shared a relieved glance.

'How can we help you then Mr Fell?' Maddie enquired with what she felt to be a touch of well-deserved self-righteousness.

'I was just wondering if you had maybe started your own investigation and you had something more to tell me?' he replied quizzically checking their faces for any revealing tells. 'Nothing then, Alex, Maddie, Ammon?' he checked them out individually with brewing suspicion.

Ammon stepped forward standing tall and defiant, 'I am afraid we know no more than you Mr Fell. She was my girlfriend and now she is not. Now I know she is safe, for me the case is closed.'

'That seems to be the case, excuse the pun.' D.I. Fell took a deep breath and exhaled in slow thoughtful analysis. 'There is something about this that just isn't stacking up for me. You let me know if you hear anything more won't you eh?'

'Serious offence withholding evidence in a police investigation, and I wouldn't put it past either of you two,' snipped Mason.

'What could you possibly mean by that Mrs Policewoman?' sneered Maddie.

'No love lost between you old school chums then eh? Come on

Mason let's go see if we can catch some real criminals.' D.I. Fell turned and headed for the front door his magnetic superiority dragging Mason with him, scowling a wordless retort in the direction of Maddie.

'Good afternoon to you all and thank you for your time.' D.I. Fell disposed of his parting words with dutiful abandon.

As the door clunked shut Maddie doubled in a release of mocking laughter, 'What an absolute twat she is. Charlotte the harlot a policeman woman? I don't believe it. Did you see her face, like she'd been sucking a lemon?'

Alex nodded and laughed in agreement, 'She was a nasty piece of work at school, wasn't she? I remember her slapping my face because I took the last apple strudel in the school canteen. Seriously though, we're going to have to be careful, she's going to be gunning for us now, isn't she?'

Ammon looked somewhat bewildered standing on the outside of the joke, 'I thought she was quite attractive my friends, especially in that uniform.'

'Give it up mate, she's rotten to the core that one, believe me,' gasped Alex trying to catch his breath.

'We all have our troubles that taint us my friends. Under that cold exterior there will be a delicate princess longing to break out, I guarantee it.' Ammon remained serious throughout while nibbling on another piece of toast which just fuelled their giddying fits of laughter to new heights.

Alex threw himself back onto the sofa and sighed long and hard, 'So, all is well again, isn't it? Oh, apart from you being dumped by Evelyn,

Ammon, sorry about that.'

Maddie took a deep breath and tutted it out tunefully, 'I'm not sure, you know? Old chubby chops thinks there's more to this, and I think he might be right.'

'Seems pretty straight forward to me,' said Alex, self-consciously searching for something he may have overlooked.

'Well my friends, only time will tell. I hope she is safe, wherever she is.' Ammon's voice was low and wistful, staring out of the window to the distant shadowy moorland, as though lost in his own self-pity.

'Ok guys!' Maddie announced with tempered enthusiasm. 'It's open mike night at the Quiet Woman this evening. Who's up for a night out?'

The boys agreed that was just what they needed after the day they'd had. Ammon and Maddie left the cottage soon after agreeing to return later so they could drive to the pub together.

Alone again at the kitchen table Alex sat reflecting on another crazy day with the gang. At least it had been a distraction from the negative thoughts plaguing him for the last few days. Being on his own right now wasn't what he wanted or needed. It was great to have Ammon back he thought, smiling out a stifled snigger as he reflected on their humorous exchanges. He wondered what had gone on between him and his father, he hadn't mentioned anything. He made a mental note to ask him later. A run now though, a shower and some dinner before their big night out.

After a quick change of clothes before he had chance to change his mind Alex was out of the door and running along the lane down the side of the cottage. The last of the day's sun played on the underside of a single layer of cloud sat perfectly parallel to the horizon. Not the most beautiful sunset he had ever seen but oddly different, to the point of being too surreal to make an acceptable photograph. His footfalls echoed as he ran between tall farm buildings. Pushing harder he became acutely aware of his breathing, deep and rhythmic He imagined blowing out an inner darkness that wanted to consume him. In the fading light, shadows flickered across the track like his own demons hiding in wait. What did the future hold for him now, he thought to himself? Something good, he whispered repeatedly with each rhythmic breath, something good.

Jumping into the passenger seat of Ammon's car Alex turned to look into the rear where Maddie was sat with a guitar across her lap.

'Are you playing tonight?' he exclaimed with surprise.

'Indeed I am Alexi-poos, or maybe I'll just wrap this around your scrawny neck you big chump.'

'Ooooh sorry! No need to get your G string in a twist Mrs,' Alex replied comically.

'Maddie is a bit nervous my friend,' Ammon cut in. 'She has not played in public for a long time, have you Maddie?'

'No, I haven't, thank you for reminding me, again!' she snapped.

'Ok be calm Maddie. Everything will be fine. You play so

142

beautifully,' encouraged Ammon. 'Where are we going to collect the music stand? Out of town and right over the bridge is it?' he continued.

'Yes, and first left after the bad couple of bends,' Maddie reluctantly instructed.

Alex took an exaggerated sharp intake of breath. 'Ooooh, bad bends Ammon eh? You know what you're like with bad bends don't you mate.'

'That was only one time, don't make me nervous my friend,' defended Ammon with a worried smirk.

Pulling up outside a row of three terraced cottages on the roadside, Alex leapt out and flipped up the front seat to let Maddie out of the back of the car.

As she got out Maddie thrust the guitar towards Alex. 'Hold that numb nuts.'

Alex stood to attention. 'Oh, I'm your roadie now am I?'

Maddie gave him a disgruntled huff over her shoulder. 'Well you couldn't make a groupie with your track record could you Alexi-poos?'

Alex chuckled to himself, safe in the knowledge she would be suffering enough without the need for any retort from him.

Strutting off to the front door of the middle house she arrived as it was being opened by a stout middle-aged lady wearing what looked, at a distance, like horned rimmed spectacles. Alex thought she had a look of Dame Edna Everidge, bar the massive hair and purple rinse. Maddie took a folded music stand from the lady, thanked her, returned to the car and slipped back into the rear seat.

'Gimmy!' she demanded pointing to the guitar in Alex's hands. Alex carefully passed it into her, flipped the seat back and jumped in shouting,

'Go go go!'

'That was my vocal coach if you were wondering,' explained Maddie briskly.

'She teaches you how to behave like a diva then does she?' teased Alex.

'Fuck off!' replied Maddie rounding each syllable with venom. 'Put your foot down Ammon, I want to get there for a sound check and something to eat before the first acts go on.'

Ammon hit the accelerator pedal kicking the automatic transmission down into a lower gear. The little car had a big engine and the resulting increase in speed threw the passengers back into their seats with an unexpected jolt. Approaching the first of the series of bad bends Alex could see the car was travelling way too fast.

'Slow down mate, this is a tight one,' he warned with a raising shrill tone.

Ammon reacted immediately but inappropriately, firstly hitting the brakes and then the accelerator, causing the car to lurch sideways, losing traction between tyre and road. The car slide broadside into the corner with all tyres screeching for grip as Ammon fought to correct the opposite lock oversteer. Maddie and Alex screamed in terror as a foreboding, solid, dry stone wall loomed up in front of them. In an instance Ammon had corrected the slide missing the wall by inches but hitting the edge of the grass verge. Consequently, the car leapt into the air coming down hard back onto the road. The sudden shock of the collision caused Ammon to add more corrective lock to the steering sending the vehicle careering in the other direction approaching the second and tighter bend over a narrow bridge. The near side front wheel hit the verge first flipping the Alfa around and slamming it sideway through a wooden fence and into the end wall pillar of the bridge. Bouncing back from the impact the car left the road completely, coming to rest precariously between the roadside banking and a tree.

Alex still in a braced position slowly opened his eyes and looked around, 'Fuck! is everyone alright?' Ammon, also still in a braced position holding the wheel suddenly burst into life, 'I am alright yes, are you both alright?'

Maddie was sat in the rear wrapped around her guitar looking at Ammon with a raging face. 'You fucking idiot, you could have killed us,' she balled at the top of her voice.

'Come on we need to get out quickly,' Ammon instructed. 'Can you open that door Alex I cannot open this one?'

Alex opened his door turning on the interior lighting, it was then he noticed the side protection airbags on the driver's side had both inflated and a dusty chalky deposit covered Ammon's hair, face and clothes. Looking around at Maddie he saw she too had a dusting of chalk from the airbag deployment.

'Are we all ok?' he repeated.

The others checked themselves and confirmed they had no injuries they were aware of.

In his state of shock, the still silence struck Alex. He realised his hearing was still in the process of recovering from the deafening explosion emitted by the airbag inflation. Leaning out of the open door he became aware of the precarious position in which the car had come to rest. Wedged between the roadside banking and a large tree the car was in effect around eight feet off the bottom of the bank with the stream shimmering past in the near darkness. The headlights were still on but shed little light on the exit route down the banking.

'Getting out might be a bit tricky guys. We're wedged halfway up a bloody tree. I'm going to have a go at climbing down.' Alex grabbed the passenger door handle and started to edge his way out of the car until he got into a position to jump the few feet onto the banking. He landed facing the banking and grappled to arrest his slippery descent down the slope to the stream.

'I'm down ok guys. Ammon, help Maddie out will you?'

Maddie was already halfway out of the car having flipped up the front seat.

'Take my guitar Alex,' she shouted, also still deafened by the air bag explosions.

Holding onto the roof of the car she leaned out to pass the guitar down to Alex. Needing to lean out a little further she stepped out onto the door sill. As she put her foot down it began to slip sideways causing her progressively and inevitably to lose balance. Spooked and in an attempt to save a fall, she dropped the guitar. Alex instinctively caught it but then dropped it as he realised Maddie was falling towards him with a piercing screech. He caught her bodily, jumping back to brace his stance. As he did so a shattering and splinting of wood accompanied by a twanging of strings inevitably hailed the demise of Maddie's prized guitar.

'Oh no no no! You fucking oaf Alex! you've broken my guitar,' she wailed.

'I've just saved you from a dunking in the bloody stream, you selfish bitch,' Alex screamed back venting injustice.

'That is enough,' balled Ammon, now out of the car and clambering down between them. 'Come on, we need to get away from the car, it might explode.'

They scrambled up the banking Ammon pushing Maddie up from behind.

'That's only in movies anyway mate,' said Alex. 'Cars don't really explode like that.'

'Well I am not hanging around to see if you are right my friend,' Ammon replied cuttingly.

Gathered at the top of the banking the friends stood looking back at the ridiculous position Ammon's lovely new Alfa now found itself. The passenger side looked fine, if you parked it at the curb side you would probably think nothing of it. Unfortunately, the driver's side bore the scars of a losing battle with a solid stone wall pillar.

'I am so sorry my friends, it was all my fault, I shall never buy another automatic car again.' Ammon was staring misfortune in the face for a second time in a day and looked on the brink of tears. Taking a deep breath and exhaling slowly and audibly his face began to change, lighting up with widening eyes and a breaking smile.

'Bollox! As you say Maddie,' he exclaimed. 'I will not let a little thing like this get me down.'

'A little thing?' Alex queried, wide eyed and grinning in amazement.

'Yes my friend. You go to the pub and I'll sort this out and join you later.' They both looked at him stunned to silence. 'No, go on, go, I will be there later, I promise.'

'No Ammon, we need to stay, the police will have to be called and they might want statements and stuff,' reasoned Alex.

'I will call them and tell them, and sort out the recovery people. It will be fine, I promise it will be fine,' Ammon insisted placing a hand on their backs and coaxing then off in the direction of the village.

'Are you sure?' Maddie checked again.

'Yes, yes, I am very sure, now go,' he insisted.

Alex and Maddie took a few steps down the road before Maddie turned back, 'I've no guitar anyway Ammon so —'

'I can help you there Maddie,' Alex cut in wagging a raised finger. 'I've got a guitar you can borrow and it's a real beauty.'

'Go on Maddie, Alex has a guitar for you. I will do my best to be there before you play, go and do it Maddie, make something good happen for me on this day.'

Ammon's calm inspiring words were enough for Maddie, turning she headed off over the bridge into the village.

As they entered the village main street Alex paused prompting Maddie's attention. 'You carry on to the pub Maddie. I'm going to run back to the cottage and get the guitar.'

14 THE GUITAR

With the guitar wrapped unceremoniously in a black bin bag Alex shut the cottage door behind him and eyed the car, deciding there and then to drive back to the pub and leave it in the car park overnight. Securing the guitar on the floor behind the front seats he started the engine, still panting from the run and hurried activity. Taking a deep breath and venting a huge sigh he flicked the headlights on and pulled out of the drive. It was a dark moonless night. Looking up at the bejewelled sky he chuckled, contemplating the vastness of the universe and the insignificance of a broken guitar. He expected to get another good tongue lashing about that before the night was over. Feeling around checking the security of the instrument a thought struck him, that he might actually want to give it to her, and how good that would make him feel He shook his head. That couldn't happen, not while it had such a strong connection with his father.

Spotting a suitable parking spot Alex pulled up outside the Quiet Woman, turned the headlights off and sat for a few moments. A couple of people arrived with instruments in cases and music stands in hand.

'Bloody music stand! We left it in the car,' he recalled. 'Oh well another thing for Maddie to fuss about.' His mind drifted as he stared out into an unknowing world beyond the confines of his metal box, until a shadow of someone passing made him jump. It was the pub landlord with a cooler box hanging low from his right hand. It was obviously of some weight as he was struggling to keep an upright posture. Alex watched as he disappeared into the shadowed darkness of the building. Speculating for a moment as to the contents of the box, he entertained himself with a few possibilities. Pies, he thought, or maybe illegal alcohol to boost his bar profits, or just a spare head for the decapitated quiet woman depicted on the pub sign.

'Ok Alex, time to face the music,' he chuckled to himself realising the little pun he'd just made.

Arriving at the door of the pub he walked past an old Ford Granada hearse being unloaded by a big bloke with a long ponytail down his back. On the side of the vehicle, gothic signwriting read 'Deadicated Sound Systems' with a mobile phone number as though engraved on a headstone. Very nice, Alex thought, nodding an acknowledgement to the big guy who was carefully manoeuvring himself and two speakers through the pub entrance whilst holding the door open with his foot. Alex grabbed the door, to a nod, smile and a mouthed thanks from the big guy.

'You playing tonight?' asked the big guy.

'Oh umm, no, this is my girlfriend's guitar.' Girlfriend he thought, he would keep that faux pas to himself.

'Nice gig case,' joked the big guy.

'Sorry?' Alex questioned, checking the guitar in its bin liner. 'Oh yes, not the best protection is it? You wouldn't believe this guitar as well, it's a real beauty.'

'Oh yeah,' the big guy chuckled politely.

'You doing the PA tonight?' asked Alex.

'Yeah, and I'm a bit behind, better get on,' replied the big guy waddling off with his burden towards the stage area.

Alex stopped a moment inside the doorway and looked around for Maddie. It was quite busy in the bar with groups of people sat around chatting in several obvious clicks. Performers and their supporters Alex assumed. A young lad was tuning his guitars over by the fireplace with his following looking on proudly. Amongst them, Alex was drawn to a striking older woman whose presence intrigued him. He couldn't place her age but thought her to be around the same age as his mother. That aside, she was still a very attractive lady with long grey hair and the minimum of well applied make up. She turned to look over in his direction He quickly turned away and searched for Maddie, feeling a little self-conscious. Spotting her he made his way through the tables to the stuffed fox corner where she sat eating.

'Oh, the guitar assassin is here at last,' mocked Maddie as Alex took a seat opposite her. 'That's not going to last long in a bin liner with you around is it?' she continued pointing disapprovingly at the black bag. 'You wanna get yourself a nuclear waste flask to have any chance of keeping that safe don't you, Mr flippin chump?'

'Ha ha Ms Gresham. Are you not just thankful that you're still alive after that bloody scary crash?'

'Oh, I know, poor Ammon.'

'Poor Ammon! He nearly fucking killed us.'

'Yeah, but you've gotta love him though haven't you?'

'Yeah, I suppose you do,' conceded Alex. 'He's not having an easy time, is he?'

'No. He's made up with his dad, it sounds like it anyway, but the old man won't give on the business issues. Apparently, he left with them agreeing to disagree, which has got to be a better place for him hasn't it?'

Alex shrugged his shoulders and tutted. 'It's a better place to start from I suppose. We can give him an ear and a shoulder if he needs it later can't we?'

'Come on then Alexi-poos what's so special about this amazing guitar then?' insisted Maddie.

'Wait till you see this,' said Alex removing the bin bag from the instrument's curvaceous form.

'Wow Alex! That is actually absolutely beautiful.' Gasped Maddie.

'Isn't it just?' agreed Alex proudly.

'Where on earth did you get it?'

'That's a long story and I'm not sure is over yet,' he mused.

Maddie took the guitar from him and inspected its immaculately crafted body. She strummed it quietly several times listening intently to the sound it returned. As she did so the big guy began the proceedings over at the stage area. Briefly welcoming everyone he then introducing the first performers, a fiddle player and a guitarist. The duo, a middle-aged guy on guitar and what must have been his twin brother on violin burst into life with cheers from the gathering onlookers. It was fast and fun, with a Celtic refrain but Alex's ear was taken by Maddie with a curious smile on her face.

'Alex,' she whispered loudly. 'You've got an admirer, over by the fireplace, the woman with the long grey hair, she can't stop looking over.'

Alex sniggered and smiled not daring to glance round for fear of meeting the mysterious lady's eyes. He didn't know why, but he was again feeling very self-conscious.

'She's a stunning woman for her age Alex, have you seen her?' continued Maddie.

'I did notice her on the way in. She's happen a bit old for me though I reckon,' he replied making light of the moment. 'Anyway, I need a drink, do you want one?'

'Get me a G and T and a pint of water please.'

A pint of water, probably for her voice if she's singing thought Alex, heading off to the bar. Making a conscious effort to compose himself he looked around randomly, but with the intent of checking out the mystery lady. She was staring straight at him. He flinched to look away but found himself compelled to return her gaze. Getting to the bar he was relieved to turn away. Who was she, he puzzled? He bought the drinks and returned to Maddie avoiding making further eye contact with the older woman.

'I'm going to wait until Ammon gets here before I go on,' announced Maddie starting to look nervous again.

Alex put the drinks down on the table. 'Ok, but don't leave it too late, will you? That's what we're here for.'

'I know that you fuck wit, I'll do my thing when it's time,' she snapped back.

'Ooooh Maddie, language please,' condemned Alex comically. He pointed at the stuffed fox on the shelf behind her. 'Mr Fox there he doesn't tolerate bad language. He only bites the heads off chickens cos he thinks they're saying fuck, fuck, fuck, fuck.'

Maddie smiled, suppressing a laugh. 'Oh you big chump Alexi-poos, sit down, listen to the music and shut the fuck up.'

The evening progressed with the big guy introducing an odd-looking couple wearing similar pullovers and thick black rimmed glasses. Alex leant forward beckoning Maddie closer.

'I think these two are the Proclaimers' parents, aren't they?' he whispered loudly behind his hand.

'I wonder if they've walked five hundred miles and then walked five hundred more to get here tonight?' posed Maddie seriously.

'No, I saw them pull up in a Renault earlier,' replied Alex.

The man was thin and tall with a wild head of hair pointing out in three directions. Across his body hung a huge ornate accordion that he played with great skill, filling the room with a wide spectrum of lush sound. The lady was similarly thin with a set of teeth a horse would have been proud of. She hunched forward, rattling and clapping a tambourine until her cue to sing neared. Stepping forward to the microphone she let go.

Maddie covered her mouth to hide a giggle as the woman's soaring vocal left the pitch on a detour around all available notes bar the right one. Alex, arms crossed, mouthed stop it with feigned disapproval.

Their attention was drawn for different reasons to the next act. This was the young man who was accompanied by the striking older woman.

While he was taking to the stage, Alex chanced a glance over at the woman. She was engrossed in supportive applause, smiling and cheering. After his first notes were played, she relaxed a little but continued her unbroken gaze, resting an expectant finger on her lips. The boy was good and Alex caught Maddie, nodding in approval.

During the performance, Ammon arrived and carefully made his way over through the audience, waving and mouthing, hi, as he took a seat with them.

'Did you get sorted alright mate?' Alex enquired moderating his voice and drawing the others in towards the centre of the table.

'Yes, the police came and he seemed ok about it. We waited for a recovery truck but when it came the man said he could not get the car out of the tree with his winch so they are returning tomorrow with a bigger vehicle.'

'So, you're not gonna get done for dangerous driving or anything?' squeaked Maddie.

Ammon sat back and smiled, raising his hands jubilantly. 'No, I told him I lost control on some wet leaves and the car skidded off the road. He just said I hope you'll be more careful in future. A real result my friends to end an awful day.'

'A result mate!' exclaimed Alex. 'You've a pile of scrap hanging in a tree back there. Doesn't seem like a great result to me.'

'It is only money Alex, the car is fully insured, and we are all ok and that is the important thing. Who wants a drink?'

Ammon took the drinks requests and meandered off through the tables to the bar just as the young guy was finishing a song. Ammon stopped for a moment joining in the enthusiastic applause to which the young musician showed gracious appreciation. He thanked everyone before pointing out his friends and family over by the fireplace.

'Thank you, aunty Sarah, for your support over the last couple of years and Mum and Dad for putting up with the racket that's been coming out of my bedroom, for most of my life, sorry. This next one is for you lot, thanks.' He dropped his head and began to delicately pluck a familiar tune.

This was received by more applause and cheering especially from his supporters.

Alex watched the reactions carefully noting the boy had provoked a nod and wave from the older woman on the mention of Aunty Sarah.

Maddie interrupted his fixation. 'He's good isn't he Alex? And I've got to follow that, bloody hell.' She slummed back with folded arms and gurning rejection.

Alex laughed and leant over to encourage her. 'I'm sure you'll be fine. Ammon tells me you're really good.'

Ammon, who had returned from the bar and was resting a tray drinks down on the table, overheard the conversation. 'You are Maddie.

You are as good as him, just different. Do not be afraid, you have just escaped death because of my rubbish driving, what can go wrong now?'

Maddie recoiled further and clamped her head between her hands. 'Ok, fine, I'll do it, I'm fine.'

The boy ended his song with a fast strum of his guitar to tumultuous applause. Maddie sat upright and took a couple of deep fast breaths in an attempt to compose herself.

'ok, ok, fuck, fuck, fuck.'

'You'll be fine Maddie. Come on get yourself together,' encouraged Alex, watching her down another gin and slam the glass to the table.

As Alex looked across the room to see the youngster leaving the stage, the big guy was wandering over, trying to catch Maddie's attention. Maddie chirped up on seeing him and donned a smile.

'Are you ready Madeline? You can give it five minutes if you want, yeah?' said the big guy.

'Yeah, ok, thanks Greg, I'll be over in a few minutes,' replied Maddie continuing to smile until the big guy, Greg, had turned to leave. Her smile then inverted into an exaggerated fear face as again she slummed back into her seat to hide behind her hands. She surfaced moments later and downed another of the gins Ammon had racked up for her.

'Guitar Alex please,' she instructed with outstretched arms.

Checking the tuning and strumming a few chords she humming a melody line. 'No music stand, bollox! I'll just have to do it from memory.'

'I could ask if anyone has one you could borrow if you want Maddie?' offered Ammon.

'No, it'll be ok thanks,' she replied with chirpy but palpable trepidation. 'I'll put the sheet on the floor and try to do without it. OK guys wish me luck.'

The boys wished her luck, standing to see her off across the floor to the stage area. The big guy met her with an obliging frown and a few words while he pointed to a microphone and two monitor speakers on the floor in front of her. Maddie nodded in response placing a song sheet on to the mesh grill of one of the angled speakers at her feet, before approaching the microphone with her head bowed. Lifting her head and looking around the audience with a warm smile she began to introduce herself.

'Hi everybody. Hope you're having a lovely evening. I'm Maddie Gresham, and, I'd like to share with you a song I wrote recently. Hope you like it.'

Alex couldn't help but smile, she looked so much more confident than he had expected and her introduction was calmly projected and engaging. Her first few notes broadened his smile even more, with the guitar sounded amazing miked up through the PA system. He was even more surprised when she began to sing. Her voice was strong but gentle with a rich warm tone that gave the words life and meaning beyond their definition. He felt the hairs raise on the back of his neck and an emotional surge that was difficult to suppress. He remembered the first time he'd seen her a few days before, but this was a different girl again. Ammon's wise words came to him, suggesting her hard exterior was a shield to protect and reject after being hurt and abandoned. They were not so different, maybe not so much of a train wreck than clash as opposites attracted.

'Told you she was good Alex my friend,' beamed Ammon grabbing him by the shoulders and shaking him with excitement.

Alex acknowledged with a slow approving nod. Listening to her song he felt he was getting a rare glimpse of the real Maddie behind the fiery mask. He listened closer to the lyrics.

'...In the candle light dancing
I see your face in the shadows
Pray you come to rescue me my love
In my dreams you're there beside me
Give me your hand to guide me
And on the breeze your soft words come to me

Breath again my love, you'll not be the lonely one
Breath again my love, life has just begun
Breath again, oh my love breath again...'

Briefly he allowed himself to believe those words were for him, before shrugging it off dismissively. In those moments of distraction it crossed his mind he hadn't checked in with the older woman for a while. He glanced across but she wasn't in her seat. He strained his neck to see around the onlookers barring his view but she wasn't there. Turning back to the stage and Maddie, he saw her, standing amongst a small crowd that had gathered in front of the stage area. That's odd, thought Alex, she hadn't got up for her young prodigy so what was so special about Maddie?

With a soaring melody line resolving and fading into silence Maddie ended her song to gathering applause. Overwhelmed she covering her mouth, speechless.

'Thank you so much, thank you.' She managed to get some words out after finding her breath and returning to the microphone.

As the applause died down Alex and Ammon got to their feet to welcome Maddie back from the stage. Alex found himself drawn into a warm and tight embrace with her, a mutual resolution of relief and celebration of a job well done.

'Wow Maddie, that was brilliant, you were great,' lauded Alex.

'Small fish in a tiny puddle Alexi-poos, but thank you and thank you for being there.'

Alex pulled back to look her in the face, her eyes twinkled and her smile was full. 'There was nothing small fish about that Maddie, it was, brilliant, really beautiful.' He paused expecting her usual put down but she just carried on looking into his eyes and he carried on looking back into hers. Suddenly and simultaneously they broke their embrace both sensing the point of noticeable intensity had just been passed. Ammon recognised their brief connection and the awkward moments that followed, prompting him to step in and hug Maddie who jumped around with him in a celebratory dance.

It was then that Alex sensed someone close by seeking his attention. He turned and to his surprise was politely greeted by the older woman.

15 THE OLDER WOMAN

'Hi there, my name's Sarah. I do hope you don't mind me coming over?'

'Hi, I'm Alex and these are my friends, Maddie and Ammon.'

'Lovely to meet you Maddie,' she said leaning in to shake her hand. 'You did a great job there my dear. That was a really lovely song.'

'Oh, thank you, you're very kind,' Maddie responded still holding Sarah's hand.

'And you are very good my dear. Is that song about a certain boy then Maddie?'

Alex and Maddie's eyes met briefly.

'Who knows where songs come from eh? They write themselves sometimes don't they?' quipped Maddie.

'I think they do Maddie, and it's a wonderful feeling when it happens like that isn't it?'

'You, perform, have performed, Sarah?' Maddie enquired.

'I have, and I do still occasionally, but that was another life really.' Her reply was a little coy and evasive but undeniably gracious. 'Now you must be wondering why I've come over, so let me get to it. I'm sorry but I must ask where did you get that guitar?'

'Alex,' said Maddie.

'It's, mine,' said Alex almost simultaneously. 'It was actually my father's. I found it in his workshop after his, death.' A flash expression crossed Sarah's face that was long gone before truly perceptible, but Alex saw it. He didn't know why but he knew he could trust this lady and needed to be honest with her.

'I'm sorry Alex,' she said with a sympathetic pause. 'I only ask, because, it was actually once mine, many years ago.'

'Really!' Alex exclaimed. 'So, you recognise it?' he continued trying not to sound too defensive but probably failing.

'Oh yes, I would know that guitar anywhere Alex. It's just amazing that it should find me again, here and now. Check the makers name on the label inside?'

Alex picked up the guitar and began to examine it. Of course, he remembered, Sarah was the name on the label.

'John Bailey, for my forever friend Sarah?' she recounted.

'Yes, it is,' confirmed Alex. 'Did you know the maker?'

'I did yes, he was a great friend for many years. Now look at the rosette around the sound hole, what do you see?'

All three of them gazed at the guitar body and the elaborate marquetry that formed the rosette decoration around the sound hole.

'Oh my God!' exclaimed Maddie. 'I see it! Do you see it? Is it your name, Sarah Haven?'

'I see it yes,' said Alex amazed he hadn't noticed it before. 'That is so clever isn't it?'

'It's good isn't it, how it's not initially obvious? John was such a clever and gifted artist. Some of his guitars are works of art and impossible to find these days. I can't imagine how your father managed to come across this one Alex.'

Sarah's emotional connection with the guitar was obvious, but what was the right thing to do? Alex pondered. Give it back to her, a woman he didn't know two minutes ago? Offer to sell it back to her? What is it worth? What would be a realistic price? He hoped that question would not be raised this evening.

'Sorry Sarah I can't help you there,' Alex answered, half in response to his own tangled thoughts.

'Drinks anyone?' Maddie interrupted. 'Can I get you something Sarah?'

'Oh no thank you Maddie, that's very kind but I'm ok thanks.'

Maddie took requests and left for the bar with Ammon close behind.

Alex felt suddenly exposed and self-conscious. He looked at Sarah and smiled, she smiled back with a strangely over familiar and unusual warmth. There was something behind her eyes that puzzled him.

'Shall we sit down Alex? There is something else I want to talk with you about my dear.'

Alex took his seat, flush with anxiety. He felt something was about to fall into place in his head and somehow this lady held the key to that. Sarah sensed his plight.

'Don't be afraid Alex, I'm a friend. Please be mine, will you? I knew it was you when you first walked in, Alex Hidde. You see, I knew your father. For quite some time before he passed away.'

'Oh my god,' he whispered in disbelief as his brains neural pathways connected fragmented facts, throwing a startling realisation into his conscious mind. 'Hidden Haven, Hidde n Haven, the sign in my father's workshop, is that you Sarah?' he choked, on what felt to be a very physical lump in his throat.

'Yes, you clever boy, it is. I knew your father very well Alex. He was a wonderful man, and I miss him so very much. Please, come talk to me tomorrow, just me and you Alex, will you do that?'

'Yes, yes I will Sarah.' His emotions were on the brink of getting the better of him; he reached out for the remains of his drink and finished it.

'Are you ok Alex,' asked Sarah trying to regain eye contact.

'Yes, I'm ok thank you.' Alex took a breath in an attempt to compose himself.

'Let's keep this to ourselves for now can we Alex?'

'I think that will be best, yes. Where can I find you tomorrow and when?'

'Come to my house, it's off the square in Shire's Muse. It's called My Haven, third on the right, set back in the corner. I'll be in all morning, so any time after nine if that's ok with you?'

Alex nodded in agreement, a little lost for words.

Sarah placed a hand on his shoulder as she prepared to go. 'I'm going to go back to my crowd now, they'll be wondering what I'm up to over here with an attractive young man. See you tomorrow Alex, and thank you.' Getting up she turned to go.

'Sarah?'

'Yes Alex?'

'Did you love him, my father?'

'I do Alex, very much.' She intentionally stressed, do, as if to say he's still here in my heart. Alex wasn't going to argue with that.

He could tell she was also fighting her emotions as she returned to the group over by the fire place. She was quickly drawn back into the group and their boisterous conversation, smiling and laughing. Returned to her world after touching his with a revelation that seemed to change everything.

Ammon and Maddie returned with the drinks in fits of laughter, talking about some guy who had tried a pick up line on Maddie and regretted it. Alex consciously tried to return to the here and now as if nothing had happened but evidently, he wasn't fooling anyone. Maddie was first to notice his distant eyes and deflated body language.

'Alex, are you alright?'

'I'm fine, I think. I've just had a conversation with Sarah that's kinda, knocked me a bit sideways.' He pulled a false smile pushing back resurging emotion.

'Sarah's lovely Alex. What's she said that's upset you?' probed Maddie.

'She knew my father. Sounds like they had an affair before his death.'

'Oh Alex, how do you feel about that?'

'Really glad actually. She is lovely, but it's sad too, like he and I missed a chunk of, good life.' He struggled for the words to express his emotional state.

'I know who Sarah is Alex. I couldn't place her at first. Then when I heard her name it started to come back to me. She was pretty big in the folk-rock scene some years back, had a couple of hits too. And get this, I went to see her with my dad when I was about sixteen, so a couple of years before he died.'

Alex looked at her slowly shaking his head in disbelief. Maddie smiled a deep empathetic smile. 'Sarah has connected us both with our fathers, how spooky is that?'

'Which is my drink?' asked Alex. 'I need to do some proper drinking now.' He grabbed his pint and downed half of it in a single gulp.

Ammon laughed but gently put a stick in his spokes. 'Too late Alex, they are closing the bar now my friend, and we have a taxi coming soon.'

'Oh Bollox! Well, here's to a crazy life that just seems to be getting crazier, as if that was possible. Ok, all for one and one for all, down the hatch, yeah?'

They laughed, clinked glasses and downed their drinks in as close to one as they could manage. Ammon drained his glass, turned it upside down and plonked it on top of his head. Alex and Maddie did not follow his interpretation of the drinking tradition and fell about laughing.

'Oh, I thought that was how you did this thing, come on my friends' he pleaded beaming joyfully. 'Ok, I'm going to check on this taxi, I'll let you know if it's here,' he continued, wondering off towards the door.

Alex and Maddie were left sat opposite each other in an awkward scene, neither knew quite what to say or do next.

Alex broke the silence. 'I'm going to go see Sarah tomorrow, and talk with her.'

'That's great Alex. I'm sure it will help you both.'

'Thanks Maddie. I'm really glad we came out tonight. It's been a bit, bizarre, but.'

'Yeah. And who'd have thought it? I'm actually brilliant and a budding diva. So move over Maria Carey and Beyonce, there's a new girl in town and her ass is as cute as any of yous bitches, Ooooh yeah!'

Alex laughed. 'You are mad, you do know that don't you?'

'Yeah, but you like it don't you?'

'Oh yes I like alright.' Their eyes connected and the awkwardness returned.

'Taxi is here you two,' came Ammon's shout from the doorway. 'Come on he is waiting.'

Alex secured the guitar on the front passenger seat of the cab and they all jumped into the back with Maddie in the middle and the boys on either side.

'Where to first Ammon,' enquired the driver in a familiar accent.

Ammon gave the driver Alex's address before turning to his friends.

'Can you believe it this man he is from Egypt, not a hundred miles from where I was raised. Is that not true my friend?' said Ammon opening a conversation with the driver.

Ammon and the driver talked more as the cab drove the short distance to the cottage, leaving Alex and Maddie to take a back seat in the conversation, politely acknowledging and reflecting where appropriate. They were both deep in their own thoughts and maybe wishing they were somewhere else.

Alex felt Maddie close to him, her side against his. A pressure she could have controlled and adjusted but she chose to stay close, he was sure of that. He contemplated her body as the movement of the car on the road played their thighs against each other. The thought of touching her and feeling her was exciting and consuming. He teased himself that she was feeling that too. As the taxi pulled up at the cottage Alex fumbled for the door handle.

'Ok guys, thanks for a great evening, see you Ammon mate.' As he moved to leave the car he felt Maddie's hand in his, he looked back at her. 'I'll see you tomorrow yeah?'

She smiled maintaining eye contact and keeping hold of his hand for just a few moments longer. 'Yep, ok, see you tomorrow Alex.'

Grabbing the guitar from the front seat he closed the doors and stood back as the taxi drove away, taking with it what seemed to be the only light for miles.

Enveloped by the darkness he looked up into the celestial canopy of distant stars and watched the vapour from his sighing breath leave his body, dispersing into the cold night air. He stood there for some time wrapped in the universe, waiting for a shooting star to hang a wish on. That was his father's line from a distant childhood memory. He'd given up hanging wishes on shooting stars years ago but tonight felt like the right time to take it up again. He stayed out there until the discomfort of his shivering body forced him inside to the warmth of the kitchen.

At the kitchen table with a cup of tea and the guitar across his lap he strummed a few chords and thought about the two women that had just entered his life. He hummed a melody line and allowed a few words to scan along with it.

'One could be my lover and one could be my mother.' He laughed at the craziness that had just flowed out of his head and slammed out a heavy riff to reset his uncomfortable thoughts. During the cacophony the sound of a text message notification from his mobile vibrated through the table. He flipped it around and swiped the screen, it was from Maddie.

Maddie - 'Hi A, I'm in my diva bed wearing my diva jimjams while my entourage are polishing the Lear jet ready for a breakfast dash to Tiffany's. What's goin down in the world of mere mortals? M Diva x'

Alex sat up and tapped out a reply.

Alex - 'Breakfast at Tiffany's eh? Do you remember the film and maybe kinda liked it? I actually prefer Texas Chainsaw Massacre x'

Maddie - 'I prefer a fish knife for my kippers thank u, I find a chainsaw a little vulgar'

Alex - 'Oooooh ever so posh aren't we dear?'

Maddie - 'Wanna talk you big chump?'

Alex – 'Go on then, when you're ready ma'am'

Alex sat back and waited for the phone to ring. He'd barely come to rest before the call came in; he answered it, nestling into the corner of the sofa.

'Good evening ma'am, how are you?' Alex greeted in a posh voice.

'Hello you big chump, I'm ok, still full of it obviously but I'll be back to doubting myself tomorrow. How are you, is more to the point?'

'Shaken and stirred, I think. Bit of a crazy night for a boy like me wasn't it?'

'Bit of a shocker alright, Sarah and your dad and all that.'

'Yeah, she's such a lovely lady though, it just all makes sense, and, it's nice to think my Dad had some happy times in his last... I'm so bitter about my mother at the moment, it's just eating me up.'

'I know Alex, you'll deal with that in time, won't you?'

'Yeah, I will, I know.' Alex's voice sunk into a silence before Maddie sensed the timing was right to pick the conversation up again.

'I've been thinking about my Dad too after meeting Sarah. It's just so...' she trailed off to silence.

'Go on Maddie tell me about your dad, I'm listening.'

'Thanks Alex.' She paused and took a breath. 'I lost him when I was eighteen, and my life pretty much fell apart. My Mum met Graham, my step father, and it was crap, we didn't get on from the start. I just felt so abandoned and my Mum couldn't see it, she was so full of him and his big important city firm. That's where the big family money came from Alex. He was a self-made millionaire hotshot arsehole with no family, so when he died mother got the lot, and now for fucks sake, it's all mine. It's mad isn't it? You'd think it would be a massive life changing, joy giving, thing, but it feels like a millstone right now. '

'I think I see, Maddie. Just take your time, that's all you can do isn't it? There's no rush is there?'

'I know, you're right. You know, I wish I could spend that money to bring our Dads back. Doesn't work like that though does it?' she fell silent for a moment before something tickled her, forcing a giggle. 'I used to have these conversations with my Dad, from being really small, they were our talks about life, the universe and everything. I still remember some of the moral stuff and little life lessons my dad slipped in here and there. It was great. An opportunity for me to just talk, about anything that was on my mind or that was bothering me, and I knew he was listening, always listening. And his responses were always considered, and usually funny, he could be so funny. As I got older the conversations became more, equal, and I developed my own opinions, which he encouraged, sometimes challenged, which was good, that made me think more critically. What happened to that me? I wish I could have been her for the rest of my life.'

Alex could hear emotion breaking in her voice, he wanted to hold her and make everything alright.

'Maddie, it's ok, those are wonderful memories. I'm not sure how you detach the pain from memories like that, about those you love. I want to remember my father without the pain, and, the regrets. I don't know how you do that.'

'I know what you mean Alex. Regrets are yours to let go of, aren't they? I've got regrets I can never let go of, because, I'll never be able to forgive myself. They'll always come back another day and start the regret loop running again and again. I hate growing up Alexi-poos, can we stop please?'

Alex laughed. 'We just have to get on with it Maddie, it's as simple as that, pick ourselves up and just bloody get on with it. Parts of us will always be young but we are people who care, and, want to grow. So, I'm afraid that means more philosophical life, the universe and everything talks like this.'

'Great Alexi-poos, tune in again next week when we will be using Occam's Razar theory to shave a fish?'

'Say what girl friend?'

'Oh come on Alex, catch up! Occam's theory basically says that the more simple a theory is, the more likely it is to be right. So, if a man is caught shaving a fish, the simple answer is, he probably needs some serious psychiatric help.'

'Mmm I see. So, if Maddie is showing signs of madness, she is probably mad?'

'Argh, you're cheating, you knew that anyway. Right! I need to sleep, my head is banging and I need my beauty sleep.'

'You don't want to get too much of that or you'll be totally irresistible.'

'Oh you charmer Alex Hidde. You know beauty is only skin deep and I still need some work on the inside bit?'

'I can help you with that, if you'll help me with mine?'

'Ok, that's a deal then. Maybe see you tomorrow?'

'Yeah, I'll let you know how I get on with Sarah.'

'Yes! Please do Alex. Good night.'

'Good night Maddie.'

They both held on the line, waiting and wanting to say and hear more, until one of them hung up, though neither of them heard the other doing so.

Alex jumped to his feet and strutted around the kitchen filled with a consuming frustration. They were just good friends he thought decisively. He'd got wrapped up in the promise of them being lovers but that conversation was about two friends, all be it two close friends, that's all it was. They were both going through difficult times, vulnerable and maybe even needy. Not a good sound basis for any kind of relationship. And a serious relationship was the last thing he needed right now. Was he over reacting, he asked himself? The truth was he was only capable of mentally putting one foot in front of the other in that moment. His hypersensitive emotions were clouding what little judgment he felt he had left to rely on. He paused at the mirror over the fireplace and looked long and hard at himself.

'A good night's sleep is what we need now. Then what will tomorrow bring eh? Another emotional rollercoaster probably, and no doubt more hidden truths.'

16 HIDDEN TRUTHS

Someone was playing a guitar, in fact 'the' guitar; its sound was so distinctive. He closed his eyes to concentrate, to focus, to locate the whereabouts of the player. Waves of sound bounced wildly around him. He could see them flashing with blinding intensity as they hit walls and ceilings. Where was this place? He looked around trying to make sense of his surroundings. He was in the carcass of a derelict building, a long-abandoned hospital. It was decaying around him, unstable and precarious, like a Jenga tower of Weetabix soaked in the milk of his emotions, weakening and twisting. He went on searching corridor after corridor with no doors and no windows as faster and faster the music played and faster and faster he ran. Making decisions which way to turn with less and less logic and more and more uncertainty. He had to get to the player before the music ended, or he would never find him. The player was his father, he knew that now. He cried out for an answer, straining to be heard. His voice close to bursting, he screamed ever louder. He'd emptied his lungs, gasping for air he fell to the ground. The player stopped playing and so ended the sound.

Alex woke shaking from the intense effort he had just expended, but it was only a dream. He could breathe normally. Everything was ok, and the air was fresh and untainted. Well, as untainted as the air in a guy's bedroom could be. The dream had disturbed him and as he slowly came around, the intensity of the emotional loss broke him. He wiped the tears from his face and fought back more. Was he ever going to find peace and solace from this torture?

It was already after nine as Alex poured milk into a mug of tea. He considered chucking it in the sink and just getting out the door and on with whatever the day was going to throw at him. Instead he grabbed an energy bar from the cupboard and sat at the kitchen table. He thought back to yesterday morning when everything had kicked off with the disappearance of Evelyn. It had been a crazy day but purposeful and distracting. The three of them were the most unlikely team but their strength together was becoming intoxicating. Alex felt a positive charge from his train of thought, he had friends around him now like he hadn't known for some time. He was reluctant to call them kindred spirits, however they were all going through difficult times and that is in essence what had brought them together.

Donning his jacket and a black beanie he set off walking from the cottage towards the village, deciding he would go get his car from the pub carpark after meeting Sarah. The walk was going to give him an opportunity to think a little more about what he wanted to know from her and how he was going to react to her admissions. There would be no hiding from the inescapable emotions that would surface in the course of bringing back the memory of his father. He knew though that she would be there to support him through those difficult bits; he would also have to be there for her. On his way through the village it occurred to him that he might literally be following in his father's footsteps. He would have probably taken this very same route on the way to one of his clandestine meetings with Sarah. He pondered how he would have made that work, the excuses, lies and not only that but avoiding suspicion in the small village community where your business was not always your own.

After entering the mews from the square Alex could make out what he suspected to be Sarah's cottage tucked away in the right-hand corner. At first it appeared to be quite modest but as he got closer the full extent of the property could be appreciated. Stretching back into a sizable plot it really was a hidden haven, he thought. Approaching the front door, he noted the nerves he had harboured for most of the walk had subsided. In their place was a sense of expectation, this was a safe house, hidden from the toils of the world outside, this was a meeting with the past in a place that would also inform his future.

Before he had reached the front door, it was already opening, Sarah had obviously seen him arrive.

'Hi Alex. Come on in.' Sarah led Alex into the house down a sparsely decorated hallway. The walls were painted matt white and adorned with a few simply framed black and white photographs. Really well taken photographs Alex noted, and probably taken by the same person. Some were portraits of which Alex assumed were folk musicians. Their evidently eccentric personalities captured beautifully by the observer.

'What do you think Alex?' questioned Sarah noticing he was paying the images some attention. 'A bit of a passion of mine, photography. Purely amateur though, won't be up to your professional standards.'

'They are really good,' assured Alex responding to her shrugs of modesty. 'I mean it, they are really good. Are they all friends of yours?'

'At one time or another, yes. It's always the kindness in someone's eyes that draws me to take their picture.'

'Well that's as good a reason as any I know,' beamed Alex recognizing her familiar warmth.

'I'll make a pot of tea, if you want to just go through to the conservatory Alex.'

'Ok, thank you.' Alex wandered through into the conservatory to be greeted by a wonderfully maintained and blooming garden that seemed to wrap itself around the indoor space with all the colours of an autumn wilderness.

'Here we are dear,' said Sarah bringing in the tea.

'That was quick,' remarked Alex.

'I expected you'd be on time...'

Alex finished her sentence in his head - like father like son.

Sarah placed a tray down on the conservatory table, two cups, a tea pot in a cosy and a jug of milk. It reminded Alex of the set up in his father's workshop that he'd noticed the last time he was in there retrieving the guitar. The guitar that ultimately brought Sarah and himself together.

'Do you take sugar Alex?'

'No thanks, not for me,' replied Alex returning from his

distraction.

They sat down on wicker chairs either side of a low glass coffee table. A brief but awkward silence followed as they both sought where to begin. Acknowledging the obvious impasse brought knowing smiles to their faces.

'I've been trying to find you Alex, for some time. I must be honest with you. All I knew was that you were living in Manchester with Michelle.' Sarah paused at his fleeting despondent expression. 'But I am gathering that that relationship has problems? I don't mean to pry, sorry Alex.'

'That's most definitely over yes, and pretty much the reason I'm here in Sterndale. Getting away from it all, and taking some time out to rethink my life.' Alex looked down at his hands clasped in front of him and prompted himself to relax a little.

Sarah began pouring the tea showing intent to lift the mood of the conversation. 'I'm sorry to hear that my dear but very glad that you are here and we've had this chance to meet.'

Alex smiled as he took a cup of tea from her. 'I'm glad to be here too. It is a bit strange though isn't it? I can't help but think you're going to tell me something, bad, sorry.'

'Oh Alex, not all I have to say is good, that's true, I wish it were, I wish things had been so different. What I can say is that the times I did spend with your father were some of the best of my life. He was a very special man.'

'How long, where you…?' Alex began not knowing quiet how to

finish.

'I knew your father for several years. We'd stop and chat in passing until.' Pausing she put her hand to her face to hide an embarrassed smile. 'It was silly really. We found ourselves going out of the way to have these chance meetings and it was obvious they weren't chance anymore. It wasn't long before we became very close.'

Alex knew it was only a matter of time before the inevitable swell of emotions would be too much to push down. He sensed Sarah was also sharing that fight, he wasn't alone this time. A question crossed his mind that helped quell the rising.

'Why didn't he leave my mother, for you? Several years is a long time isn't it?' He carefully unfolded the questions so as not to upset her.

Sarah took a breath and sighed thoughtfully, looking for the words in a blurred space between them.

'That's where it becomes more difficult Alex. Things got complicated when he confronted your mother. She knew, you see, for a long time, but she wouldn't let him go. Alex, she had some hold over him, something that made it necessary for her to keep the marriage going. She didn't care about him, just the money she would lose if he left too soon. You know your father worked for the government?'

Alex nodded in agreement. 'I did yes, he worked in intelligence, but I'm not sure what he really did.'

Sarah continued, 'Now I don't know all the ins and outs, he told me it was better that I didn't. He was due a payment, for his involvement in some work with a foreign government, and that had to remain out of the public domain for political reasons. Your mother found out about it and threatened to expose him. It would have ruined him and probably worse, I don't know, it certainly scared him. I don't know if that payment has been made yet, but it will go to your mother now, I'm sure of that. So you see, he was trapped with her. It wasn't all bad Alex, we saw each other most days, we just couldn't live together as we wanted to, until he could sort out the mess.'

Alex shook his head slowly in disbelief. 'So, she knew all along?'

'Yes, and it was then that your father discovered she had been having an affair with that man from the horticultural society.'

Alex huffed, 'That doesn't surprise me one bit. He's a dodgy character I reckon.'

'He is Alex.' She paused before dropping a bomb into Alex's already tormented state. 'This is really hard for me to say, and it probably sounds crazy Alex but, I think they had something to do with your father's death, I really do, and I haven't known what to do about it. I'm so sorry Alex.'

Her words sent a bolt of pure shock to his core. The hollowing fracture tore into him with deafening reality.

'Oh my god, that can't be true, it can't be.' Wrestling with the suggestion it struck him that she could well be right, his mother could be capable of such a thing.

'I can't handle this right now, if that's right we need to do something, but, it is only a suspicion, that probably can't be proven.'

Sarah came over and sat next to him, holding him by the shoulders, her silent empathy calming his building rage.

'I'm so sorry Alex, I didn't want to upset you. I just knew you would want to know. I couldn't keep it from you, and yes, it is only a suspicion, but it feels strong enough for me to need to share it with you.'

Alex sat head clamped in his hands trying to take in the destructive possibility. 'I can't take this in Sarah, I can't handle it right now. I need to think about this.'

'I know Alex, and I'm sorry, I had to let you know my suspicions. Your father talked about you a lot you know. He understood why you kept away, and he knew that one day you would be closer.'

'I think I knew that too,' chocked Alex. 'It's too late now though, he's gone and I miss him so badly.'

'Oh Alex, I know, I miss him too, I miss him like life its self.'

They shared their tears in a tight embrace both in the knowledge that they had found the only person that could possibly ease their grief.

Alex conceded to himself that he could not remember ever being held in such a warm loving embrace in all his life, not by his mother or anyone. He struggled to recall the last time he was held by her, he couldn't even imagine ever wanting to. Her significance in his life amounted to no more than the emotional scars he now sought to heal and if the suspicions were true, she needed to be dealt with, appropriately, but how?

Sarah slowly broke from their embrace and sitting back from Alex held his hand.

'Can we get through this together Alex, please? I would love you to be around, you are so much like him you know.'

Alex sat up and composed himself. 'Yes, I'd like that.'

'Thank you, Alex. I'll make some more tea. You will stay a while longer won't you?'

'Yes, I will, if that's alright.' Alex felt shell shocked like he had never known. What do you do and how are you meant to react to such a notion? For now, he must put this to one side but he would have to find out the truth. There was no way this could rest in him and not be resolved. It was a rage so deep and frightening it would have to be vented somewhere somehow.

Sarah returned from the kitchen with a fresh pot of tea and a bottle of Macallan Single Malt Whisky.

'I know it's probably a bit early, but I thought a little tipple in our tea wouldn't go a miss, what do you say Alex?'

'I'm not going to say no right now, thank you,' countered Alex holding up his cup for Sarah to splash in a dram or two. 'The sign I found in my father's workshop Sarah, was that for here?'

'Hidden Haven? Oh yes, that's what your father called this place when we first talked about living together.'

'And the guitar?' Alex paused watching a smile fill Sarah's face. 'He went and found that for you, didn't he?'

'He did Alex. I didn't know until I saw Maddie playing it, and then of course seeing you there as well, you can't imagine how I felt. I told him about it, about the guitar and how I'd lost it, well, stupidly trusted someone with it. I didn't know he'd go and try to find it, it's amazing, truly amazing.' She covered her mouth a moment as she fought the surge of emotions but gracefully defied it with a sip of tea and a smile.

'It's your guitar then Sarah, you ought to have it back really,' announced Alex without question.

'I don't know Alex, it's not that I've got a lot of use for it these days, and Maddie plays it so well. Maybe you'd want to give it to her?'

'I did think of giving it to Maddie, but that was before I knew the truth about it. Why don't you play anymore Sarah?'

'Oh, that's complicated Alex and not a story I want to go into right now, if that's ok?'

'Of course, I'm sorry, didn't mean to pry.' Alex backed off politely.

'We have so much to talk about Alex, we'll come back to my dreary past another day. Anyway, Maddie seems a little sweet on you I'd say. Are you two an item?'

'Now look who's prying?' joked Alex. 'Well, we've had our moments but I'm not sure we are right for each other really.'

'That's a shame, she seems such a lovely girl, and she has a beautiful voice. Are you good friends then?'

'That's a good question, we get at each other now and again, but yes I think we are becoming good friends despite that. In fact, all three of us have become pretty close since we came together over this missing girls thing, sorry, have you heard about that Sarah?'

Alex went through the whole story of meeting Ammon, the missing girls and their ill-fated quest to find Anna. Being with Sarah felt very natural to Alex and time passed quickly as they talked on into the late morning. He still had to check himself, being with this beautiful lady who had all too briefly been his father's lover, but it felt good and right and he was drawing strength from it and that was just what he needed right now.

Turning to give Sarah a last wave Alex walked off up the drive and back into the mews. The glow of sharing some time with her was holding a lid on the disturbing, damning suspicions directed at his mother and her henchman lover George Chapman. He knew the underlying sadness that was a denied future with his father and Sarah would always be there, but his blessing for today was that he had found Sarah and she had found him. Taking his phone from his pocket he tapped Ammon's number and waited. There was no way he was going to mope about for the rest of the day, he needed a distraction.

Ammon answered the call with his familiar and grounding, 'hello my friend.'

'Hi Ammon mate, what you up to?' jibed Alex boisterously.

'I am just collecting a hire car. They are giving me a hire car from the insurance while they sort out the Alfa.'

'Wow mate! They're hiring you a new car and they expect to get it back in one piece?'

'Ha, very funny my friend. As you know I am an extremely good driver, but just not of automatic cars in tight corners. Anyway, this is small and white and has a gear stick, and, it probably does not go fast enough to get worried in corners, so it is perfect.' Ammon was sounding incredibly chirpy

'That's great Ammon, I'm only kidding mate. What you up to today? I could do with some company and a bit of a distraction.'

'What is going on my friend? Are you ok? I was going to head back to Manchester later but there is no rush, I will come round to yours now if that is good with you?'

'That's great. I'm on my way back now. I'm ok, I'll tell you when I see you ok?'

'Ok Alex, I will see you shortly.'

'Don't call me shortly.'

'Sorry, what Alex?'

'See you later mate.'

'Ok see you later, goodbye.' Ammon's voice faded but Alex could hear a conversation between him and someone in the background as he was being shown around the car, Ammon hadn't disconnected the call. Alex chuckled to himself and tapped the end call button. That felt better, he had his distraction for the rest of the day and maybe, between them, they could even come up with a plan.

17 A PLAN

Looking out of the kitchen window Alex studied the light on the distant moorland as it played through gathering clouds. His thoughts, chaotic and aggressive were fuelling a building gut felt anxiety, compelling him to pace the kitchen searching for something to break the loop and distract him. This was ridiculous, he thought. He needed to calm down and get a grip. Thankfully Ammon would be there soon. Picking up his camera flight case he placed it down on the table and opened it. He took out a camera body, turned it on and went through a series of checks he often did to ensure the shutter and aperture mechanisms were functioning correctly. It always made him feel like he was servicing his weapon, this was his sniper rifle, his weapon of choice. Taking out his large zoom lens he snapped it into place on the camera body and pointed it out onto the distant hill side. Pulling the zoom the autofocus zipped into action instantly bringing the image into sharp focus. Scanning along the top of the tree line he could pick out the odd bird in flight. Dropping it down into the foreground he caught a rabbit darting in and out of the hedgerow. Lowering his sights further found a flower head, filling the viewfinder, stamen clearly visible. He wished he could pull the trigger and blow the head off the damn plant. That would be the way to do it, a high-powered rifle from a distance, a thud and blood before the target had even heard the gunshot. But where would he get a high-powered rifle around here today? You'd struggle to get a sink plunger never mind a lethal firearm.

Two sharp knocks at the door broke the silence and Alex's disturbing fixations. Ammon let himself in with his usual greeting.

'Hello my friend, how are you?'

Alex grinned and shrugged his shoulders, 'I'm ok mate. A mixed day really, how about you?'

Ammon looked on puzzled and concerned. 'I am good Alex, you are troubled though, I see that my friend.'

Alex nodded and turned to put the kettle on. 'Let's have a brew. Do you fancy some toast?'

'I will never say no to toast,' declared Ammon rubbing his hands together. 'Have you got the lime marmalade as well?

'In the fridge with the butter. Come on! You should know where it is by now, you've nearly finished the jar singlehanded.'

Ammon opened the fridge door. 'This fridge reminds me of my new hire car, white and the light comes on when you open the door. What is it you say my friend? It cannot pull the skin off a rice pudding, but it can fight its way out of a paper bag, but only just.'

This got them both into instant fits of laughter further heightened by Ammon's impromptu but hilarious car driving dance in front of the open fridge door.

'Where did that come from mate?' Alex questioned holding his sides in pain from laughing.

'I do not know. I have been feeling good today. Thankful to be alive maybe. Did you go to see Sarah this morning?'

'I did yes. It was good. Emotional, as I expected, but just really nice to get to know her.'

'So, what has got you troubled my friend?' Ammon probed.

Alex's face dropped with a sigh and a familiar knot tightening in the pit of his stomach.

'Sarah,' he started slow and weighty, 'thinks that my mother and her bloke had something to do with my father's death.'

'What?' exclaimed Ammon. 'Do you think that can be true?'

Alex fought for words confronting the painful revelation again. 'Yes, I'm thinking that more and more, and I don't know how to handle it. What do I do Ammon, if it is true?'

'That is what you need to know, if it is true Alex.'

'But how? She's not going to admit it to me, is she?'

'No but she will admit it to someone who does know it to be true,' said Ammon cryptically.

'What on earth are you talking about?'

'If we can get her to admit it in a conversation with her bloke, and we can record it, then we have the evidence, don't we?' Ammon continued getting a little excited.

'Are you a secret agent Ammon or are you talking hypothetically here?'

'No, I am not a secret agent my friend, but I have equipment that can make us so. You see I brought with me some surveillance equipment. It is things that our company sells, remote cameras, microphones and monitoring devices. We can set it up at your mother's house and see if we can get her to confess.' Ammon was getting visibly excited.

'What are you doing with kit like that Ammon?' quizzed Alex with amused surprise.

Ammon paused. 'I brought it to help solve the missing girl crimes, and Evelyn disappearing. I thought it might be useful, you never know do you my friend?'

'That takes being prepared to a whole new level mate. Have you got your boy scout's covert surveillance badge then, and your exploding waggle?' mocked Alex still stunned by Ammon's suggestion.

'We can go do it now if you want my friend? We will need to pick up the kit, it is at Maddie's house, but we can go and set it up and then you will have your answer. If there is no one in the house that is of course.'

Alex contemplated the plan and the frightening reality that could be the outcome. 'Shit Ammon, this is serious stuff. Can we really do that?'

Ammon reassured him with sobering clarity. 'You need to know Alex, and we have the means to do that. Be brave my friend, you have to know.'

'Ok Ammon, let's do it, you're right I do need to know. How is it going to work then?'

Over the now customary tea and toast they put together a plan. After planting the bugging devices that afternoon they would try to provoke a reaction whilst listening-in that evening. Ammon would call the home phone purporting to be a blackmailer who has evidence that Mr Hidde had been killed in suspicious circumstances. He would be intimidating and hang up with the parting line, I will call again soon be ready if you know what's good for you.

Sat in the car outside Maddie's house, Alex and Ammon familiarized themselves with the bugging equipment, fitting the devices with mobile phone sim cards and testing the microphones. Alex took two of the bugs and wandered off a few yards away from the car talking into them as he went. Ammon waved and beckoned him back.

'All is working loud and clear Alex,' confirmed Ammon. 'Let us go see if we can plant them.'

Parking the car a discreet distance away from the Hidde family home they carefully approached the side gate looking for signs of anyone home.

'There's no cars in the drive so I'm guessing they're out,' whispered Alex checking around for any possible onlookers.

'So, the key is hidden under a plant pot is it my friend?'

'Always has been, let's see if it's still there,' replied Alex sneaking down the side of the house to a row of pots near the conservatory door.

'Gloves, no finger prints yeah?' said Alex taking out a pair of yellow Marigolds from his pocket and putting them on.

'Why did mine have to be pink Alex? I hate the colour pink,' moaned Ammon.

'This isn't a bloody fashion show, just get on with it and don't go knocking anything over,' scorned Alex playfully trying to inject a little calming humour into the proceedings.

Tilting each pot in turn Alex looked up at Ammon, his face showing the mounting disappointment of each unsuccessful forage. Slowly lifting the final pot, barely able to look he groped around under it and stopped. A smile came slowly to a relieved face as he pulled a rusty key from the dirt under the pot.

'Looks like mother might have forgotten this was here, lucky, lucky, lucky,' celebrated Alex. 'This should be the key for the back door, round here Ammon.'

Alex scurried off around the conservatory to the back door. Cleaning the key on his jeans he checked its condition and picked out a couple of rusty fragments from the indentations that made up its unique profile. Looking around once more to reassure himself they were not being overlooked, Alex offered the key to the lock and slid it in. It fitted, now it just needed to turn and...

'Bollox! It's not working, it's not the right key,' he exclaimed slamming down the handle and pushing the door in frustration. At this the door flew open clattering against the inside wall.

'Shhh,' signalled Ammon looking around in fright.

They stood there for a few moments checking the disturbance hadn't attracted any unwanted attention then quickly entered. Closing the door behind them, Alex led Ammon into the house and through into the kitchen.

'This is where they will spend most of their time I reckon, so a good place for one of the bugs,' said Alex looking around for a hiding place.

Ammon took a bug out of his pocket and stretching up dropped it inside one of three porcelain flower shades that made up the ceiling light. 'That will be perfect. It will pick up sound from the whole room. Now where else?'

'Nice one!' praised Alex wishing he'd thought of it. 'The conservatory I reckon, that's where the old trout watches TV and relaxes.'

Walking into the conservatory Alex looked up and immediately recognised the ceiling light as a perfect place for the second of the bugs. Pointing smugly to the light he gestured to Ammon. Ammon laughed as Alex pulled up a chair to help him reach the higher lamp shade.

Alex grabbed Ammon by the shoulder as a sudden noise startled him. They both froze, senses heightened listening for further movement. With the sound of the front door opening came his mother's impatient voice.

'Bring those things in George, don't leave them in the car you fool!'

Alex pulled Ammon after him tip toeing out of the conservatory and round to the back door where he reassessed their escape route.

'We can't get past the conservatory, they might see us,' whispered Alex through gritted teeth.

They listened intently as his mother wandered through to the conservatory followed by a crash of something falling to the floor and the legs of a chair screeching on the wooden surface. Alex and Ammon stared at each other with wild grins recognising their minor oversight.

'Who put that bloody chair there?' screamed Mrs Hidde. 'George! I've just tripped over a damn chair. What did you go leaving it there for you stupid man?'

Alex nodded in the direction of the back door and they both slipped out closing it firmly but quietly behind them. Dropping down on all fours they carefully crawled under the conservatory windows and round to the side of the house where they held up waiting for George to finish unloading the car. After hearing a car door slam and then the front door close shut they ran for it, Ammon clearing the front gate in a single bound. Alex approached the gate in full flight with the intention of jumping it. Miss timing his pace he and was forced to swiftly but silently open the gate and close it behind him before carrying on after Ammon. Regrouping at the car they laughed out their relief on successfully completing their covert operation. Back safely inside the car Ammon took a small hand held monitor from his pocket and turned it on, switching it between the installed bugs they had left in the house. Conversations came through with reasonable clarity, Mrs Hidde still cursing at George who was pleading his innocence regarding the chair that had obviously caused her to take a tumble.

'That's great, thanks Ammon. Phase one completed, phase two later and then what the fuck is phase three? I only wish I knew.'

'We will cross that bridge when we come to it Alex. You will have an answer later for better or for worse. I am going to turn the monitor off for now so we do not drain the battery in the bugs, is that ok Alex? We will listen in again when we get back to your house and make a call, yes?'

'Ok Ammon. Let's get back then mate.'

'More tea and toast my friend?' enquired Ammon.

'Yes, my insatiable friend, more tea and more toast. Oh, can you stop at the Spar for some milk? I'm nearly out.'

Leant against the kitchen worktop Alex stared into the toaster, lost in his thoughts and struggling to come to terms with what they were about to do. How would he react if he heard a confession of guilt from his mother, a clear unequivocal admission that she caused the death of his father? Just the suspicion of it was crushing enough. He had to know, he had to know. Repeating those words swung his precarious mood into anger mode, from which he knew he could muster all the energy he needed to get this job done. Alex brought a plate of toast and two mugs of tea to the kitchen table and sat down opposite Ammon who was playing around with two monitoring units.

Ammon pointed to each of the monitors in turn. 'Ok, this is set to pick up from the kitchen and this one is the conservatory.' He sensed Alex's apprehension giving him space to ready himself.

Alex played with his mobile phone, lining it up with the monitors and a note pad on the table. His OCD behaviour was a distraction but only that. He would have to engage with this undertaking sooner or later, if he wanted to know the truth.

Ammon turned on the monitors one by one and looked at Alex for a cue to begin. The early evening news could be heard from the conservatory television on one of the monitors and the sound of someone humming over the clinking of pots and pans on the other. Alex pictured his mother in the kitchen, preparing dinner wearing one of her hideous flowery aprons. George was in the conservatory watching the news. A cough followed by repeated throat clearing confirmed this. As he thought of these people going about their evening rituals, he couldn't help but feel sorry for them. In a few minutes he could have the power to destroy their lives just like they had destroyed his and his father's, and Sarah's. If these accusations were nonsense, all would stay the same, his father would still be gone and suspicions will have been just that, suspicions. Within all this he wanted to believe Sarah. She wasn't some neurotic crazy woman. She was intelligent, sensitive and graceful. If she had serious suspicions then he wanted to and had taken them seriously.

Ammon reached across and gently took Alex's wrist. 'It is time to be brave my friend, I know this will be difficult for you, I am ready if you need me.'

Alex looked across at him taking several deep breaths in an attempt to quell his raging nerves. 'I'm going to call her Ammon.'

'What! Alex that is not our plan. Are you sure?' questioned Ammon gripping his wrist tighter.

'Yes, I'm sure. It has to be me. It's me that needs to know. I just need to get her thinking I know more than I actually do, and see if that gets a reaction, gets them talking.' Alex picked up his phone in both hands and tapped it on his chin as he focused on what he would say and how he was going to say it.

'You do not have to do this Alex; I will do it as we planned.'

'No Ammon, it's ok, I need to do this. Are you ready to record?'

Ammon nodded, fingers hovering over the monitor buttons. 'Remember you must be well away from the monitor so you do not create a screeching feedback loop with the bugs.'

Alex got up and headed off to the living room. 'Ok, I'm as ready as I'm ever going to be, here goes.' He hit the call button and waited.

'I can hear the phone ringing Alex,' shouted Ammon. 'Good luck my friend.'

'Hello.' His mother's usual chirpy posh telephone voice answered.

'It's Alex.'

'Oh! Alex, what do you want?' Her tone changed, scornful and bitter. 'If it's about the other day don't bother apologising, it's too late for apologies, you've burnt your bridges here young man.'

'No, I've not called to apologise mother. It's something else, far more serious than that. I've heard something that has deeply disturbed me and I want to… share it with you.'

'And what would that be Alex, come on I haven't got time for your nonsense right now.'

A moment of fury rose in him and the control he fought to maintain lost out to a desire to shock a reaction out of his mother with the delivery of an atomic bomb.

'You killed my father. That's what I heard mother.' Alex held his breath waiting for a response in that eternal adrenalin filled moment of reckoning.

'What?' came a notably delayed response. 'Where did you hear such nonsense? How could you possibly believe such lies and untruths, you stupid boy?'

He calmed his tone in an attempt to sound as menacing as he could. 'I'm not stupid mother. I think you need to be very careful. You don't know what I know and I'm going to get to the truth.'

'You don't know anything, there's nothing to know. Who have you been talking to? That whore in the village no doubt. You can't trust a woman who steals a married man from his wife of nearly forty years.'

Alex ended the call rushing back into the kitchen to hear the fallout from his baited bomb. Over the monitors they could hear Mrs Hidde moving through the kitchen and into the conservatory where George was watching the television. Her voice was shrill and distorted the sensitive microphones.

'George! George! That was that little bastard Alex on the phone. He's claiming he thinks I had something to do with his father's death. Where in heavens can he have got that from? That fancy woman in the village I don't doubt.'

'Calm down dear.' Came the relaxed and reassuring voice of George. 'I told you they will never be able to prove anything. The Oleander in the tea is practically undetectable in my formula. I'm a botanist and chemist dear, they'll never be able to prove anything…'

Alex and Ammon grabbed each other's shoulders across the table in celebration of their defiant moment, but it was short lived. Alex withered in Ammon's grasp, falling to the table head in hands he wept uncontrollably. Ammon tried his best to console the inconsolable. Stepping back, he decided all he could do was to give Alex the time and space he needed to release his pent-up emotions. Retreating to the kitchen Ammon took out his tablet computer and booted it while he put the kettle on to make another cup of tea.

18 ANOTHER CUP OF TEA

Alex sat staring at the table through sore eyes, still lost in his own thoughts. Reality was the sound of a spoon rattling around the sides of a mug of tea. Ammon put the cup down in front of him taking a seat opposite.

'Where are you my friend? That was a painful truth for you, and a very serious crime, you have to think about your next move.'

Alex clenched a fist and put it to his mouth contemplating a reply that wasn't yet fully formed. His internal barometer swung slowly but erratically between rage and unreachable grief, making his thoughts difficult to process and externalise.

'I just don't know right now Ammon. I can't make sense of it. I feel like someone's put my whole life, and some dodgy crime novel, in a bloody food blender.'

Ammon caught a brief chuckle. 'Sorry my friend, you can still make me laugh even when you are so torn up. Take strength from that please, you are hurting deeply but you must rise up and do what is right for the right reasons.'

'Thanks Ammon, yeah, I'm getting there mate.'

'I had a look on the internet. This Oleander he mentioned, it is a plant, a bush, a very common ornamental bush. It contains chemicals called cardiac glycosides, which can cause cardiac arrest. This man George is a chemist so he has known how to produce this and refine it. We need to get our hands on some of that and then we have a case to take to the police.'

Alex nodded in affirmation. 'Yes, I agree, and I think I know where I could find some of that poison, but not just now. I want to talk with Sarah about this and make sure we go about it in the right way.'

'Ok, it is your call my friend,' said Ammon picking up his phone. 'Oh, I have missed a call from Maddie. I had it muted when you spoke to your mother. I have a text message too.'

Alex grabbed his phone. 'I've got a missed call from her too. What does your message say?'

'Hold on I will just...' Ammon tapped through to his message inbox. 'She says - Answer the frickin phone bone head, outside QW, seen something suspicious, will call back soon - What do you think that means Alex?'

'That means she's been pocking around on her own again and who knows what?' Alex was exacerbated by what he saw as her repeated recklessness.

'Shall we go find her Alex? She could be in danger.'

Just then Alex's phone rang. He quickly hit the answer button and turned on the speaker. 'It's Maddie,' he confirmed to Ammon. 'Hi, what you up to Miss Marple?'

Maddie unsurprisingly retaliated with a sarcastic tone. 'Oh, hi Alex you big arse. I have actually been sleuthing, yes. While you guys have no doubt been eating toast and supping tea like the big puffs you are.'

'Well yes, we've had a brew or two, amongst other things. What's your latest deductions?' Alex replied equally cutting.

'Ok, suck this up and swill it about a bit Inspector Clouseau. Why would the pub landlord take a tray of food across the square to the cellar under Evelyn's lodgings?'

'I don't know, why would the pub landlord take a tray of food across the square to the cellar under Evelyn's lodgings?' parroted Alex.

'It's not a fucking joke you dingbat. It looks suspicious to me. I wanna know who's down there?'

'It could be anything Maddie. It sounds odd fair enough but there is probably some logical explanation. How do you know it was a tray of food, how close were you?'

'It looked like a tray of food, with a cloth over it,' she insisted.

'It could have been cheese that he was putting back into storage, or anything. If I remember rightly there's an old cold store down there where they used to store beer kegs from the pub, not sure if they still do but…'

'Ok, I was just trying to revive this Anna thing, I'm looking for clues anywhere and everywhere, and anyway he's a dodgy looking character, never liked him.'

'He's an ok guy Maddie. Just because he gave us a ticking off for laughing at his stuffed fox doesn't make him bad and Ammon says he was good to him while he was staying there, so.'

'Ok, ok. So, what have you boys been up too today anyway?'

'I'll tell you tomorrow Maddie. I might need your help with something.'

'Oooh, Intriguing Mr Poirot, I'll speak to you tomorrow then, byesy bye.'

'Good bye Maddie,' echoed the guys in unison.

'She has a point,' considered Ammon. 'We have lost sight of the Anna case. She is still missing and we have no leads or anything.'

'We are not likely to Ammon. The police have basically warned us off and yes, we have no clues or anything to follow up. That's why Maddie's going around coming up with any crazy nonsense and anything that looks vaguely out of the ordinary.' Alex had got it into his head he must stop any escalation of Anna fever starting up again. He had bigger problems to solve and much closer to home.

'Fancy a beer my friend? I have some cans in the car,' offered Ammon, vying to change the subject.

The guys opened a couple of cans and helped each other steer the conversation away from the hard stuff that had dominated the day. Alex consciously strove to turn the conversation away from himself, cueing Ammon to reveal more about his situation.

'Maddie tells me you have made up with your father?'

'Yes, my friend, yes, I think he missed me, that and my mother tearing a strip or two off of him while I was away. That is all though, he still will not see my concerns about the business. I had to stop pushing, I could see it was going to come between us again. I have been thinking, maybe it is time for me to go my own way, and start my own business.'

'Well that's great Ammon, what would you do?' encouraged Alex.

'I'm not sure yet, how about a private detective agency?' Ammon beamed a cheeky grin and he and Alex laughed out loud.

'And why the hell not eh? Apart from the fact you have no previous experience, don't smoke a pipe or wear a funny hat,' joked Alex.

'I will go shopping for a funny hat first thing tomorrow my friend, if that is what it takes. Will you join me as my side kick partner Alex?'

'As long as we can get a tasty fast motor and I do all the driving, I don't see why not.'

A knock at the door suspended their sleuthing dreams, followed by Maddie letting herself in.

'Hi Guys, was bored so I thought I'd come check out what you losers are up to. Nice, a couple of beers and,' she stopped to sniff the air, 'A few rounds of toast if I'm not mistaken.'

'Wow Maddie you are ascending into the realms of super sleuth with that kind of deduction-ing,' quipped Alex.

'Not sure there is such a word as deduction-ing Alexi-poos, but I'll let it go this time as this isn't a round of Countdown and I'm not Rachel Riley,' teased Maddie superciliously.

'You're not? Oh, that's a shame I quite fancy Rachel Riley,' admitted Alex.

'Charming, as though I'm some sort of ginger minger not worth a second glance,' protested Maddie strutting a couple of catwalk paces across the room.

'Sit down and have a beer you crazy broad,' insisted Alex resisting her taunting.

Ammon opened a beer and passed it to Maddie as she took a seat at the table.

'Thanks Ammon,' she said double taking Alex. 'Are you ok?' She continued tenderly, checking Ammon open mouthed as Alex's head dropped.

'We found something out today Maddie, a bitter sweet victory that has caused Alex a lot of pain.' Ammon's voice carried the weight of what they had uncovered.

Maddie sat in silence looking between the guys for further disclosure.

'I am going to leave you to talk my friends. I have to make some calls, ok?' said Ammon softly, picking up his car keys from the kitchen worktop. 'Take care of him Maddie, I will see you later.'

It wasn't until Maddie heard his car pull out of the drive that she ventured into gentle enquiry. Alex delivered the shocking news on the edge of his emotional control, Maddie grasping both of his hands and holding them tightly in hers. The unbelievable gravity of the facts beggared her belief as Alex revealed the events of the day up to the startling admission over the monitor.

'So, it's all recorded, George's words about the poison in the tea?' stuttered Maddie.

'Yes, Ammon got it all on tape here,' said Alex pointing at the monitoring devices. 'And I think I know where to find some of that tea and the poison. There could be some in my father's workshop.'

'We need to go get it before it's tampered with and have it analysed by someone,' insisted Maddie.

'All in good time Maddie, I just need to think about this more.'

'What is there to think about? There's no time like the present.'

'No, please Maddie just leave it for now. I know you're trying to help but I just need to get some things straight in my head first.'

'Ok Alex, I'm sorry, it just seems like an important detail that—'

'Maddie!' insisted Alex.

'Ok, sorry. Do you want me to stay or would you rather be on your own right now?' she enquired sensing Alex's descending mood.

'I think, I just need to think, sorry, thanks Maddie.' He looked at her with obvious appreciation.

Getting up to go Maddie moved close and kissed him on the forehead. 'You know where I am if you need me, ok?'

Alex looked up and smiled through painful emotions. 'Thanks

Maddie.'

He watched her leave questioning his want to be alone. Moving over to the sofa he grabbed a fleece throw, wrapped it around himself and collapsed into it. The jumbled array of thoughts flitting around his consciousness gave way to a half sleep and dreams. Twisted versions of reality, anxiety and all too painful truths played out on the familiar stages of his dreamscape.

A sleep and many dreams later he woke to the sound of his phone ringing, it was Maddie.

'Hi Maddie, you woke me, I was asleep.'

'Sorry Alex, you're not going to like this.'

'Where are you Maddie? What are you doing?'

'I'm in a wardrobe with a tea caddy.'

'What! What the fuck are you up to Maddie?'

'Calm down Alex, I need your help my knight in shining armour. I'm in the wardrobe in your dad's workshop, I've got the tea caddy but they must have seen me and they're wondering about outside. That George character came in here and looked around so I'm a bit trapped.'

Alex couldn't help but laugh. 'Maddie you crazy broad, what the hell possessed you? I'm on my way, just stay there until you hear from me again, ok?' Grabbing his jacket, he dashed out of the house and into the car. Seeing his Bluetooth earpiece in the centre console he turned it on and slipped it behind his ear. Revving the engine hard he dropped the clutch and roared out of the driveway onto the road. Fumbling with his phone during his overly aggressive driving he reconnected the call with Maddie.

'...Ok, I'm on my way Maddie. Are you still in the workshop?'

'Yes, George is poking around with a torch. I'm out of the wardrobe and just keeping out of sight.'

'Right, keep your head down I'm coming up to the lane now, I'm going to try a distraction,' shouted Alex throwing the car into the lane with tyres screaming into the stillness of the night. Accelerating hard towards the house he yanked the handbrake on and spun the wheel hard right. The car slewed round sideways with another piercing screech as he rammed home first gear and planted the throttle hard to the floor. He was there and gone in seconds, hopefully heard but not seen.

'Is that you Alex? All that noise? George is running up the path to see what's going on,' relayed Maddie from the workshop.

'Good, right, run for it towards the bottom of the garden. I'm coming up the access road to the electric substation; it runs along the back of the house. Get on top of the wall and be ready to jump. I'm turning my lights off.'

'Jump! Alex what the hell are you wanting me to do? I'm coming up to the wall now.'

Alex was there out of the car and ready when Maddie climbed on top of the wall wearing a black balaclava. Muting an uncontrollable laugh, he beckoned her in a low voice.

'Come on, jump!'

Maddie looked around before leaping faithfully towards Alex. She landed in his arms pushing him violently against the car.

'Are you ok Alex?'

'Yes, yes, get in the car, come on.' He stretched and groaned briefly as he recovered from his role as a human airbag, before jumping in himself and driving off at speed down the lane.

'You crazy woman, what do you think you're doing?' condemned Alex.

'You a favour, maybe?' responded Maddie defiantly.

Alex shook his head and laughed. 'You shouldn't have.'

'But I did,' she said pulling the tea caddy from inside her jacket. 'We need to get this analysed asap, here, I'll put it in your glove compartment for now.'

'Thank you, Maddie,' said Alex reluctantly. 'I could have got it myself with a lot less fuss though.'

'Yeah, but wasn't that fun,' roused Maddie opening the car window and shouting out, 'Woooohoooo! Bonnie and Clyde ride again.' Maddie kept her head out of the window as the car sped along, her fulsome ginger locks flowing around her face. Giving Alex a cheeky grin she looked up to the night sky. 'Wow! Alex look at this sky.'

Alex took a glance upwards, she was right, it was another glorious star filled canopy above them, unspoilt by any light pollution out here in the middle of the Peak.

'Drive up to Hillhead Tops and let's sit out under the stars Alex,' suggested Maddie.

Alex pulled into the large parking area at Hillhead Tops and parked up close to a bench near the edge. Here you could see for miles across the dales and beyond. As viewpoints go this was recognised as one of the best in the area and was always packed with tourists in the good weather. Maddie jumped out of the car and postured for to Alex to join her. They both slouched down on the bench rolling their heads back to take in the heavens.

'Look at that Alex,' she marvelled. 'It just makes you feel so small, so insignificant. The light we see from some of those distant stars set off before humans even existed here on earth. It's amazing isn't it?'

'It is yes. We ask some big questions about what's out there don't we? I often think we maybe don't ask enough questions about what's in here,' he said pointing to his head. 'The human condition Maddie, love and hate, war and peace, prejudice and tolerance. We're still wired in the same way as we were at the dawn of civilization but the world is a very different place, still fragile and infinitely diverse but now we have the power to destroy it.'

'Very profound Professor Brian Cox, can you go and say that again silhouetted against the night sky in a lovely deep voice. Now he's hot for a prof.'

'Your joking, he's old enough to be your father,' teased Alex.

'No way, when I was born, he was nowhere near old enough to have baby gravy swimming around his little man bags.'

Alex spluttered not able to get his laugh out fast enough, having to double up to avoid internal injury. Maddie was powerless not to join him and they rolled around tears streaming down their faces for a good couple of minutes. In the chuckle punctuated stillness that followed they stared skywards unable to catch each other's eye for fear of losing control again.

'Laughter is a pretty powerful therapy isn't?' declared Alex. 'After today, I wasn't sure I was ever going to laugh again.'

'Don't forget friends Alex, we are always here for you, you know.'

'Thanks Maddie. I can't believe what I have to do now. I've got to turn my mother in to the police, what craziness is that?'

'What was your father like Alex, do you mind?' questioned Maddie softly.

'He was a good man. I just never got to really know him as well as I'd liked. I think he despaired of me as a teenager. He was always fair though, and calm, and did his best to guide me I suppose. He wasn't around as much as I think he would have liked to have been, with his work. I have great memories of him, just doing interesting things and having fun as a kid. My relationship with my mother has always been crap for as long as I can remember. The others, Michael and Carolyn sailed through school no trouble, then I came along and blotted her score sheet. I think my father did his best to moderate things but he just wasn't there enough to have much influence, and when the poor guy came back from trips, he got it in the neck from her so, I just got out as soon as I could. Always missed him though, and we shared some good times when I came back on the odd occasion.'

'You've been to see Sarah I take it?'

'Yes, this morning. She's really lovely you know. I can't believe how close I feel to her. I suppose I've never really been able to share my father's loss with anyone before.'

'I'd like to get to know her too Alex, if I could?'

'I'm sure she'd like that. You share the music thing don't you so, somewhere to start eh?'

They sat close and silent, Alex conscious of every breath he took and feeling the pull to be closer to her. That primitive human magnetism was at play but she didn't seem to stir at all. There was no sense of reciprocation, like misaligned poles keeping them from final contact and that irreversible touch. There were too many clouds and not enough sun to make things grow here and besides this was a friendship he didn't want to complicate right now. He shivered uncontrollably making him aware of the creeping cold driven into them by a gathering breeze.

'Yep, come on Alex time to go, I'm getting cold,' announced Maddie jumping up and heading for the car.

Driving back there was a quiet awkwardness in the car that Alex couldn't fathom. Was he missing something or was he still playing with magnets? Whatever it was he had to break it.

'What you up to tomorrow then Maddie?'

'Not sure yet. If it's a nice day I'll take Clyde out for a trot around the bridleways, but apart from that not sure yet, just chill maybe.'

'Shall we see if Ammon wants to meet up in the pub for a drink, in the evening maybe?' suggested Alex.

'Yeah, let's do that, I'll ask him in the morning. He's no trouble you know, out there in the guest room.'

'I don't suppose he is, he's a good guy,' said Alex as they pulled up at the end of Maddie's drive.

Maddie opened the door and raised herself to leave the car but stopped to look back. 'Good night Alex,' she said with what he thought to be a little longing; hesitating he missed the moment and she slipped away out of the car.

'Good night Maddie.'

She looked back, pulled her hair away from her face and smiled briefly before turning and walking away up the drive.

'Good night Maddie,' he whispered again under his breath. That smile said something but what it was he could not decipher. It was lost to him, hidden away in a deep dark place.

19 A DEEP DARK PLACE

Bound to a chair and gaged, all Alex could do was watch the proceedings of the court unable to plead his case. The judge sat stern faced behind his bench, the corners of his downturned mouth visibly quivering with rage. The prosecuting lawyer strutted across the floor barking the facts to a terrified jury. How had it come to this? The tables had turned against him, he was being accused of the murder of his father and this man had the evidence to convict him. Straining his neck to look around the bindings that held him he saw his mother and George smug and grinning as their devious conspiracy played out. The lawyer concluded, making it plainly clear to the jury that there was only one outcome for this heinous crime. Alex screamed to be heard as he was brutally manhandled to his feet by two thuggish police officers; then all was quiet. The judge rose, the whole court followed. From one side of the room a figure appeared wearing a long black hooded robe. Alex sensed it was a woman and someone familiar. She was carrying an elaborate velvet cushion, upon which was a black cap. This couldn't be, they could not sentence him before the jury had made their decision and it was wrong, it was all wrong. He made attempts to move and shout but was unable to make himself heard through the gag. As the hooded figure placed the cap on the awaiting judge's head Alex could see it was Maddie. She gazed through him in a trance like state before turning and bowing her head. In a cataclysmic eruption of earth-shaking wrath, the judge raised his gravel and roared his verdict,

'Take – him – away.'

The grating roar of stone on stone rumbled beneath him and he was falling, plummeting into an eternal black abyss to oblivion.

Alex woke with a start, braced in the foetal position. He rolled over and lay on his back breathing deeply. It was another crazy dream he thought, this was becoming an almost nightly occurrence. That morning he woke slowly, struggling to open his tired eyes and motivate himself to rise. As far as he was concerned all the events of the previous days could have been a dream. Piecing together reality was a painful experience that left him withdrawn and hollow. He knew he had to get up and get moving to break out of this debilitating cycle. Rushing down a quick breakfast he was out of the house and marching down the lane in the direction of Sarah's house. He had to make a start however painful it would be, and in his mind he had decided that she must be part of it. Internally he rehearsed how he would break the news to Sarah, that her suspicions had been proven and he imagined her reaction and the inevitable emotional outpouring. Maintaining a furious pace, he strove to focus through the minefield of facts and emotions that swirled around inside his head, until a sudden realisation forced him to stumble to a halt. Why would he want to put Sarah through all that, the facts and the bitter twisted nature of his mother and her accomplice? It was breaking him, why would he want to expose her to it? Turning around he sauntered tentatively a few paces back then stopped and turned again. Should he tell her? Nothing was clear anymore. All that seeming clarity he'd left the house with had fragmented around him, and a different perspective prevailed. He was hanging his head but a new confidence was building and about to put a spring back into his step as he headed back to the cottage.

Clasping his phone in his jacket pocket he was strangely expectant of a call from Maddie, he just hoped it wouldn't be another misconceived and ill imagined lead in the crumbling case of the missing girls. He'd replayed last night's parting scene with her over and over in his mind trying to stack up the implicit and explicit meanings in tone of voice and body language, but his jury was out with no conclusions. He forced a half-faked shudder, consoling himself that he had escaped lightly. There was some chemistry at play between them but he needed to be careful that it didn't blow up in his face. When the call came, he was not far from the cottage He took it with the genuine intention of sparing her a lecture or his usual sarcasm.

'Hello Mrs Bond I was expecting you.'

'Were you, oh?' replied Maddie whispering and seemingly oblivious of his humorous intent. 'Now, don't go off on one Alex, I need you here now. I'm across from the Quiet Woman in the church yard.'

'Maddie what's going on, what are you up to? You're whispering, that's not a good sign.'

'Listen Alex, get yourself here as soon as you can. I've just watched the pub landlord going into that cellar again with more food,' insisted Maddie.

'How do you know it's food Maddie? We've been through this

yesterday.'

'Yes, but this is different, I've found out something else and we need to check this out Alex. Ammon's on his way, trust me just get here ok.'

'Ok I'm on my way,' conceded Alex setting off running towards town, phone still at his ear. 'How long has he been in there?'

'About five minutes, I'd say. I'm thinking we wait until he comes out and then see if we can get in. Ammon reckons he can do that. Anyway, just get here, I'm in the churchyard behind the wall.'

Somehow, he felt he needed to take this seriously, what else did Maddie know? Was the landlord really their man? It seemed too close to home to be true. This man had been right under their noses and interviewed by the police on several occasions relating to the disappearance of Anna and later Evelyn. They knew Evelyn was in London, so who, if anyone could be locked in the cellar? Surely not Anna?

Approaching the square Alex slowed to a walk, deciding he must appear to be just strolling through so as not to draw attention to himself. Nonchalantly he walked on across the square catching Maddie and Ammon peering over the church wall beckoning him.

'Ok, what's going on Maddie?'

'Keep a look out Ammon while I fill in Mr Pudding head here,' started Maddie showing her frustration at his lack of faith. 'Nobody has heard anything more from Evelyn, right? No Facebook activity? Nothing.'

'Yeah,' acknowledged Alex.

'Well I think there's a good reason for that. I was checking out Evelyn's Facebook message this morning and decided I'd have a go at tracing its source, and, it wasn't sent from London, it was sent from a device on the pub's Wi-Fi network.'

'That doesn't mean to say it was the landlord. It could have been a guest. What about the car, you tracked her car to London?'

'Well, it's not moved since, so, I don't know about that, but we need to check this out.'

'I think she might be on to something here my friend,' affirmed Ammon dropping his head below the wall as Maddie resumed watch duties. 'We will get in there when he has left and find out for sure anyway.'

'The vicar! Get behind the tree guys,' warned Alex in sudden panic. He'd been sitting with his back to the wall facing the church and seen the vicar walking in through the back gate down the side of the building. The three of them lined up behind a tree with Alex at the front peeping round to check the vicar's whereabouts. As he got closer it became obvious to Alex they would need to move around the tree to stay out of sight. Reaching a hand behind him he guided the others with him as he shuffled sideways to maintain their cover.

'He's gone in the front door, coast clear guys,' relayed Alex. 'Not sure how we'd have explained that one away.'

Before they had chance to return to their surveillance position Ammon had noticed movement outside the lodgings. 'He is out and crossing the square!' he exclaimed in a loud whisper.

'Shit! We nearly missed him, thanks to the vicar. I hope he doesn't go making a habit of it,' smirked Maddie.

'Cassocks!' corrected Alex.

'Ooooh there's no need for language like that Alex,' denounced Maddie.

'Vicars wear cassocks.' Alex was trying to keep an eye on the development in the square but recognised he was being side-tracked by an inappropriately excited Maddie.

'It is Bill Palmer alright,' confirmed Ammon as they watched him disappear down the side of the Quiet Woman.

'Ok boys let's go and check out his cheese,' announced Maddie through a smarmy grin.

'What!' said Alex.

'Remember, that's where he keeps his cheese collection according to you Alexi-poos,'

Ammon sniggered, slapping Alex playfully on the back. 'You walked right into that one my friend, so funny.'

'Ok you two jokers, there's a good chance that you're both well wrong about this so let's go check out this cellar and see who has the last laugh. And anyway, Maddie if you think you're on to something why the hell are you making light of this? If there is someone down there this is not going to be fun, is it?'

'Sorry Alex, I know, you're right, it's just a bit too scary isn't it?' Maddie's mood changed, taking Alex's arm and moving in close to his shoulder.

She'd been hiding behind her humour again Alex surmised. He recognised he was sharing that fear, driven by his own chilling apprehensions.

Reaching the building they checked around for onlookers. Fortunately, the door was not easily visible from anywhere other than their recent position, behind the wall in the church yard. A short stairwell of some six steps led down to the door which was sturdily built in well-aged oak.

'Ammon, over to you,' said Maddie gesturing towards the door.

Ammon stepped forward swinging the small rucksack he was wearing to the floor and opening it. Studying the door lock, he pulled out two slightly different tools. Deciding on one of them he returned the other to the bag and approached the door.

'Where did you get the lock picking kit Ammon?' asked Alex.

'This was my father's business when we first came to Britain, but now we just sell the equipment. I am not a great expert, but let me see what we can do,' replied Ammon working the tool into the mechanism.

Alex and Maddie looked on, continuing nervously to check around for onlookers.

'What do we do if there is somebody down there guys?' posed Alex.

'I really don't know,' was Maddie's only offering, her heightened anxiety evident and her focus elsewhere.

It was taking more time than they expected for Ammon to break the lock, but neither Alex nor Maddie expressed any desire to hurry him. He looked like he knew what he was doing and they were determined to give him time without the added pressure their impatience might bring. With a sudden clunk they both turned to see the door open and Ammon beckoning as he stepped inside. They descended a stone stairway down to the left, their footfalls noticeably muffled in the strange deadness of the acoustics. A strong musty smell hung heavily in the air as they penetrated the darkness, slowing to feel their way down each step one at a time. Taking out his phone and activating its flashlight Ammon scanned around the room allowing them to make out its contents. The first thing that struck Alex was the carpet covering all the walls, evidently the reason for the lack of reflected sound. In a blinding flash the room was illuminated by the flickering start-up of florescent lighting, taking all but Maddie by surprise.

'That's better boys, I found the light switch,' she sighed with a mix of pride and relief.

The room was filled with various bric-a-brac including a variety of stuffed animals and bar equipment. A workbench covered the length of one wall with tools and assorted devices hung above it. In a far corner an arched stone corridor led further into the cavern-like space.

'Nothing particularly odd down here then guys,' declared Alex nervously.

Ammon and Maddie marched off down the corridor leaving Alex to follow.

'Another door here, and more of this rubbish,' reported Ammon twisting the door handle and pushing. 'This door is locked as well.'

'Hold on!' demanded Maddie. 'Listen! I thought I heard a voice. I did. Fuck! Somebody's in there.'

'I heard it too.' Ammon concurred pushing at the door. 'Who is in there?' he shouted.

A muffled reply could be heard and this time they all made out the voice. It was Evelyn screaming desperately for help.

'Come on, get this door open,' asserted Maddie frantically kicking and beating the door. 'Evelyn, it's Maddie, hold on, we're going to get you out,' she shouted through cupped hands.

Their pounding made no impression what-so-ever on the solid, tightly fitting door.

'Give me room,' insisted Ammon trying to employ his skills again on the ominous looking lock.

Alex and Maddie continued shouting through the door in an attempt to communicate with Evelyn. Stopping and listening intently after each effort they debated the possible interpretations of the returned muffled replies, with only minimal success, such was the soundproofed quality of the room.

Incredibly this lock fell to Ammon's efforts in less than a couple of minutes. The three of them storming it open to reveal Evelyn bawling with joy at seeing them, floods of tears filling her sore, fearful eyes. They all embraced her deeply, Ammon wrapping himself around her pitiful form and comforting her with his tenderest words.

'What has he done to you Evelyn? Are you ok?' he implored.

'I'm ok, I'm ok, he hasn't touched me, he's mad, he's insane, he comes and talks to me about crazy things. I was so scared, so scared. Just get me out of here before he comes back,' she cried shaking with fear.

'Yes, come on let us get out of here. I shall see that Mr Palmer regrets what he has done here.' Ammon spoke through gritted teeth his anger evident but controlled.

As they turned for the door a sudden ear-piercing boom reduced them to cowering under shielding arms, eyes tight shut. Fragments of something pinged an array of tones off every surface around them. Alex felt a couple of them bite at his legs and back reminding him of being shot by a friend's air pistol years before. Stepping away from the source of the blast, Alex turned to see the pub landlord in the doorway, shotgun in hand and casually trained on the shell shocked friends. He stood in silence waiting for them all to take note of his presence. There were protests from the bewildered group and strong words cursed at him but he remained unnervingly calm with an expression no more unusual than if he had come to take a drinks order.

'Now, what's going on here?' he enquired.

Ammon stepped forward posturing aggressively. 'Put down the gun Bill and let us out of here now.'

'Step back boy, or, I'll blow your head off,' Palmer pointed the shotgun up into Ammon's face with every apparent intent of discharging it again.

Ammon stepped back, raising his hands. 'Now come on Bill, this is crazy, you are just making more trouble for yourself.'

'Think so do you. I think it's you lot that's found trouble, get back against the wall.'

Alex backed up towards the wall behind them finding his arm around Maddie's shoulders drawing her back with him. Ammon stood in front of Evelyn his reluctance to follow Palmer's demands obvious, and seeming to Alex, dangerously confrontational.

'No, Evelyn, you're coming with me,' asserted Palmer beckoning her forward from behind Ammon with the shotgun.

'No Bill. Take me if you want a hostage, take me,' begged Ammon.

Palmer grabbed Evelyn and pulled her towards him. 'What would I want with a hostage? Get back boy,' he threatened lifting the gun to Evelyn's head. 'Back against the wall the lot of you, or this will get messy I can promise you that.'

Alex felt a tug from Maddie as she too sought to show some resistance. 'You won't get away with this you evil bastard, let her go,' she screamed, pulling forward against Alex's restraint.

'So how did you get in here then eh?' questioned Palmer kicking Ammon's rucksack and checking its contents. 'I see, very clever.' He picked up the rucksack, taking it with him as he dragged Evelyn back through the door, slamming it hard behind them.

The cold hard echoless thud of the door seemed to draw all the air from the room. In that fearful silent moment it crossed Alex's mind that he had been imprisoned himself, before he'd had the chance to see his murderous mother and her accomplice where they belonged, behind bars.

20 BARS

Alex and Maddie charged the door screaming every obscenity they could muster, pounding and kicking desperately in a vain, hopeless attempt to break out. That was until they noticed Ammon's unfazed response. Standing behind them with a big smile beaming from his face, he was holding something in his hand. It was the lock picking tool he had used on the cell door.

'Palmer did not check very well, did he my friends?' Ammon chuckled. 'I put this in my pocket when we entered the room.'

Alex punched the air defiantly, grabbing Maddie for a quick celebratory dance. 'You flippin beauty you, get this door open mate and let's go get after that son of a bitch.'

Ammon got to work on the lock prompting Maddie to raise a pending concern. 'Tell me that that is the same lock tool for the outside door as well Ammon - please?'

'I am afraid it is not,' he replied reluctantly, maintaining focus on picking the lock.

'Oh shit!' screamed Alex. 'So, we're still trapped when we've got out of here!'

Ammon turned briefly with a serious look that said it all. 'One thing at a time my friend, we are not beaten yet, that man is not going to get away with this.'

'Why didn't you guys take me seriously when I saw him the other night?' despaired Maddie. 'Instead of your bloody cheese store nonsense. We could have had him arrested yesterday.'

'Yeah?' countered Alex. 'And we could have been in here since yesterday too. Come on Maddie, we couldn't suspect someone just cos they walked across a road with pie and chips and a bottle of Irn Bru can we?'

'Don't be such a fucking arse Alex!'

'That is enough both of you,' intervened Ammon abruptly. 'We need to be together to get through this. We will find a way out, we have to.'

A silent pause in hostilities was broken with the click of the door lock releasing. Ammon turned and put a finger to his lips. 'We need to be careful now, we do not know if he is still here, ok?' he whispered.

Slowly opening the door to a pitch-dark corridor, it was obvious Palmer was gone, taking Evelyn with him. Ammon turned on his phone's torch app and wandered off to find a light switch. Alex and Maddie followed, entering the main cellar room to the flicking of fluorescent tubes strobing their motion as they buzzed into life.

Ammon ran off up the stairs to the outside door and returned shaking his head. 'We are definitely not going to get out of that door, it is solid. We need to find another way. Let us search and see what we can find.'

Maddie looked around erratically, unable to let go of her frustration. 'This is a solid stone underground cellar, what the hell are we supposed to be looking for? I say we run around in circles until we get puffed out, what do you say boys?'

'I'd say you need to be a bit more positive Maddie,' asserted Alex. 'We just have to get out of here, and fast. Who knows what he'll do with Evelyn, and you can bet he's not going to be bringing us chicken in a basket and a pint of lager shandy any time soon.'

'Here, here,' agreed Ammon straining to pull down a section of carpet from the wall.

'Can we not use any of these tools to break through the door?' suggested Maddie smirking at a strange looking device she'd picked up from the work bench.

'I have not seen anything I think could do any damage to that door but we must keep looking,' encouraged Ammon.

'I don't suppose anyone's tried their mobile for a signal, have they?' asked Maddie holding up her phone.

'Not a sausage,' scoffed Alex. 'If this was a cold store it could even be lead lined.'

'I reckon these tools are what one would use when practising the art of taxidermy,' suggested Maddie. 'Which is apt isn't it? As we are currently stuffed!'

Alex considered rising to her comment, but after a brief hesitation withdrew the idea to avoid another conflict and maintain his focus on finding a way out. Every wall was built of large stone blocks and the ceiling of huge oak boards. Scouring the place from top to bottom he could see no way out other than the formidable cellar door that looked like it was capable of taking a direct hit from a cruise missile. The frantic and optimistic searching was beginning to fade to a desperate but sullen realisation that escape from this place was not going to be easy, if possible at all. When eyes met there was panic behind them, even Maddie had become quiet and withdrawn after resorting to hammering on the outside door with anything substantial that she could find. Ammon had switched his attention from scouring every wall and ceiling to rooting through the tools that littered the work bench and several boxes underneath it, taking some interest in the occasional item and examining it in the hope of sparking some inspiration. Alex nervously tapped a finger to his lips as he too continued looking around for some obvious chink in the apparently inescapable chamber. Moving back into the cell where Evelyn had been incarcerated, he studied a small vent on one wall up near the ceiling. It was far too small to be of any use but was the only possible link to the outside he had found in the whole place. There was no other sign of any other ventilation, but, if the rooms had been built as a cold store then that would be expected. A chilling claustrophobic sensation gripped him as he contemplated the worst, shaking it off he returned to the others to seek some reassurance.

'Any ideas Ammon? This is getting serious, what are we going to do?'

Ammon paused his rummaging to respond but didn't turn. 'I do not know my friend, but we need to do something, this place is so solid, everywhere you look there is stone or massive oak beams. It is a prison but for one simple but very secure lock on that door up there.'

'Is there any way we can pick that lock without your tools?'

'The lock in that door with the iron frame will take a big battering ram to make an impression on it I am afraid my friend. And the lock, even with the tool, is not easy.'

Maddie joined them back from another visit to the door. 'I can't believe there's no mobile signal even right next to the door, it's ridiculous!'

'There's not even a great signal in the square at the best of times, so it's not surprising really is it?' recalled Alex taking his phone out and staring at no bars of reception until the screen timed out. 'Shame there's no letter box you could stick it out of.'

'Yeah, you could glue it to a long stick and play a recorded message of us idiots screaming help,' joked Maddie.

'Hold on guys I might have an idea,' declared Alex. 'If we could get a phone outside the building we might be able to get a text message out. Come and have a look at this vent in the other room Ammon,' he continued, leading them into the room in which they had so nearly been imprisoned. 'If this is vented to the outside, we might be able to get a phone up there. What do you think?'

Maddie looked on quizzically. 'How you gonna do that then?'

'If we can break this vent and force something up and outside, then we can maybe push the phone up on a stick or something. It's got to be worth a try hasn't it?' encouraged Alex.

Ammon and Alex dashed back into the other room to look for anything that could be used to break into the vent. Alex returned almost immediately with a pair of long nosed pliers. Dragging a chair over he jumped up, slammed the pliers into the grill and began riving at the thin metal vanes. In only a few seconds he had managed to break one off, and quickly moved on to the next. After a little more work there was a hole about the size of a generous letter box where the vent grill had been.

'Turn the light off Maddie please, I want to see if there's any light getting down here.'

With the room pitch dark, he waited a few seconds for his eyes to adjust. 'Nothing, I can't see any light, it's probably blocked off,' he concluded.

Maddie turned the light back on as Ammon entered with a long metal rod.

'Where the hell did you find that mate?' exclaimed Alex pleasantly surprised.

Ammon sported the metal rod like a spear with a broad grin lighting up his face. 'It was part of the bench, holding the legs together.'

'Just what we need mate,' said Alex, his optimism rekindled. 'Ram it up the hole and see if we can break whatever is blocking the way.'

Almost running at his target, Ammon thrust the rod up into the hole forcing it as hard as he could to a point where it jammed tight between the rim of the hole and the back of the vent shaft. Heaving on the rod he formed a bend in it and was able to force it further. He did this several times until he could gain no further progress. 'We need something to knock it up,' he suggested racing off to find a substitute hammer.

Following him, Alex offered a solution. 'There's a small anvil under the bench Ammon. If we can swing that together we'd get some fair umph into that rod, I reckon.'

'Let us give it a go my friend,' agreed Ammon as they carried the anvil between them.

'What the...' started Maddie as they entered the room with the hefty chunk of iron.

'Can you hold the rod please Maddie, and we'll swing this thing into it like a big hammer,' instructed Alex, panting under the exertion.

Maddie grabbed the rod and held it firmly at arm's length giving the guys room to manoeuvre into position. On a count of three they swung the anvil back and forth before a combined explosive effort brought it into ringing contact with the rod. The first blow saw a short movement as the other end of the rod was heard to come up against something hard and metallic in the vent shaft. A second blow rendered much the same sound but with no movement of the rod, followed by the same again for the third and fourth hits.

'Rest, rest,' insisted Alex prompting them to drop the weight to the ground and shake out the fatigue.

Maddie kept a firm grip on the rod giving it an assessing wiggle. 'Whatever it's hitting up there is pretty hard, you might just be wasting your time and energy.'

'Might as well use it up now and reduce the lingering death that faces us if we don't get out of here!' scathed Alex not in any way ready to accept the inevitable truth of his own words.

'Again,' Ammon interjected sensing another round brewing between them.

Taking a few deep preparatory breaths, the boys took their positions on either side of the iron mass. Further hard metallic thuds followed a series of five more blows to the end of the rod after which they rested again, both visibly struggling for breath.

'Come on guys, one more big one eh?' encouraged Maddie.

'Right, this is the one Ammon, ok,' Alex proposed championing a fierce determination.

Checking each other's eyes to share the intense build-up of energy they picked up the weight again. This time prepared to give it every last offering they had. Two perfectly timed swings creating momentum were followed by a roaring chorus of released power focussed on the obliging end of the rod. The resulting familiar unyielding sound provoked more roars of defiance and another precisely delivered blow. This time the sound was different. A sense of something giving imbued the returning change in tone. Yells of pending success spurred on another swinging build up, this time higher and with even more purpose. With the last screams of strength channelled into that blow another explosive contact was made. The imparted energy this time was enough to break through, driving the rod upwards at such a rate that the boys could only jump aside as the anvil left their hands and slammed to the floor. Maddie jumped away with a shriek of surprise bracing herself as she fell back against the wall.

Without a moment's hesitation Alex ran over to inspect the vent, craning his neck to look up into the void. 'Daylight. I see daylight! Yes! We've bust the bloody top off. Phase one complete, now we need something to get a phone up and out of the top.'

Ammon was already onto the task, heading off into the main cellar room. Alex stayed to wrestle with the steel rod, to retrieve it from the vent shaft and get it out of the way. It came out eventually with a sudden release that nearly took him off his feet. Peering up again he beckoned Maddie over.

'I reckon we'll be able to get a phone up there, what do you think?'

'Who should we message if you do get it up there? Old cheesy chops Fell and his plod mates?' enquired Maddie.

'Yes, I think so, we need them to stop the pub landlord as soon as possible, and he'll probably be able to get us out of here.'

'Ok, I'll work on a message while you boys sort out the stick thing and all that stuff.'

'Great. I'll go see what Ammon's up to.'

'By the way Alex,' started Maddie. 'Why are we calling him the pub landlord? It sounds like he's a comedy act, it should be something like evil murdering bastard.

'Well it's certainly got a ring to it,' smiled Alex as he left the room.

Working away on the bench Ammon had found a reel of fencing wire that he had doubled up and was twisting to make up a sturdy rod on which to mount a phone, he had already formed a cradle at one end to sit the device in.

'That's looking good mate,' said Alex getting excited his plan was coming together. 'Maddie's working on a message for D.I. Fell. I think he's our best bet of getting out of here and stopping Palmer.'

Ammon agreed, 'Let us hope he gets to Evelyn before anything bad happens. Come on, I am done here, let us try this thing out. Whose phone shall we use?'

Maddie was still busy typing in a message on her phone when the boys returned into the prison room. She looked up and grinned betraying her apparent lack of confidence in what she had written.

'Ok, see what you think of this then.

"URGENT SOS – Myself, Ammon and Alex are trapped in the cellar under the lodging house opposite the Quiet Woman pub. Bill Palmer has kidnapped Evelyn and was holding her here. We came to rescue her but Palmer caught us and has taken Evelyn and locked us down here. Palmer has a shotgun and is dangerous. Please help. Maddie Gresham."

What do you think?'

'It's fine,' conceded Alex, not entirely convinced but sensibly declining to challenge. 'Looks like it'll be your phone to go up the vent then Maddie.'

Maddie had no objection handing over the phone to Ammon who placed it in the cradle and tightened the wire around it. With the phone in place he unlocked the screen and touched send on the messaging app.

'Ok, so the message is sent, but will not go while the phone is down here, but it will retry again when it finds a signal up there, I am hoping.'

Moving over to the vent Ammon began carefully threading the device into the shaft and upwards towards the surface. 'I think that is it outside. All we can do now is wait and see if we can hear the tone of a reply.'

They waited in silence for some time, but heard no response to the message. Ammon eventually lodged the wire device into the vent hole so he didn't have to hold it any longer and suggested they take it in turns standing by the hole to listen out for a message notification tone. Instead of sharing the duty Alex and Maddie closed in on Ammon, eager to hear a response that would mean their freedom was a step closer.

'There's one obvious thing that's concerning me now boys,' whispered Maddie. 'What happened to Anna? What has he done with her and the other girls? I really dread to think.'

'I know, it did cross my mind,' replied Alex. 'Why is he imprisoning these girls and what has he done with them? It's just weird. And he was so, matter of fact about leaving us here and letting off that shotgun was...'

'He doesn't seem to have had any sexual interest in Evelyn. She said she was ok and he hadn't touched her, so what is he about?' Maddie pointed out moving into the room and looking around at the minimal furnishings. 'She was down here, alone for, what? Three days? She must have been terrified the poor thing. How horrible is that? And Anna, was she here? I can only think the worst.'

Alex shook his head contemplating what fate may have come to the lovely Anna. 'Now we are down here, and if this messaging idea doesn't work we are in trouble. I can't think how we can get out of here other than through that door.' Looking around he had noted there was a small amount of food and some bottled water, but that wouldn't last long. He tried to remember the estimated times associated with surviving without food and water. Four days came to mind regarding water, so it didn't matter how long they could go without food. With the water they had, could they survive a week? And when would they deteriorate into a state where they no longer had the energy to work on escaping this prison? Could they really be trapped and potentially die so close to home?

Ammon, who had been pretty quiet until now suddenly spoke up with great resolve. 'If no one comes soon I will find a way out of here. We will attack that door and not give up until we have broken it down my friends. I have to get out and I have to get my hands on Palmer. He has to be stopped.'

Alex and Maddie shared a look of both hope and fear, weighted precariously on a balance, which for the moment was tipped in their favour, partly on the back of Ammon's obvious determination. In the lapsing of time Alex's thoughts drifted to the door and wood and carpentry and inevitably the memory of his father. He knew a bit about wood working but wished he'd paid more attention to his father's attempts to teach him his impressive and extensive skills in carpentry and general DIY.

21 DIY

It had been over half an hour since the phone had been raised into the vent shaft, they had heard no reply and hope was fading amongst the three friends.

'There should have been some response by now surely,' reasoned Alex. 'Let's get the phone back down and check we haven't missed anything.'

'Yes, come on Ammon get it back down here,' agreed Maddie.

Ammon nodded, reached for the wire and pulled. 'Oh, it is jammed,' he exclaimed pushing and pulling gently on the wire trying to free it. When that didn't work, he gave it a good firm tug. At this the wire released and came back down the shaft. It was obvious from Ammon's face that the phone was no longer attached and sure enough the wire was retrieved with no phone in the cradle.

'Oh shit!' snapped Maddie. 'We don't even know if the bloody message was sent now.'

Ammon's face read sad disappointment and frustration. 'I am so sorry Maddie. Shall we try another phone? Mine is out of battery because I have used the torch so much, so it will have to be yours Alex.'

'Ok let's give it a go, my reception isn't good here though but, yes, let's give it a go,' agreed Alex.

With another message scripted, Alex's phone was mounted in the cradle and sent up the vent shaft. This time they had agreed to give it a few minutes and bring it back down to check if it had sent. On the first return and inspection no network connection had been made and the message was still in the out box. Subsequent tries yielded only the same result. After several attempts they decided to leave the phone up in the vent in the hope it would eventually find a signal before the battery failed.

'So that's that idea exhausted,' Alex conceded 'We need another plan guys.'

Maddie slumped back with her head in her hands. She was evidently emotional and Alex noticed tears welling in her eyes. He immediately went over, knelt beside her and put his arms around her.

'I'm sorry, I'm getting scared now. And the thought of those girls and what has become of them, it's just all too real and horrible,' she sobbed.

'We're all scared Maddie, but we are going to get out of here, aren't we Ammon?' comforted Alex.

'We are, yes,' said Ammon reiterating his defiant confidence. 'Come on Alex let us have another look at that door.'

It really was a brute of a door, with thick oak panels and an iron frame it looked impregnable. They considered using the anvil to bash away at it but there was little room to swing it in the confined space at the top of the stairway. Unwilling to let go of any hope they purposefully descended the stairs in search of inspiration and a tool or something that could be used to break out. Maddie joined them ascending the stairs to look for herself. Her immediate and flustered return startled the boys as she ran into Alex's arms.

'There's someone at the door, I thought I heard a key turning. It'll be that nutter coming back for us.'

Gripped with fear they braced themselves for another uncertain confrontation

Sure enough, the sound of the door opening was followed by footsteps as someone made their way down. The voice they heard next was not what they expected.

'Madeline Gresham, Alex Hidde are you down there? D.I. Fell to the rescue, you might say.'

The friends erupted with joyful relief as D.I. Fell stood before them with a huge grin on his face. Celebrations were tainted a little by the appearance of detective constable Charlotte Mason, who stood at her boss's shoulder with a contemptuous curl forming on her upper lip. That aside, attention was focussed on the detective inspector, all three poised with the obvious question.

'Tell us, have you got Palmer, is Evelyn safe?' urged Maddie.

D.I. Fell held a hand up in a request for calm. 'We are standing back from the public house and have Mr Palmer under surveillance. I'm currently waiting on an armed response unit before we can make an arrest. He's armed and dangerous so we can't take any chances.'

'Ok, we'll need statements from you lot,' announced Mason. 'And I think we are going to want to know why you've persisted in interfering in a police investigation.'

'Not now Mason,' asserted D.I. Fell in a calm patronising tone. 'Let these people at least get out into the fresh air. We will need statements but we can do that later at the station.'

Mason's bottom lip dropped as she aimed a disdainful stare at the D.I. After which Maddie caught her eye with a smug grin, visibly riling her even more.

D.I. Fell gestured with a nod towards the stairs. 'Come on, let's get out of here and not disturb this place any more than we need to. The crime scene chaps will be here shortly.'

Walking up into the light of day and with D.I. Fell apparently on their side, a calm satisfying relief came to Alex. It all seemed now to be a mere formality. The apprehending and ultimate arrest of Palmer was in the hands of the authorities. His own unresolved issues with his mother, supressed during the ordeal of the last few hours now flooded back into his consciousness as his eyes adjusted to the glaring sunlight. He had half expected to emerge into a full-blown police operation, with cars surrounding the pub and officers wandering about to the tune of crackling two-way radio conversation but that was not what greeted them. In the immediate vicinity there was one young officer nervously keeping watch over the Quiet Woman, and a guy holding a tool bag who D.I Fell introduced as the locksmith employed by the police to crack the lock on the cellar door. Ammon went over to shake his hand and thank him.

'How long did it take you to pick that lock my friend, it is a tricky one is it not?'

The locksmith smiled and nodded a wink at Ammon. 'It is, but they usually don't take more than a couple of minutes.'

Ammon looked across at his friends, shrugging a grin in acknowledgment of the expert. Alex recognised Ammon's inferred shame at the length of time it had taken him to pick the lock but he had no complaints, smiling as he shook his head.

'If it wasn't for you Ammon, we wouldn't have got in there, and we wouldn't have found Evelyn. But we did get in there and now Palmer is going to get what he deserves.'

'Not all he deserves my friend,' snarled Ammon under his breath. The intent in his eyes saying far more than the words.

D.I. Fell approached them following a brief conversation with the young police constable who was keeping a watch on the pub. Apart from him, Alex could see no other police presence in the square, he assumed there must be more officers scattered around the village.

'Ok you three, I've organised a car to take you down to the station so you can start on those statements we'll be needing from you.'

Maddie turned to the others with some indignation before squaring up to the detective. 'I think we would like to stay around until we see Palmer arrested, if you don't mind Mr Fell.'

Fell pursed his lips and frowned in thought for a few seconds as

Maddie eyed him with her most persuasive stare.

'I would say that was totally inappropriate sir,' piped in Mason. 'This lot have interfered in this investigation more than is appropriate, and I think—'

'Where do you get off chocolate Charlie, the Mars bar queen?' cut in Maddie abruptly but holding back on a fully charged bitching attack. 'If it wasn't for us the Derbyshire police wouldn't be on the brink of arresting a potential serial killer, so put that on the end of your truncheon and stuff it where the sun don't shine.'

'How dare you!' replied Mason flustered and scrambling for words. 'Carry on like that, Gresham and I'll arrest you for, for - obstructing a police officer in the course of his, or her duty, and the Mars bar rumours were not true, they were made up by you and your nasty crowd of elitist toffee nosed—'

At this point D.I. Fell intervened with a barely perceived smirk of amusement teetering in the corner of his mouth. 'Now, now, that will be enough of that. You ladies appear to have some history and I'm not going to let that get in the way of police business. As for you staying around here until an arrest is made that could be some time—'

'D.I. Fell sir!' The officer on watch broke in excitedly. 'The suspect sir, he's out with the girl, and they're heading towards his Land Rover. He's got a gun sir. A shot gun sir.'

'Oh shite,' groaned the D.I. under his breath. 'Mason, call the fire-arms guys and find out how far out they are. Woodcock, follow at a distance we need to know where he's going.'

'I think he's seen us sir,' replied constable Woodcock reluctantly.

'Can you not surround him Mr Fell,' suggested Ammon, compelled to do something to stop him getting away.

'Sorry lad, three officers don't even make a circle. And besides, he's armed and we are not going to take any chances or partake in any heroic acts, is that clear Ammon?

Moving into a position where they could observe the goings on in the pub yard, they saw Palmer bundling Evelyn into the passenger side of the Land Rover before moving around to the driver's side. As he did so he looked over to the assembled group and waved the shotgun. It appeared he had indeed seen them, and decided to make good his escape.

Decisively D.I. Fell leapt forward into full view of Palmer, radio in hand. 'Move in all cars, move in all cars,' he yelled down the radio while waving signalling gestures to both ends of the main street.

At this Palmer jumped in the Land Rover and sped away towards the rear gate of the yard up to a small bridge over the stream that ran behind the public house. Stopping short of the gate, he paused a moment then reversed back a couple of car lengths before crunching the vehicle back into first gear and racing towards the gate with the obvious intent of breaking through it. The first attempt yielded minimal damage to the gate so a repeat run followed with an increased run up.

'You said there was only you three,' declared Maddie.

'I know my dear, but he now thinks the roads out of town are blocked so he's going to attempt to head off across country and hopefully buy us some time,' replied D.I. Fell smugly.

'Sir,' interrupted Mason. 'I've just spoken to the fire-arms team. It seems they've been involved in an incident with a B&Q delivery truck outside Buxton.'

'Bugger! Looks like we're going to have to DIY this job then doesn't it?' quipped the detective. 'Come on Mason, fire up the Skoda Fabia. We're going to have to take chase.'

The second attempt at the gate saw it clatter to the ground under the wheels of the Land Rover as it slipped and slid up into the soft mud of the field. Siren blaring and blue lights flashing Mason and D.I. Fell took chase, heading towards the gate at some speed. At this point Alex was already across the main street behind the police vehicle and heading for the gate, Ammon and Maddie close behind him. With Palmer now making progress across the field the police car crossed the pub yard and hit the soft ground on the small incline up to the bridge. Almost immediately it began a careering slide sideways. Mason's frantic fight with the steering did little to correct the vehicle's course as the driver's side front wheel found the edge of the bridge, beginning an inevitable topple into the stream where it came to an abrupt halt at a precarious angle in the shallow flowing water. Alex and Ammon looked on the hopeless scene uncertain of what to do next, whilst Maddie struggled to contain her roars of laughter at this seemingly ridiculous attempt at a pursuit. Running over to the car to offer their assistance to the police officers Alex noticed P.C. Woodcock approaching on a motorcycle, peeling off from the others he ran over to him.

'Can you get after them on your bike mate, you've got some decent off-road tyres on this thing?' he shouted over the sound of the bike engine.

'I can't ride off-road. I've only just passed my test three weeks ago,' replied the young and seemingly naive constable.

'Get off and let me have a go then,' shouted Alex assertively grabbing the handle bars.

'Oh, ok then,' submitted Woodcock offering Alex his helmet. Alex declined the helmet and jumped on the bike, revving it aggressively. As he pulled up alongside the stricken police vehicle, Ammon and Maddie were trying to help D.I. Fell out of the passenger door to shrieks of panic from Mason. She had found herself helplessly pinned under him against the driver's side window, with Maddie still chuckling as she held the door open. Due to the D.I.'s not inconsiderable girth, they were struggling to get the cursing man out of the vehicle.

'I'm going after him,' shouted Alex.

Maddie looked around and paused a moment as an idea seemed to flicker across her face. 'We'll head him off, now go, and take care Alex, don't do anything stupid.'

Alex smiled through a nervous glare. Kicking the bike into gear he ploughed forward up into the field showering mud behind him. Palmer was some distance ahead now, finding better grip on the lesser gradient and drier ground further up the field. Alex battled on, pitching his body around to stay upright as the bike slid violently from side to side on the soft earth. Gradually finding the better ground, the bike with its chunky tyres came into its own picking up speed and closing in on the Land Rover. Standing up on the foot pegs Alex opened the throttle, riding the bumpy terrain with reasonable ease. In his haste to catch up with Palmer he hadn't thought through what he was going to do when and if he eventually did. Thinking realistically, he could only keep his distance and the gun toting landlord in his sights. He probably hadn't even noticed he was following him. That notion was dispelled almost immediately when Palmer veered off to the right and slowed down, with the gun being shaken out of the driver's window, he was obviously signalling him to back off. Throttling back and returning to the seat, Alex slowly rode out to the left and then back in towards the rear of the Land Rover to keep himself far enough back to discourage Palmer from taking a shot at him. This slow pursuit carried on for a while with Palmer veering left and then right before he lurched forward and sped off towards a closed gate in a tall drystone wall. Without slowing the Land Rover crashed through the gate slewing immediately left and out of sight. Alex slowed further as he approached the gate which now lay flattened in the muddy opening. Moving out to the right, he could see Palmer driving off at speed, he revved the engine and headed for the gap. As he did so the Land Rover was thrown around broadside to the right with the gun pointing straight at him. His instinctive reaction was to hit the brakes and change direction. A shot rang out as he fought to keep control of the motor cycle. The pellets pinged and twanged off the frame and tank. Like needles he felt them bite into his right side. Wet tyres running over the gate lost all traction, dropping him to the ground. His right leg shrieking with pain was now trapped under the bike.

Alex lay still as the Land Rover drove away, shock masking the full extent of his pain. A heady mix of emotion and adrenaline surged and waned through his system, throwing images around his head in a cascading slide show. Anna, Maddie, Ammon, Sarah, his mother, the events of the past days, were interspersed with black and white flashback visions of his father and a tangle of poignant moments that had brought him to this emotionally intense point in his life. In a breath, his fleeting trip fused back into the here and now. He had to get up and get after Palmer, he'd started this and he was going to see it through, whatever that meant. He tried to move but couldn't. Within him the mechanism to do so was being overridden by an internal desire to feel no more pain and to rest in this void. If he moved, what other trauma might he discover had beset him? He lay motionless as if frozen by a self-preserving paralysis. He pushed to break its hold and to fight back the emotional tide that was raging through him. He knew what he had to do, for Evelyn, and Anna, and for Sarah and the memory of his father. With each breath it was becoming all too much for him to cope with. What he needed right now was good to arrive, over the hill, like the coming of the cavalry.

22 THE CAVALRY

A growing certainty that his friends and the police would be that cavalry gave Alex a renewed strength. Consciously he ran a systems check over his uncertain physical and mental state. There was pain but it was bearable, he might have hit his head. That was an unknown but tentatively he began to move, hoping beyond hope that there was no further trauma he hadn't been conscious of. Confidence gaining, he slowly got to his feet and lifted the bike back under him. It seemed ok, he kicked it into life and looked around for the Land Rover. Pointed towards the distant target heading up the other side of a small valley he revved hard and launched himself towards his prey. Picking his way down the steep hillside, he found he was catching up at a considerable rate. The bottom of the small valley was predictably boggy, but a well-chosen path found him picking up speed again on the lesser slope going up the other side. Nearing Palmer's vehicle Alex began considering his distance, was he in shot gun range? He was no expert but judging by the previous shot and what he suspected to be embedded in his body it was something small like a birdshot pellet. He reckoned he'd been hit from around seventy-five metres, not in killing range for that type of shot but as he could confirm bloody painful. Opting to stay at seventy-five metres plus, he approached his adversary. Palmer had slowed and seemed to be deliberating which way to go, or perhaps his next move. Up here on the top of the hill the ground was undulating with various small valleys emanating from the reasonably flat top plateau. Partitioning with dry stone walls created a maze of gateways that Alex knew reasonably well from exploring as a child. To make his getaway Palmer would have to negotiate this maze and find his way to the small track to the west of the town, that would take him to a multitude of potential routes out of the area. No doubt this is what he was planning, knowing that the police would not be able to cover all the roads. Circling around the enclosing walls, it was becoming apparent that Palmer was in fact struggling to find his way out. Alex realised that he was heading away from the gate that led over to the track. The circling continued like some old Western movie dual. Alex imagined dramatic spaghetti western music playing. He was the Good, Palmer the Bad, and the Ugly was probably still to come. Aware that Palmer could make a move at any time he chose not to close in on what he considered an undoubtedly dangerous cornered prey. It would be a big mistake to come up against this mad man's gun again. With a sudden whirring and surging of transmission noise, the Land Rover was off, leaving a cloud of black exhaust smoke behind. The chase was back on and gathering speed. Palmer was now making for a gate that Alex was certain led in the right direction off the hillside and towards a possible escape. Nearing the gate, it was obvious to Alex that the Land Rover would have to cross a narrow drainage ditch close to the wall, Palmer was heading for it but had he seen it? Alex suspected not and he was right. The inside wheels of the Land Rover found the edge of the ditch. The rear of the vehicle snatching violently as it toppled sideways coming to a sliding, grating halt on its passenger side. All four wheels spun up as engine revs soared wildly, there was no way Palmer was going to get any further in this floundered vehicle. This changed things completely, what would Palmer do now, cornered and on foot? Alex kept his distance. Within a few seconds of the Land Rover going quiet the driver's door was thrown open and Palmer emerged shotgun in one hand whilst dragging Evelyn out with the other. After helping her climb down from the high side of the toppled vehicle, he stood defiantly with the shotgun to her head beckoning to Alex. He had no choice other than to move in closer, Palmer was obviously considering his options but what was he thinking? If he was after the bike, he would have to make that difficult for him. Turning off the ignition he took the key, dropped the motor cycle to the ground and stepped over it. Still at around his predefined safe distance he stood his ground and waited for a reaction from the gunman. Palmer looked around before returning his stare and beckoning again. Alex was beginning to feel he maybe had the upper hand. Taking the key off its ring he began to walk slowly forward raising his hands. Nearing Palmer he made clear exaggerated movements as he put the key in his mouth, he wasn't going to give up the bike easily.

'What you doing boy? Give me that key,' snarled Palmer dragging a distraught Evelyn closer to himself and the gun.

'Come on Bill, you're not going to get away now,' pleaded Alex. 'There's an armed police team surrounding the area, they'll shoot you down on sight if you put up a fight.'

'I've got the girl here, they'll have to give me what I want. I've got you too boy, I can do you in to show I mean business. It's not over for me yet, not by a long shot. Excuse the pun.' Palmer was calm and showing no signs of feeling threatened by the situation. Evelyn had her hands bound, shaking, distressed and sobbing.

Alex could see a glint of a mad man in his eye, he needed to play on that if he could. 'Why are you collecting girls Bill, is it a hobby?'

'What's it to you boy? Give me that key.'

Alex feigned a swallowing action slipping the key into his cheek. 'Sorry Bill, you'd be an easy target for the police marksmen on a bike anyway, wouldn't you? Be much better with a helicopter, you could negotiate for a helicopter. You've been collecting some lovely girls haven't you mate, what do you do with them?'

'I can dig that key out of your stomach if I need to boy, but you might be right, a helicopter, they'd have to get me that if they want this girl alive, and then a plane out of the country.'

'Are the girls like pets or something. You feed them and keep them well by all accounts?' continued Alex, thinking of more and more weird distracting questioning.

'I like quiet women,' announced Palmer.

'Oh, like the pub sign?' probed Alex.

'That's who I want them to be, it doesn't always work but that's who I want them to be, yes,' admitted Palmer casually.

'So where are they now, the other girls Bill?' asked Alex trying to be as matter of fact as he could.

'Where are the police boy? I want to get that helicopter sorted out. They'll have to do that for me or this girl will get it.' Palmer reverted firmly back to his present situation.

'They'll be here soon, I'm sure they'll want to help you with the helicopter Bill. You've got bargaining power with the girls haven't you? So, the girls Bill, where are they?' persisted Alex.

'I've given them the greatest gift, the greatest gift anyone can give.'

'What's that Bill, what did you give them Bill?'

'Eternal life, I gave them eternal life, my quiet women.'

'Wow Bill, you can do that, you can give people eternal life? That's amazing.'

'I can, I've done it for all the animals in my care and I've done it for my quiet women.'

'Anna, Bill, Anna the bar maid, did you do it for her? She was beautiful, wasn't she?'

'She's my favourite, beautiful girl Anna, my ultimate quiet women. I think I did my best work with her.'

'So, Bill, the pub sign is, kind of inspiration then, would you say?' continued Alex starting to feel he was on to something far weirder and macabre than he dared imagine.

'I buy them the finest dresses, they're expensive you know. Anna is so close to perfection, I don't know if I can do any better.'

'You started with the animals then, the taxidermy, yeah?'

'Oh no it's far more than that boy, you're not understanding, it's giving them eternal life, beauty that lasts forever.'

The realisation was building, a realisation Alex was reluctant to accept but it was there in this mad man's admissions. Eternal life for him was preserving human beings. The girls were his taxidermy projects. He was making them into the quiet woman portrayed in the pub's sign. For Alex, the horror of this man's deeds was overwhelming, but in the midst of this face off Alex had to put that to one side and keep the negotiation going until the cavalry arrived. His hopes of someone getting here in time were beginning to fade.

'You must be very proud Bill, of the girls, are they on display, in cases or something?'

'You won't find them, they're not for other's eyes boy. When the police get here you know I'm going to have to do you in don't you?'

'Is that wise Bill? You'll only have two shots in that shotgun, you might need more during your escape.'

A fleeting image in his peripheral vision broke Alex's total focus on Palmer. Determined not to give away the distraction and arouse suspicion, he continued to maintain eye contact and the conversation with Palmer. Mopping his brow with the back of his hand in a feigned need to wipe away sweat, he disguised a brief glance over the wall behind Palmer. It wasn't the cavalry but it was Maddie and Ammon on a bloody big horse, Maddie's horse, the big hunter Clyde. They had approached on the other side of the wall both mounted on the magnificent beast.

'I've got more cartridges boy, more than enough.'

'But reloading Bill, they'll take you out, one of those snipers with a

254

high-powered rifle, they'll take you out, won't they?' Alex felt himself waffling and aware he could be giving away his friends on horseback beyond the wall. They had moved in closer to see where Palmer was before circling back a distance out of view.

'I wouldn't go worrying about me boy. There's one in the barrel for you. That's what you need to worry about.'

Alex raised his hands as though exasperated and looked around. 'Bill, they're not here yet are they? You still have chance to get away without hurting anyone.'

What Alex thought he saw during that opportunity, was Maddie looking like she was lining the horse up to jump the wall, was that even possible? It was a pretty high wall. Was he managing to hide his nerves? He'd done a pretty good job to this point, making the negotiation as natural as possible. Palmer was certainly beginning to look more suspicious. He'd glanced over his shoulder, but not seeing anything his attention returned to Alex.

'You know Bill, I know the way off here, if you want to go we could get down to the track and you could be on your way.'

'They're coming aren't they boy? It's nearing your time. If they find you dead, they're going to think twice about dealings with me aren't they eh?'

Alex swallowed nothing in his tight dry throat. Every nerve ending frayed and screaming fear. What could his friends do against this mad gun toting murderer? If he could, he would have called them off and out of harm's way. He was right Maddie had lined up the horse to jump the wall, what the hell were they thinking? As the horse began its gallop towards the wall, he caught Maddie's frightened but focused gaze. Palmer looked around again but not seeing or hearing anything over the masking sound of the facing breeze turned back to Alex.

'So, you stuffed girls for your own perverted pleasure then you fucked up freak?' screamed Alex in an attempt to keep his attention.

The next moments were as surreal as any he could have imagined. His eyes widened in awestruck surprise as the horse and riders appeared, leaping over the wall in full flight. Palmer noticed Alex's stunned expression and turned raising his gun. With the horse bearing down on him he jumped to one side, away from Evelyn. It was in that same instance that Ammon was making his move, launching himself from the back of the horse he soared towards Palmer like a Kung Fu missile. His movements were fast, accurate and ultimately ruthless. Kicking the gun with his left foot he knocked it aside where it discharged harmlessly with a thunderous boom. In the same heartbeat his right foot connected with Palmer's jaw sending him flailing to the ground where Ammon landed astride his reeling body. Palmer thrust up a hand to protect himself. In a flash, Ammon grabbed his wrist, putting his arm in a lock from which he was powerless to escape, placing a foot on the back of his neck for good measure.

On seeing Palmer restrained Alex's attention was drawn to Maddie and the horse which had landed badly not far from him. Stumbling as its front hoofs fought for traction Maddie had been thrown forward off the poor animal's back, falling hard in front of its crushing gallop. Clyde's instincts wouldn't allow him to trample her but he was fighting to recover his stride. Miraculously he passed over her without making contact, leaving her slumped, motionless body lying helplessly on the ground. Running over to Maddie, Alex turned to see Ammon content in his restraining of Palmer but now with Evelyn wrapped around him. Though he recognised her need and sought to console her, he was still plainly full of a rage, but managing to stop short of giving Palmer what he thought he really deserved. Alex dropped to his knees besides Maddie's unconscious body. Carefully taking her head in his arms and held her close.

'Maddie, come on, are you ok?' his emotions broke his voice as he kissed her forehead. Stirring she began to come round and opened her eyes.

'Clyde Alex, is Clyde alright?' she murmured in her dazed state.

'He's ok, he's ok Maddie,' Clyde was on his feet but noticeably limping on a delicate front leg and snorting his displeasure.

'And Palmer, did Ammon get him?'

'Yes, he's half breaking his arm and he's wearing Evelyn around his neck. Keeping up the warrior ancestry I reckon.'

'You're amazing Alexipoos, do you know that?' said Maddie.

Her conscious smiling face almost choked him but he fought it off and laughed. 'That was one incredible jump missy, two up as well. It's you that's amazing and that crazy flying Egyptian,' praised Alex full of pride for his friends.

Maddie looked up into his eyes her face lit up with a beaming smile. 'Maybe we need each other Alex, what do you think?'

'You be careful lady, you've just had a bang on the head.'

'I know what I'm saying, and I know you feel the same way you big scaredy cat.'

Flustered, Alex tried to kerb her advances. 'Don't go making me say silly things here that you'll make me regret when you come round later.'

'Oh, come on Alex say something silly, like you love me, cos I know you do.'

'How do you know that?'

'I can read you like a book Alex Hidde. Are you going to admit it?' She flinched with pain as she attempted to move.

'Take it easy Maddie, you fell pretty hard, I was worried about you.' He held her tighter restraining her attempts to move.

'Were you worried cos you love me Alex? Are you?'

Alex paused, took a long hard look into her eyes and smiled. 'Yes, I'm worried because I love you Maddie. There, I've said it, where's your punch line eh?'

'No punch line. There is no punch line Alex.'

'I've got some tough things to sort out Maddie, I'm gonna need you, it's going to be hard.'

'I'm here Alex, we'll get you through it. Now, are you going to kiss me?'

They lingered in the tender moment, but it was taken from them before their lips could meet. D.I. Fell and company had arrived with five armed police officers fully kitted out in body armour.

'Well, looks like it's all wrapped up here gentlemen,' announced the D.I. addressing his group of disappointed looking action seekers. 'You might as well get back and fill in your insurance claim form lads. And do remember next time, blue lights and sirens don't give you supernatural powers, a forty-ton truck will always win.' His sarcasm was met with an assortment of scowls and grumbled comments.

Three of the armed officers relieved Ammon of his restraining duties, dragging the dazed Palmer to his feet and handcuffing him. He didn't say a word or show any concern or remorse as he was marched off escorted by the armed police.

'What was the gun shot?' questioned D.I. Fell. 'It was that that led us here, to a far more pleasant scene than I expected I must admit.'

'I'm not sure you'd believe me Mr Fell,' began Alex shaking his head. 'But, it was Ammon that disarmed Palmer and the gun went off in the process. He's an evil and twisted man, you're not going to find any of those girls alive, he told me what he'd done with them.'

'Ok Alex, we'll evaluate the details later. Let's just concentrate on getting everyone off this hillside safely first eh?' D.I. Fell's voice was low and conveyed a compassion that gave the situation a fitting gravity. This was a moment to celebrate the capture of an, until now, unknown serial killer but it was also a time to remember there were victims who had suffered an horrendous fate at the hands of this truly disturbed individual.

Ammon and Evelyn joined Alex as he helped Maddie to her feet. She was bruised and battered from the fall but protesting she was ok to walk unaided. Suspecting she may have cracked a collar bone, an injury Maddie confirmed she had suffered before when falling from a horse, Alex fashioned a make-shift sling to hold her arm up and close to her chest. There wasn't a lot said verbally as they regrouped, but their faces said it all. Evelyn never left Ammon's side on the way back to the police vehicles and beyond. D.I. Fell had arranged for the group to be met by an ambulance and taken to the local hospital for a check-up. Maddie being Maddie, insisted she must take her horse back to his stable before any such thing, so Alex led Clyde with Maddie holding him for support as she hobbled alongside. To her delight the massive stallion seemed to have recovered well from his heavy stumbled landing. He was now walking with no signs of the limp he had developed after the jump.

'I think we deserve a drink my friends,' announced Ammon.

'You certainly do mate. You did actually save my bacon back there, again! A nice cup of tea would do me,' said Alex.

'A good stiff gin and tonic for me,' added Maddie.

'I'll join you there for sure,' chuckled Evelyn.

'Gin and Tonic eh?' queried Alex. 'What is it they call that stuff? Mother's ruin?'

23 MOTHER'S RUIN

Over the distant hills the last embers of a waning autumn sun painted a glorious fringe on the underbelly of a broken layer of cloud. Alex stood outside the cottage gazing at the photographic opportunity he was missing as it faded before his eyes. Behind him, the sound of the police car that had taxied him home swirled and refracted amongst the trees as it drove away into the silent backdrop of evening. He stood silently, reflecting on the day, its images stacked like the photographs he would have taken if he could have been detached from it all - but he wasn't. A numbness had set in during the interviews with D.I. Fell. The repetition of his experience created a distance from the events as they became facts on a sheet of paper underwritten with his almost reluctantly scrawled signature. Four hours in A and E hadn't helped matters, especially as he couldn't sit on his shotgun pellet ridden back side without significant discomfort. Maddie had cracked a collar bone. He'd recognised that, but a flippant comment from the paramedic about his sling work had shot him down in front of her and robbed him of a huge chunk of the gallantly he thought he'd earned. After all he was a spectator when it came to the final showdown, with Ammon taking the landlord down in such a spectacular fashion. The police seemed to have found this movie like action scene hard to believe, rewriting that section of the statement over and over to capture the details. On the way out of the police station, Alex had chuckled to himself after seeing the desk sergeant in mid Kung Fu pose, obviously retelling the tale to his assembled colleagues. More disbelief had followed with Alex's account of Palmer's admissions about the fate of the other girls, including Anna. Though potentially devastating he'd not found the time to process the reality of these confessions, choosing to allow his post traumatic mind to push them down, for now. Pain and indignity would be his abiding memory of the visit to the hospital. Removing every pellet embedded in his right buttock and thigh, even though punctuated by humorous and encouraging repartee from the medical staff, had been nothing less than embarrassing. To top it off his moment with Maddie had been lost in the business of the day. He contemplated what that simple communion had meant, and if it actually had been the turning point that he'd thought. Only time would tell, but he could only see himself being shot down when she retrospectively withdrew her outpouring of affection.

Going into the cottage seemed like a retreat from what should have been some sort of celebration that evening. In the confusion of the police station, the friends had been separated and before he knew it he was heading home in a police car having missed any opportunity to organise a get together. Patting his pocket, he confirmed he'd lost his phone in the commotion of leaving the cellar at the lodging house, creating another hurdle to communicating with his friends. As for when they could gather again at the Quiet Woman for a drink, that was another unknown. The place was in darkness as he'd passed in the police car. Finding the door key in his pocket he slid it reluctantly into the lock, opened the door and dragged his heavy legs into the house. With the door closed behind him he caught a fragrant smell in the disturbed air, it was familiar he thought, floral but not from the garden. It was his mother's perfume; his mother had been in the house. Normally he wouldn't have questioned that, but after the recent revelations he knew his curiosity was more than deserved. He looked around but found nothing moved or taken or anything else that concerned him, maybe he was mistaken. Deciding to ignore the possible scenarios he had begun to concoct, he entered the kitchen and grabbed the kettle. Watching it boil, his thoughts drifting over everything and focussing on nothing in particular. He breathed in the steam as he waited for the always overly long interval between boil and pop-like click as the kettle's mechanism finally accepted the obvious. Throwing a tea bag into a cup he poured hot water onto it, watching the bag swirl around in the fragrant whirlpool.

***

It wasn't until late the next morning that Alex's mother returned again to the cottage, George being the first to discover Alex's motionless body strewn across the kitchen floor, as he peered in through the window. All conquering George marched into the house with Mrs Hidde cautiously following behind.

'Oh my poor boy,' she chocked in the realisation of what they had done.

'Come on my dear, it was what you wanted and as good as what he deserved thinking he could expose us, the little bastard,' corrected George casually.

'I know. But he was mine, as unwanted as he was.'

'Well let's just call it a late termination then my dear, one sip of that stuff would wipe out a herd of wildebeest,' quipped George.

Walking over to where Alex lay, his mother bent forward slightly to look closer. 'Have you checked if he's, actually, dead?'

The shock that then confronted her was as unexpected as it was surreal. Alex spun himself around and sat on the floor facing her.

'Not dead mother, no, but you do make a lousy cup of tea, you fucking evil bitch.' Spitting out all his supressed rage he shook with a surging rush of adrenaline.

In a vicious panic George was upon him, having picked up a chunky glass vase en-route. Now it was held above him ready to descend with lethal force onto Alex's skull. Sat on the floor he was powerless to respond, instinctively closing his eyes and lifting his arm for protection. A loud thump followed and then a moment of silence. Opening his eyes slowly and looking up a new scene met his bewildered gaze. George was flat on his back with Ammon towering above him, the vase firmly in his grasp.

'Lovely vase Mrs Hidde, shame to see it broken,' remarked Ammon with a huge grin directed at the dumbstruck woman.

From behind his mother, a familiar voice approached reading them their rights as her hands were taken behind her back and secured in cuffs. He'd expected her to have a lot to say for herself at this unreal and disturbing time but she said nothing, just glared at him with an expression he didn't recognise in her. Before he'd got to his feet, she was being escorted out of the house to the sound of vehicles grinding to a halt on the gravel of the driveway, whilst George's groaning carcass was being manhandled across the floor. Ammon grabbed Alex and pulled him close. Whether he'd got up too quickly or the overwhelming emotions had taken his legs or a combination of the two, Alex was on the point of flaking out.

'Are you ok my friend?' enquired Ammon helping him over to a chair at the kitchen table.

'I think so,' replied Alex in a thin croaky voice. 'Maybe a cup of tea and some toast is what I need mate.'

'Always up for that my friend,' replied Ammon.

'You got to old George just in time eh?' whispered Alex, beginning to get some colour back in his face. 'So saved my life just the three times then, is it?'

'You are so very welcome my friend,' beamed Ammon. 'Oh, and I did not kill you in my car accident.'

Alex smiled and scoffed a brief laugh, 'Oh, yes, you didn't kill me in your car, thanks mate. How could I forget that?'

Approaching footsteps turned their attention towards the open front door and D.I. Fell entering the kitchen. 'Well, you'll be needed down at the station again you two,' announced the detective. After a brief pause he spoke again, his tone was clear and sympathetic. 'In your own time Alex, just take your time, and bring your friends. This is a time for friends, and you've got some good ones here.' With that he tugged down on the lapels of his jacket and composed himself before heading out to the waiting vehicles.

***

Peering into the cup Alex watched the tea bag spin to a stop, turning the water slowly tea coloured. Rhythmically breathing in the rising steam, he filled his palette with the soothing smell of tea, until, along with the usual aroma he caught a hint of something else. Dropping the tea spoon to the tiled floor he grabbed his car keys and was at the front door before the metallic ringing of spoon on terracotta had decayed. From the glove compartment of the car he retrieved the tea caddy Maddie had clumsily appropriated from his father's workshop, opening the lid he took a good hard sniff. The same subtle hint of something other than tea permeated his nostrils. It was the poison, the Oleander, and it was in his tea in his kitchen. Dashing back into the cottage, he threw open the cupboard door above the kettle and took out the box of tea bags, carefully opening the lid he stared in. Magnifying glass, he muttered to himself as he flew around the kitchen drawers in a rapid and random search. Finally armed with the magnifying glass he returned to the box of tea bags and took one out for closer inspection. What he saw confirmed his suspicions. Along one edge the bag had been opened and delicately resealed. He concluded to himself that his mother and botanical bollock brained George had been there with the intention of poisoning him in the same manner as his father. His first reaction was to laugh but that only briefly masked the fury that quickly rose within him. Hammering his fists on the counter top he fought to bring his delirious rage under control. Powerful emotions flooded his dwindling reserves of rational thought. He knew he needed a plan, and he knew he needed his friends. With no phone that meant going out. He'd go to

Maddie's, and see her and Ammon.

Maddie opened the door to a distressed but silent Alex.

'Come in Alex, are you alright?'

Ammon was at the door in a flash, realising something wasn't right.

'What has happened Alex? Are you alright my friend?' He took Alex's shoulders and walked him to a chair at the table.

'They tried to poison me. If I hadn't...,' lost for words Alex dropped his head. 'They'd have poisoned me just like they did my father.'

'How did you find out Alex?' enquired Maddie sharing an opened mouthed gaze with Ammon.

'My tea bags have been tampered with. They have the same smell as the tea in the caddy from the workshop.'

'Okay!' barked Ammon. 'It is time for a plan to catch them in the act my friend.'

'Let me get you a cup of t..., coffee Alex?' offered Maddie.

'Yes, coffee please Maddie, thanks,' replied Alex returning a vague smile.

***

Alex and his friends were sat across a desk from D.I. Fell, again. 'So, I'm sorry Mr Fell that we didn't let you in on the plan until it was nearly too late, but, we just wanted them caught in the act, with all the evidence you would need. We didn't know how much of what we had was going to be admissible in court.'

'A fair argument Alex, but, we have procedures for these things and for you to take the law into your own hands was stupid and reckless.' Fell drove home the point with a beat of his pen on the desk, then sat back fostering a brief thin smile. 'As it is, I'm going to overlook your amateur sleuthing antics in light of the obvious grief this has brought you, and for that you have my deepest sympathy.'

'What will happen to them, my mother, and George?' asked Alex, the question visibly unsettling him.

The detective replied bluntly but kindly, 'That is for a court of law to decide Alex, but, the charges will be attempted murder and of course, without a doubt, premeditated murder in the case of your late father. They will both get considerable prison sentences, I can assure you of that. I believe you have siblings Alex? They will need to be informed. There will be a lot of things to sort out with solicitors and so forth, a busy and distressing time for you all I'm afraid.'

'Thank you,' tendered Alex. 'You've been very fair and considerate throughout all this.'

D.I. Fell raised his eyebrows along with a wry smile before rising from his seat. 'Don't expect the same if I see you in here again with more of your amateur sleuthing antics. Now, get out of my sight before I have to lock myself up for imitating someone who gives a damn.' Offering his hand Alex took it and shook it firmly, Ammon and Maddie followed thanking the D.I. as they exited the office into the corridor.

Alex walked out into the carpark winged by his two best friends. 'So, just the fallout from the biggest bombshell of my life to sort out now then eh?'

'We'll get through it Alex,' reassured Maddie taking his hand.

'I think we could do with a good drink my friend,' suggested Ammon putting his arm around Alex's shoulders. 'There is an old Egyptian proverb that says, time is like a river, you cannot touch the same water twice, the flow that has passed will never pass again. Let us drink to the past with our eyes ever on the horizon my friends.'

'Hey Alex! That reminds me, guess what I've heard?' announced Maddie. 'Well, the brewery has given Crazy Claire and Arnold the Quiet Woman to manage until they find a new landlord.'

'You are joking, aren't you?' laughed Alex.

'I am not, and, the open mike session tomorrow night is going ahead as usual, so, party time Wooohooo!' Maddie grabbing the boy's hands and danced them across the car park towards Ammon's car.

'That's great. We need to get Sarah out to that then,' Alex suggested. 'It's going to feel strange now though isn't it, after everything, going back to the Quiet Woman?'

24 THE QUIET WOMAN?

Alex pulled focus on Maddie's pouting face across the table by the stuffed fox. Through the lens of the camera he could study her discreetly, every twinkle in her eye, every freckle, every sexy turn of her mouth. She'd scrunched her hair forward around her face, playfully throwing pose after pose at the camera like a working model. If he'd had his heart rate monitor running on his sports watch, it would be showing an error message. But Maddie wasn't an error, she was a beautiful collision and if he lost his no claims bonus he didn't care. If, that is, she really meant what she'd said after the fall from her horse. He snapped off a couple of shots and beckoned Sarah into the frame.

'Two more beautiful ladies my camera has never captured,' enthused Alex.

'Oh, you charmer Alex Hidde,' Sarah replied patting her hair in feigned modesty.

'More drinks my friends,' announced Ammon depositing a handful of glasses to the table. 'Have you seen, Arnold is behind the bar? Not as quick at pulling a pint as descending a steep hill, I must say. Claire keeps slapping his bottom every time she passes him, they are having a ball behind that bar.'

Following Ammon, Evelyn appeared with even more drinks, to join the friends around the table.

'So, Evelyn,' began Alex inquisitively. 'Some loose ends I think need clearing up, your car for one, why did it end up just off the M25, and, who sent the Facebook messages?'

'He sent the messages. He took my mobile and did it right in front of me. And my car, apparently, he drove it down to a scrap dealers in London and had it crushed, then came back on the train. They caught him on CCTV cameras at the stations. He was such a creepy guy in that cellar, oddly though a perfect gentleman too, but to be sure a total head case.'

Ammon sat forward to address the group. 'Well I too have a loose end that is now tied up.'

'We don't need to know your personal problems mate, but go on,' joked Alex.

'No seriously, the body we found, we know it was this Richard McGuire yes? Well he was looking for his daughter who went missing, she was another of Palmer's girls, and, he has admitted that he took the man out to look for his daughter and pushed him into that hole where Arnold found him.'

Sarah gasped and covered her mouth. 'That is terrible, the poor man. What a horrible story. And you three are the reason he was caught. I hope he never sees the light of day again.'

'Here, here,' agreed Maddie.

'When are you doing your song Maddie?' asked Ammon.

'Well actually it's not one of my songs I want to do, it's one of yours Sarah,' replied Maddie coyly.

Sarah looked surprised and a little puzzled. 'One of mine, really?'

'Yes, I hope you don't mind but I found it on the internet, in fact a video of you with your band at the Royal Theatre in London. It's "By the Morning". It's such a lovely song. Would you join me please Sarah? I've borrowed another guitar, so you can play yours.'

'Thank you Maddie. It's been a while, but hey, why not,' conceded Sarah raising her glass.

Maddie did nothing to hide her excitement, whooping and clapping, 'Woohoo brilliant, thank you Sarah.'

The atmosphere was buzzing in the Quiet Woman. Whether it was just a coincidence or morbid curiosity that had brought people out, the place was as busy as Alex could remember. There were some old faces he recognised dotted around the bar, and spurred on by the larger than life personality of the temporary landlady, all seemed to be having a great time of it too. The big guy, Greg, was running the open mic again, wearing a Quiet Woman t-shirt, Alex noted. He wondered where on earth had he got that from? The subject matter with the headless girl was right up his street though, for a guy whose daily transport was a large black hearse. It occurred to him that this place was now going to become infamous with Palmer having inadvertently put it on the map. For all the wrong reasons, but in all probability this once humble village pub could now be a little gold mine. Looking around at his friends he couldn't help but feel that this might be their last night out together. Ammon and Evelyn were going to Ireland to catch up with family after her ordeal, and he hadn't thought about his future beyond sorting out the family home and all the nonsense that would inevitably throw up.

'Alex, check out the fox behind you.' Maddie yelled across the table bringing him back from his reflecting with a dizzying jolt.

He turned and let out a convulsed laugh at the scene before him. Someone had gone to the trouble of dressing the fox up in a huge black afro wig, floppy velvet hat and sunglasses, with a cigarette placed casually in the corner of his mouth. Around him had been placed an array of bright yellow chicks in various poses, probably robbed from one of the other displays that littered the room.

'What do you reckon Alex, Jimmy Hen-tricks the juggling fox eh?' Maddie was in a glowing mood. No doubt she would sober up when the call came for her to take to the stage for her performance, but for now she was just enjoying the company and the moment.

When the call came, Alex could see she was looking pretty nervous as the ladies got up and headed for the floor to encouraging applause from the gang. Sarah whispered something in her ear that seemed to perk her up, and by the time they stood in front of the microphones and behind their guitars she was beaming with apparent confidence. After they had both strummed through a quick tune up, Maddie stepped forward to introduce them.

'Hi, good evening, we're going to do one of this lady's songs, you might know it, and you might know her, Sarah Haven ladies and gentlemen.'

A ripple of polite applause rose from the audience suggesting there were a few who clearly did know the accomplished lady.

Alex suddenly felt huge apprehension for them, they hadn't practised together, how long was it since Sarah had sung this song and did Maddie know it well enough? He needn't have worried, after a brief intro a wondrous blend of rich female voices filled the room, a surge of pride saw him fighting back a surprise tear, he shrugged it off coughing discreetly and swigged a mouthful of beer. Taking his camera he moved out into the room to capture a few shots of the girls together. Lifting the camera to his eye he saw Maddie looking back at him down the lens just as they reached a seemingly familiar chorus.

'I'll be yours by the morning, if you'll just keep me close tonight.'

Coming out from behind the camera his spontaneous smile was returned. Was she singing to him? He had thought that before only to be left feeling like a fish having taken an un-baited hook. Glancing at Sarah he picked up on a knowing look, backed up further by a subtle wink in his direction, she could see what was going on, couldn't she? The performance from the ladies was magical and by the end of the song the onlookers were wanting more, a rowdy applause keeping them on the stage and feeling guilty to walk away. Finally, Sarah took the microphone and delivered a graceful acknowledgment.

'Thank you so very much. We are going to go now and let the next act come on, but we will be back, maybe next time after I've done some well needed practice. Thank you, enjoy the rest of the evening.'

From the midst of the crowded room Alex began to move towards the girls leaving the stage. Seeing Maddie frantically scanning the room he grasped the notion that it was him she was looking for. When their eyes met he was nearly certain. When she headed for him his certainty blossomed. Questioning nothing he embraced her and went to kiss her cheek only to meet her lips with tingling surprise. They were in their own little world now, all around was a blurred backdrop to their moment.

'I'm letting down my deflector shields Mr Spock, that song was for you.'

'Nothing like a Star Trek chat up line to get a guy going, the song was brilliant, you were both amazing, I'm so proud of you.'

'Can we be together Alex? Do you think that can work?' Maddie's deep gaze into his eyes spoke to him of her insecurities and reluctance to give herself to someone again.

'We could give it a try, I suppose. You keep those shields down and keep reading me like a good book you can't put down and... what do you say?'

With a searing violin intro, the background came to life around them as a rousing jig erupted from the band that had taken to the stage.

'I say yes Alexipoos,' shouted Maddie. 'Hold me close and dance with me please.'

Celebrating their assignation with joyful laughter, they waltzed off into the crowded dance floor with no thoughts of past or future, just the gift of the present.

During the applause at the end of the song Alex took Maddie's hand, pulled her close and pointed over to their table where Sarah sat alone. Without a word they went back to join her with the intention of making a fuss of her. Soon after Ammon and Evelyn returned to the group of friends and the real revelry began.

At the end of the evening the friends were invited to stay on after all had gone and the doors had been closed. The evening of drinking fuelled the party atmosphere which was playful and exuberant, beginning with an over animated Alex re-enacting the grizzly encounter with the bikers at the bar. Under some modest duress Ammon was persuaded to demonstrate his bar stool wielding skills to rapturous applause from their hosts Claire and Arnold behind the bar. When Alex suggested they all propose a toast, Ammon was the first to raise his glass.

'I would like to propose a toast to toast,' he broke off to hysterical laughter, mainly from Alex. 'I'd like to propose a toast to toast, and a good cuppa tea, because it has supported us through some really difficult times.'

'To toast!' chanted the high-spirited company.

Next Maddie got up. 'I'd like us to drink to my horse, Clyde, for being a brilliant launch pad for our own Egyptian interceptor missile in the shape of the lovely but highly dangerous Ammon.'

In the laughter that followed Evelyn got to her feet, she waited a moment for their attention.

'The toast for me is easy, it's to my rescuers. I owe you my life, thank you so very, very much.' Choking on her final words and with tears on her cheeks, Ammon was quickly at her side.

'And with that,' started Sarah. 'I'd like to toast the good in all of you selfless people, taking on all you have for others and bringing the lovely Evelyn out of that horrible nightmare. To the rescuers.'

Glasses clinked in a sobering refrain from the frivolous evening's activities, each of them aware of what could so easily have been a totally different outcome.

'Alex,' prompted Maddie softly.

'Err, just to my friends. The unlikely friends I made on what was going to be a short escape from my ferrr-fractured, life back in Manchester. Thanks for your support and inspirational, if not misguided, can-do attitudes. Be assured I will always be there for you, thank you.'

'Especially for me please, Alex?' checked Maddie.

'Ho ho!' celebrated Ammon. 'At last you two are finally a couple? I have been watching you pushing each other away since the first time I saw you bickering together, you crazy people, that is so wonderful my friends.'

'To crazy people,' toasted Alex leaning over to kiss Maddie on the cheek.

Claire, fascinated by the story of the three amateur sleuths wanted to know more about their adventures since meeting with Arnold. As they recounted the events that had led to Bill Palmer's arrest all three of them marvelled at the exploits and highs and lows they had shared. Sat around the bar in the partially lit room, the tales began to take on a chilling aspect as they pondered the fate of the girls, voices were lowered and a respectful silence followed, until Alex had a question.

'Claire, have the police finished their search of the pub? Did they find anything?'

'Yes, they took all sorts of things away but they've obviously not found any trace of the girls or they'd have said, I'd have thought,' replied Claire.

I'm surprised they haven't closed the place down,' interjected Sarah in disgust.

'So they didn't just rip the place apart then?' questioned Maddie with some surprise.

'No, they left a lot of, like finger print powder everywhere but they didn't take the floor up or anything like that,' continued Claire.

'Palmer's done some work around the place hasn't he recently?' posed Alex.

'He has, yes,' replied Claire. 'He's done a lot of work upstairs and he's finished one of the bedrooms, it's been decorated completely, he's made a nice job of it too.'

Alex was keeping his thought processes to himself, but their probing nature was obvious. 'I reckon he's done more than decorate that room, there was a builder's skip outside here for a few days recently wasn't there? Claire, can we go and have a look at the room?'

Looking at Arnold, Claire paused before nodding her approval. 'Of course you can, yes, come on I'll take you up, is everyone coming?'

No one stayed in the bar, they all followed Claire up into the private quarters to the rear of the pub. Ascending the stairs without a word the building's soundscape accompanied them, creaking floorboards and variously pitched footsteps drummed to an irregular rhythm. The aging structure felt almost on the brink of swaying under the weight of the group moving through it. Reaching the door to the bedroom Claire stopped and waited for the group to assemble. Pushing the door open she stood aside as they all entered. Maddie switched on the lights before walking in but the meagre single low wattage bulb did little to illuminate the space.

'What is it you think you're looking for lad?' enquired Arnold.

'The police may not have taken up the floor but they also don't seem to have checked the walls either have they?' Alex didn't get a response, he wasn't looking for one as he moved around the walls knocking on them and listening to the returning tone. Ammon joined him, then Arnold and Maddie added to the dull, hard, thudding ensemble, until, a hollow beat rang out amongst the rest followed by silence as all faces turned to Ammon.

'It is hollow here Alex, behind this wood panelling,' he confirmed.

'That's where you would expect to find an alcove isn't it, at the side of the fireplace?' theorised Alex. 'It all looks very original though and solid.'

A sudden click turned everyone's attention towards Maddie. 'It's another light switch,' she announced clicking it on and off. 'But it doesn't seem to do anything.'

'Yes it does,' said Evelyn pointing at the wood panelled wall. 'It's lighting up behind that wall, can you see it? It must be a hidden room or something.'

'Where can we find some tools, Claire?' asked Alex.

Before Claire had finished what she was saying, Alex and Ammon had left the room and were running down the stairs on their quest for the tools to help them investigate what was behind that wall. The boys returned to the room where Arnold, Claire, Maddie, Sarah and Evelyn had gathered together speculating fearfully what might be revealed. Ammon wielding a pick axe and Alex a digging spade which he thrust into the wall between the wooden boards. A couple of blows with the spade saw it buried into the wall up to its shaft, in the same burst of activity Ammon had penetrated the boards with the pick axe and was levering against the side wall. Alex also began to lever at his side until the boards could be seen to move away in one connected section.

Alex took a breath and looked across at Ammon. 'A couple more tugs is going to bring this wall down Ammon, are you ready? Everyone move back.'

Sure enough, a couple more good efforts saw the top of the wall pull away far enough for the two guys to get their hands in behind the upright timbers. With a foot against the outer walls they heaved together one last time, it was enough to bring the whole wall down, forcing them to jump back to avoid it as it collapsed to the floor.

'It's a window, or something,' said Alex straining his eyes to make out what was behind the glass panel in front of them. 'Turn that light on again Maddie.'

When the light went on what they beheld took their breaths instantly, audibly and completely. Behind the glass now fully illuminated stood the headless figure of a woman, perfectly dressed in a long flowing pale blue gown, her hands in front of her clasping a handkerchief exactly as depicted in the Quiet Woman pub sign. Like a display in a museum every detail was precise and elegant. Her skin soft and white had the tone of living flesh, her form beautifully proportioned and lifelike. This was the landlord Bill Palmer's handy work. Alex immediately recognised that it was Anna stood before them, the beautiful young woman with whom he'd become smitten the year before. The next words Alex was to speak came from a place he was unaware of, he had no control over the route they took as they weaved their way through complex neural networks to the part of his brain that would eventually signal his vocal chords to tighten and deform as a lightly expelled breath passed over them during the normal unconscious process of speech. When his lips finally moved, he was as surprised as anyone to hear the words that came out.

'Holy shit! The quiet woman, stuffed and mounted…'

The End

ABOUT THE AUTHOR

Michael Bealey lives in north Lancashire close to the Lake District national park with his partner Helen and their dog Baron Von Bramble, an energetic young Sprocker Spaniel. He enjoys the great outdoors, walking, running, climbing and mountain biking along with his writing, photography, guitar and singing as well as daily walks with the Baron

Discovering early in life a love of writing, but strangely not reading, he would regularly fill countless pages with partially illegible scrawl when given the opportunity during English lessons. The resulting feedback was probably not the most encouraging.

His first real creative outlet came when he and fellow school friends formed a rock band. Alas he's not yet taken a self-penned hit to the top of the charts but enjoyed several fruitful song writing partnerships with fellow musicians over the years.

From song writing came poetry, both serious and comic. This is where he loves to show off his rather quirky sense of humour, likened by a close friend to Spike Milligan meets Vic and Bob. The Quiet Woman has comic moments and large characters but not the more wacky edge you'll find in some of his writing.

A chance arose to write in his work life when a career change took him into learning and development. Initially involved in the production of training material he was later drawn into the design and writing of experiential learning tasks for team events and training sessions.

His curiosity in people and their development has been a great privilege and pleasure to him for more than two decades. He cites interesting life experiences from his professional and personal life as the pool from which he draws his characters and breathes life into their stories and interactions.

Michael sincerely hopes you enjoy this book. He's also hoping there will be at least a few more.

Printed in Great Britain
by Amazon

23554852R00165